P9-CFX-794

The Missing Piece

The Missing Piece

John Lescroart

THORNDIKE PRESS
A part of Gale, a Cengage Company

Dismas Hardy.
Thorndike Press, a part of Gale, a Cengage Company.

Thorndike Press® Large Print Core.
The text of this Large Print edition is unabridged.
Other aspects of the book may vary from the original edition.
Set in 16 pt. Plantin.

**LIBRARY OF CONGRESS CIP DATA ON FILE.
CATALOGUING IN PUBLICATION FOR THIS BOOK
IS AVAILABLE FROM THE LIBRARY OF CONGRESS.**

ISBN-13: 978-1-4328-9212-8 (hardcover alk. paper)

Published in 2022 by arrangement with Atria Books, a Division of Simon & Schuster, Inc.

Printed in Mexico
Print Number: 01 Print Year: 2022

Again, and always,
to Lisa Marie Sawyer,
the love of my life.

All rising to great place is by a winding stair.

— Sir Francis Bacon

Part One

1

The customer cut a fine figure, an attorney in a thousand-dollar business suit. Like the werewolves of London, his hair was perfect, full and speckled with just the right amount of gray, for the ever-crucial gravitas. Apparently deep in thought, he was twirling his empty wineglass around on the circle of condensation that had formed in front of him at the bar.

His bartender, the eponymous owner of Lou the Greek's restaurant, a popular watering hole of the legal community just across the street from San Francisco's Hall of Justice, took the twirling as a cue and moseyed on down to his only customer.

" 'Nother one, Wes?"

Wes Farrell considered for a short moment before he shook his head. "Better not, Lou. I've got to drive home in a while. Two glasses of wine at lunch is too much."

"For what?"

"Well, driving comes to mind."

"So get an Uber."

"And pay for parking overnight in the lot out there? Forty bucks per any portion of the day, plus the Uber home and back? We're talking a hundred bills here. That's an expensive glass of this fine wine."

Lou shrugged. "Okay. So. Maybe not an Uber. But even if you drove, so what?"

"What do you mean, so what?"

"I mean, you're Wes Farrell. You get pulled over, you tell them who you are, though they'd probably already know that anyway. They tell you to have a nice day and send you on your way."

This brought a dry chuckle. "Nice fantasy, Lou, but I don't think so. More likely is one of the city's finest pulls me over and says, 'Hey, didn't you used to be Wes Farrell the district attorney?' And I go, 'Yeah,' and he says, 'Well, you're not anymore.' And he writes me up anyway. I get tagged with a DUI and then I'm well and truly screwed."

"That'll never happen."

"It might if I have another glass of wine."

"That's a hell of a lot of burden to put on a six-ounce pour."

"It is. I know. It's a bitch. But there you go." Farrell gave his glass another quarter turn, threw a glance up at the ceiling, came back to his bartender. "Ah, what the hell, Lou," he said. "Hit me again, would you?"

He didn't get pulled over on his drive back to his office on Sutter Street, but he felt guilty the whole time he sat behind the wheel. After all, he was in fact the former district attorney of San Francisco, the chief prosecutor in the city and county. His administration hadn't exactly broken new ground in granting leniency to people who drove under the influence, and he wouldn't expect any mercy if he got himself pulled over with a heat on.

Still, he'd gotten himself without incident into his sacred parking spot in the garage under the Freeman Building, where he was a partner in the law firm of Freeman, Farrell, Hardy & Roake. Taking the elevator up past the ornate and even regal reception lobby, he made it to the third floor unmolested.

As usual, the place was deserted. No one, it seemed, except himself, liked working in splendid isolation up here. Even his efficient and intuitive secretary, Treya, whom he shared with his partner Gina Roake, preferred working on the bustling second floor where most of the firm's business got done.

The only door on this floor opened to his

outsize, well-lit office, which he'd furnished — another of his trademarks — with a man-child's sensibility. Heavy on games and sports paraphernalia, the space was nobody's idea of a successful lawyer's office. Featuring a full-size Ping-Pong/billiards table, a foosball game, two Nerf baskets, a dartboard, a couple of enormous television sets, a chessboard, and three soft brown leather couches with two matching chairs, the office sported exactly zero signs of files, no law books.

Farrell didn't want to intimidate clients. He wanted them to feel at home. He always made it a point to show each of them one of his nearly trademark goofy/funny/rude T-shirts that he infallibly wore underneath his white button-down shirt. (Today's message: *Qualified to Give Urine Samples.*)

Okay, not really that funny; he'd admit it. But they all spoke to him in one way or another and he wasn't about to abandon an approach that had served him so well for so long.

Closing the door behind him, he absently picked up one of the Nerf basketballs from the Ping-Pong table and shot it toward the hoop across the room, missing by about three feet.

It was all the encouragement he needed

to cross to the nearest couch, take off his suit coat, and get horizontal, hands behind his head. His eyes hadn't been closed even for a minute when the natural law of the universe kicked in and his telephone rang.

With a deep sigh, he forced himself up. He was a slave to his landline and probably always would be (although he was getting better and better at ignoring his cell phone when it rang or buzzed or strummed or whatever the hell else it could do). But the landline was an imperative going all the way back to his childhood. Ignore it at your own great peril. He picked it up before the second ring, said his name into the mouthpiece, and was rewarded by Gina's voice.

"You're there."

"I am."

"You wanted to talk to me?"

"I did. Still do. I would have called you in a couple more minutes. I just got in from the Hall. But since you called me, I intuit that this might be a good time."

"You intuit that, do you?"

"I do."

"If I've said it once, I've said it a thousand times — intuition rules." She sighed. "I'll come up. I could use the exercise."

They each took one of the comfortable

brown leather chairs and rearranged them so that they faced each other. Gina settled herself and spent a couple of seconds looking around the room, finally coming back to Wes and making a face. "You know," she said, "I haven't been up here in a while and, no offense, but it could use a little freshening up. You ever think about getting an interior designer up here and turning it into a real office?"

Wes didn't have to consider even for a second. "Never not once. This is a real office, my dear. It's just a different kind of real. Less intimidating, user-friendly and all that. My clients love it up here. Besides, I don't want them thinking that my fees are going to interior decorating. That would send the wrong message."

"Which would be what?"

"That I'm doing it for the money, and not for love and justice."

Gina chuckled. "Oh yes. God forbid they think that. I know for me and my clients, it's all about the love. I don't think they really notice the office décor downstairs. At least in a negative way. They probably even want me to have a nice office so they know they're dealing with a professional person."

"Actually," Wes said, coming forward in his chair, "that's kind of what I wanted to talk to you about."

"Being a professional person?"

"Well . . ." Wes remained silent, his face closing down. He let out a heavy, perhaps angst-laden breath.

Gina took a quick beat at the abrupt one-word change in tone. She looked over to meet his eyes and then, reaching out, laid a hand on his knee. "Hey," she whispered, with real concern. "Are you all right?"

Wes took another deep breath, again let it out heavily. Scratching at one side of his mouth, then the other, he finally shook his head. "I don't know. Not so good, I think. I feel like I'm in the middle of . . . maybe an existential crisis, if that's not too fancy a term for it. I just don't know if I'm going to be able to go on doing what I'm doing." He broke a small smile. "Sorry."

She waved off his apology. "Did something happen?"

"Not one something, I'm afraid. Several of them." He sat back and put an ankle on his knee. "I went down to the Hall this morning because it was my day to take conflict cases." These were usually cases with more than one defendant, so both of them couldn't be represented by the same attorney (or by lawyers from the public defender's office) because of conflict of interest rules. "Lots of business, right?"

"Bread and butter," she said.

"So I'm sitting there in the courtroom this morning and I'm listening to all these defendants coming through the pipeline and it occurs to me, not for the first time, that I'm not even slightly inclined to help protect their civil rights anymore. I mean, you know me, Gina, I like to think I've got an open mind on this stuff. I know how the system works. But I've spent most of the last ten years as the DA, prosecuting these people, putting them away because by and large they completely deserve it. I've just gotten to the point that I think these defendants who got themselves all the way to arrested, then guess what? They're guilty. They undoubtedly did something, and sometimes what it was is pretty damn bad. Heinous, even. And even if it's not exactly what they were charged with, so the fuck what? Undoubtedly they broke some law, so why do I want to go to work for them and try to get them off? So they can just go out and do whatever it is again?"

Gina's face had hardened down. She had spent close to forty years as a defense attorney and she knew the job — its perils and emotional pitfalls — inside and out. "You're not working to get them off, Wes, at least primarily. You're trying to make sure they get a fair trial and sentence. Otherwise . . ."

"I know, I know. Otherwise we're living in a police state."

Gina sat back in her chair and nodded. "Sadly, that is mostly true."

"And is that really the worst thing in the world?"

Gina shook her head in sorrow. "Actually," she said, "pretty darn close. On so many levels you don't even want me to start. You arrest people without any evidence, or you start charging them for crimes they didn't commit, then believe me, the whole world falls apart. People who didn't do anything start getting arrested for whatever reason, or no reason, or because somebody in power doesn't like them."

"Yeah." Wes nodded. "I know, I know."

"Well, thank God you still know that. Maybe there's hope for you yet."

"Why do you think I wanted to talk to you? I told you it was a crisis. At least as far as the firm and me are concerned. The sad truth is that I'm not at all sure that I want to defend these people anymore. I don't believe what they say. I've got no patience. I don't want to hear it. I start believing these defendants, next thing you know I start to care too much, and I just don't think I can do that anymore. What I really want is to put those bad people away, not help them get back on the street where they'll just do it again, whatever it is."

Gina sat back in her chair, her brow creased, her lips pursed.

"Now you're mad at me," Wes said.

"Not really. More sad than anything else. I mean, I know you realize that the basic problem we have as a society is poverty and lack of education, and that's what drives —"

"Please." Wes held up a hand. "I know. I've heard every variant on that before. All the bad stuff that happened in everybody's childhood so that they're screwed up forever and it makes them commit crimes when they grow up. My problem, though, is the crimes themselves, the victims, the people who get hurt or worse than hurt. At some point, doesn't a person with an admittedly sad and pathetic background become responsible for what he does?"

"Sure, and then they should be punished. But there has to be a process to make sure they're not railroaded, that they're charged with a crime they actually committed."

"Okay. I can even buy that. But my point is that I don't know if I can defend them anymore. That's all. I'm thinking we at the firm . . . I mean, we're basically a defense team, and I just don't know if I'm comfortable on that team anymore. When they started assigning those conflict cases this morning . . . okay, I know I signed up to be on the list and it was my day to get the cases, but I almost ran to get myself out of the courtroom before the judge could assign me. I just couldn't do it."

"Yeah, well, that's understandable. But you know, if you get yourself involved with somebody who's legitimately innocent —"

Wes snorted. "That's exactly what I'm saying, Gina. There aren't too many of those truly innocent people that I'm likely to encounter out in the real world, and pretty much none that I'd believe."

"You wait. It could happen anytime. Meanwhile, you don't want to do anything precipitous. I believe in my heart that you belong here with us on the side of the angels. You just need to find something — some important case worthy of your talents."

"Talents? Ha."

"You've got 'em, Wes. Don't kid yourself. We need you here."

Wes broke a small smile. "Well," he said, "thank you. And in the words of the great

Ernest Hemingway, 'Isn't it pretty to think so?' "

"More than that," she said. "Just give it a little more time. Take a day off. Hell, take a month off. Don't go chasing any business. Let it come to you."

"Hah," he said. "As if."

2

Paul Robespierre Riley lived in an upstairs garage apartment off Balboa Street at Forty-Third Avenue, in the Richmond District well along out toward Ocean Beach. The garage was the property of his father, James Pickford Riley, who was also the owner of the house to which the garage was semi-attached. James had recently retired after forty years as a Muni bus driver and was now living on his pension and social security, and that was it.

When Paul had gotten out of what was supposed to be life in prison without parole four months ago, in mid-December, he'd approached his father, with whom he was crashing anyway, and asked if he could rehab the space above the garage, where he would live; he'd put in electricity, water, HVAC, and plumbing.

Once it was done in record time and Paul was ready to move in, James — not exactly scoring points as a caring father extraordinaire — decided that since this was now a bona fide rental property with some real value, he could and should be charging $2,500 a month, which, though Paul thought it exorbitant, was a steal by San Francisco standards. If Paul hadn't been his son, he probably could have gotten $3,000. Or even more.

Paul had argued about it, of course, but James had countered — even though it was his garage and he shouldn't have had to explain anything about it — that it clearly wasn't fair that Paul, an ex-convict with few real job skills, should think he could live rent-free in one of the country's most expensive housing markets. He was now free, white, and closing in on thirty; his father thought that he ought to be able to figure out how to make things work.

The real problem, of course, was that Paul didn't have a livable income. In theory, the state owed him $50,000 for each year that he'd spent in prison, but he hadn't seen any of that money yet. The state was disputing his claim. They said he wasn't actually innocent, but had been cut loose because of legal errors in the trial. The DA couldn't go forward and try to prosecute him again for the same crime after all this time, so he was a free man, but that didn't make him an innocent man — only a lucky murderer who got away with it. It was somewhat to very unclear when, if ever, the checks would begin to arrive. Meanwhile, even after he got the job busing at the Lily Pad, a restaurant sponsored by one of the nonresidential offshoots of San Francisco's Delancey Street project — the country's leading self-help organization for former substance abusers and ex-convicts — he still made only $500 or so a week in tips.

Paul wasn't a genius, but he could figure this out; even working full-time, he was still well short of his monthly nut.

And basically this situation was what had led him back to burglary, which had been his specialty before he'd gone down.

Surprisingly, it seemed that everybody he talked to in the ex-convict community had bought into breaking into cars as a way to augment their income because it was common knowledge that the San Francisco Police Department had adopted a policy that it no longer investigated car break-ins. Unless you had some real juice somewhere in the city's bureaucracy, the cops wouldn't even take a report. They'd tell you to go online and file a report for your insurance yourself.

But low-risk as car burglaries might be, they were also fairly unproductive — recoverables tended to include iPhones left in cars, charging wires, Bluetooth and other high-tech, low-budget nonsense — and then you had to have a way to pawn or otherwise get rid of this stuff with lots of competition in your way.

By contrast, the simple break-in to an empty house often yielded veritable treasure troves of easily fenced jewelry, watches, cash, credit cards, and even — almost always — alcohol as a special bonus for a job well done.

On this Tuesday afternoon, with fog blowing in and providing cover on the ground, Paul got back to his apartment and turned on the heat and the lights. On the way home from his lunch shift at the Lily Pad, he'd stopped by Haight Street, which he'd cased a few days before. For a block littered with NEIGHBORHOOD WATCH signs, there wasn't anything in the way of security, or even neighbors watching out for people like him. He was dressed relatively nicely from the Lily Pad, and no one seemed interested, if they even saw him, as he walked confidently to the back of one of the empty houses, slipped on some surgical gloves, and broke a pane of glass in the back door. Piece of cake.

Now he emptied his pockets onto the bed — the huge haul today consisting of twenty-plus gold necklaces, half of these holding gemstones . . . ten rings with diamonds and, he guessed, emeralds . . . a Rolex Presidential watch . . . a couple dozen earrings — more diamonds and more emeralds. Finally, he unrolled the cash — $1,800 in hundreds from the upper underwear drawer — and just stared at it in disbelief.

People, he thought, were so dumb.

From his jacket pocket, he pulled out a half-size bottle of Grand Marnier, which he'd seen before but had never tasted. Now he unscrewed the cap and took a good pull — oranges with a kick. Great stuff. He took another sip and placed the bottle on the table next to his bed.

What a good day!

Below him, he heard a heavy tread on the outside stairway that led up to his unit.

His dad, no doubt, coming to check up on how he was doing in terms of rent. He'd been a few hundred short last month and Dad wanted to put a stop to that as soon as he could.

The idea suddenly struck Paul that maybe he could trade some of today's take, avoiding the always dangerous independent secondary markets and pawnshops and getting his dad off his ass at the same time.

But there was no sense letting James see how big today's haul had been, so he tried to shove it all under the pillow.

Behind him, the knock on the door.

"Just a sec. Dad?"

"Hey. Paul?"

Something about the old man's voice seemed wrong, but Paul was excited about his new plan to trade some of the jewelry as part of the rent. So without thinking, without suspicion, he opened the door.

He almost had time to realize that it wasn't his father on the landing after all. He almost had time to slam the door shut. To register that the guy had a gun coming up on him.

But in the event, the gun went off and took out the back half of his brain, and Paul didn't have time for anything else.

Ever again.

Two San Francisco homicide inspectors — Ken Yamashiro and Eric Waverly — were on their way out to a crime scene on Clement Street, a surprising second homicide on the same day in the suburban Avenues, when they got the dispatch call about what would turn out to be Paul Riley. Only about three blocks away.

But at the moment, it was just another report of a gunshot and a 911 call apparently from the victim's father saying that his son was dead.

Yamashiro, at the wheel as he always was lately since he didn't trust his partner to drive, acknowledged the call and told the dispatcher that they were rolling on it. In fact, they were almost there as he spoke.

Waverly, on the passenger side, threw up his arms theatrically. "Hey, hey, Ken. Wait," he exploded. "We're already — aren't we already moving on another thing?"

Yamashiro flashed him a quick and vicious smile. "Now we got two. Good for us. Active cases are insurance against getting laid off."

"Yeah, but —"

"No buts." He pulled over to the curb, then into a driveway, and turned off the engine.

"This is all fucked up, Ken. What about the Clement thing? We ought to —"

"Hey. We're here now, dude. Check it out. Crime Scene will just dick around the other place for a few hours anyway since that's the homicide that got called in first. Out here we get the inside track, inspectors on the scene. Faro" — Inspector Len Faro, chief of the Crime Scene Investigation unit — "and his gang won't even get here until dinnertime, if then. This way it's all to ourselves here. Pristine scene."

"Ya-fucking-hoo."

"Well, yeah, you want to get technical. Ya-fucking-hoo. Anyway" — he pointed to the house — "this is the address, unit in the back." He unhitched his seat belt. "You coming or not?"

"Goddamn."

"Okay. Stay back here then." Yamashiro knew that they were going to have to have a talk, another talk, their tenth or eleventh, about their future together as a homicide team. It couldn't go on like this, not much longer. Ken had just about had it with Eric and his chronic pain, his drugs, his anger, his guilt, the divorce.

Tiring, to say the least.

And now fresh on a hot scene, Waverly still was sulking, slumped down in his seat.

Leaning back in around his open door, Yamashiro barked out, "Are you coming, Eric? Last chance. 'Cause I'm going. Now."

Waverly swore again, but undid his seat belt and reached for his door handle.

Yamashiro came up the driveway and around the back of the house where the outside staircase ran alongside the garage; seeing a figure seated on the top step with something shiny in his hand, he hugged back into the shelter of the house itself. With his badge in one hand and his weapon in the other, he risked another look up. "Police!" he yelled. "Stand and put your hands up. All the way up."

The figure called out, "I'm the one who called you guys. My son's been shot dead. He's inside here."

From behind him, Yamashiro heard his partner's frantic tone. "Drop it!"

"It's a cell phone, you dickheads. It's what I called you with."

"Yeah?" Waverly said. "Well, put it down. Slow. Slower."

Yamashiro half-turned. He whispered, "Easy, Eric."

"I'm going easy. If I was going hard, he'd already be dead."

Swell, Yamashiro thought. Peachy.

The man called out, "I'm standing up. The phone's on the step."

"I see it." Yamashiro came out from the side of the house. "We see it. Come on down. Hands in the air."

"Jesus," the man said. "You guys."

When he got down to the driveway, hands still over his head, the two inspectors came up and patted him down. He wore hiking boots, very worn blue jeans, a green and black plaid shirt, and a Patagonia goose-down vest, unzipped.

No weapon.

His driver's license identified him as James Riley of the same street address.

"Really," the man said when the inspectors finally stepped away. "I'm his dad. I called you guys. He's shot up there."

"Okay," Yamashiro said. "Sorry about this. Anybody else up there?"

He shook his head. "Just Paul."

"Did you call an ambulance?" Waverly asked.

His mouth tightened. "Ain't no need."

Waverly said, "You sure of that?"

Riley gave him a flat stare. "Why don't you go up and check me on it, Officer? My son's got half his head blown off. If there was any question, I would have called an ambulance first. Don't you think?"

Waverly cocked his head. "You getting wise with me?"

Yamashiro backed his partner off with a palm, stepped between the two men, who both seemed about ready to duke it out. "Let's go on up," he said.

When Yamashiro stumbled upon Paul's

haphazardly hidden loot, part of it still showing at the edge of the pillow, he straightened up and said, "Well, whatever this was, it wasn't a robbery." Lifting the pillow, revealing the rest of the haul, he whistled. "Big day at the races."

James Riley moved a couple of steps into the room. "Those bills, that roll," he said. "That's mine. I lent him that this morning. He was looking at buying a bike, a motorcycle. He must not have gotten around to it. But I can take that now and get it out of the way."

He started to take another step toward the bed, but Waverly pulled his gun again and got there first. "Don't you touch a goddamn thing! Back up!"

"But it's my —"

"If it is, you'll get it back in due time." Pointing the gun, Waverly pressed him back toward the door. "All the way out. All the way, I said. This is a crime scene. Nobody touches a goddamn thing."

"Yeah? What did you guys just do?"

Waverly raised his gun and pointed it at Riley's face. "We investigated and just got some evidence, although that's none of your business. So you, now, get back and stay out, I'm warning you. And shut up while you're at it."

Just then, Yamashiro heard from dispatch, explaining that all the available uniforms were tied up at the earlier homicide on Clement Street and asking if he and Waverly could hold the fort until some of those units got free.

Yamashiro said, "Sure," although watching his partner's increasingly erratic behavior, he was beginning to doubt that that was true.

Meanwhile, James Riley stepped backward onto the door's threshold. "That money's mine," he said.

"I'm sure it is," Yamashiro said. "But what's with this jewelry?"

"I don't know about any jewelry. Paul was getting into collecting stuff."

"This is a pretty good collection, if he was."

Riley shrugged. "I couldn't keep up on everything he was into. But that roll of bills —"

"Yeah," Yamashiro said. "It's yours. I made a note of it. Meanwhile, you got any idea of what happened here?"

Suddenly, that simple reality seemed to slam into James Riley, deflating his entire demeanor. His shoulders sagged with the weight of it. "Jesus," he said. "That poor kid." He went down into a squat in the doorway. "He should have been more careful. He should have been on the lookout."

"Lookout for what?" Yamashiro asked. "Had he been threatened?"

"I don't know. He never told me. But it only made sense he would have been, right? I mean, he'd only been out a few months, since December."

"Out of what?"

Riley looked from one inspector to the other. "Avenal," he said.

"Your son was in prison?"

Riley nodded. "Eleven years. That's what I'm trying to tell you. He just got out."

"What was he in for?" Yamashiro asked.

"They said he raped this girl. And killed her. Dana Rush. Which he never did. Neither one, the rape or the murder. Like he said all along."

"So how'd he get out?" Yamashiro asked. "Eleven years for rape and murder sounds a little light. He get paroled?"

"No. He was in for life without."

Waverly said, "So how . . . ?"

"The Exoneration Initiative, that's how. They didn't have any of Paul's DNA where it happened. He got convicted because some neighbors identified him running away from the scene with a knife. But years later, the Exoneration Initiative got a hold of his case, so they started looking the way they do and they went through all the DNA samples at the scene and identified some DNA from another guy, Deacon Moore, who by that time was in prison for guess what? Another rape and murder. So they went and talked to Deacon, and he confessed. You guys really don't know about this? It was all over the news."

"Yeah," Waverly snorted. "In our spare time."

Conciliatory, Yamashiro said, "Must have stayed under our radar. So bottom line is they let him out?"

"They had to. He didn't do it. They proved it. It was fucking Deacon Moore all along. But bad luck, Deacon's DNA wasn't in the system back when they charged Paul, so they never put it together. And he — Paul — he winds up doing eleven years for something he flat didn't do. How's that for justice? How's that for the system working? And now" — he gestured down to his son's body — "look at this." His voice seemed to break. "Look at this."

Yamashiro asked, "So do you have any idea what went down here? You said he'd gotten some threats?"

"I don't know that for sure. I thought he might have. But that doesn't matter."

"Why don't you let us decide what matters."

"That's the thing, though," Riley said. "I do know what happened here."

"What do you mean?"

"I mean I know damn well who killed my son. I saw him coming down the stairs after the shot. I looked out the back window when I heard the bang and there he was, clear as a bell, even through the fog."

Yamashiro raised his eyebrows. This was unexpected. "You're saying that if we get our hands on a suspect, you could identify him?"

"Why wouldn't you be able to get your hands on him? I know who he is."

"What do you mean, you know who he is?"

"I mean it was Dana Rush's father. Doug. I know him from the trial when he attacked Paul and then came at me. He was fighting for the death penalty the whole time. He's crazy."

"And you're saying," Waverly asked, "this guy Doug Rush shot your son?"

Riley nodded. "I just said. He must have. I saw him coming down the stairs."

Waverly exploded. "Jesus Christ. You never thought to lead with that? We got a murderer running down the street with a gun in his hand and you know who it is, but it never occurs to you to tell us? Unbelievable. Did you try to stop him?" Waverly asked. "Did you chase him?"

"No. I ran up here to see about Paul. Then I called nine-one-one."

Yamashiro asked, "So why would this Doug Rush want to kill your son, sir? If he'd just been declared innocent and let out of prison . . ."

" 'Cause he didn't believe it. He had it in his brain that Paul had done this stuff to his daughter and nothing was going to change his mind. So when they let him out, completely exonerated because it really had been Deacon Moore . . . well, you can see what he did."

"And you're sure it was him?"

"Pretty damn sure. It couldn't have been anybody else."

Waverly pressed. "You'd be willing to testify to that?"

"Of course I would. The son of a bitch. He killed my boy."

3

Wes Farrell might not have wanted to defend guilty people anymore, but he still had clients from before this epiphany had kicked in, and his core belief beyond the daily frustrations with these clients and the system was that he had a duty to represent them and to provide them with that old cliché, the best defense the law allowed.

One of those clients, Aaron Ewing, now sat in a chair across from where Wes had boosted himself onto the Ping-Pong table. The meeting had started out pleasantly enough, with Aaron coming around to deliver in person the final payment — $14,000 — for services rendered in his defense.

Normally, for obvious reasons, Farrell and most other defense attorneys demanded that their clients pay their legal fees up front. But Aaron's father, Bryce, had known Wes since they were both in college, and when Bryce's son got charged with attempted murder and assault with a deadly weapon, he'd come to his old friend to handle his son's defense and Wes had cut him some slack on the pay schedule.

Aaron was thirty-two years old, lanky and large. A wedge of dirty-blond hair fell over his forehead. He hadn't shaved in a few days and his pale-blue eyes did not exactly brighten up either his expression or the room. In another day, when Wes had been the district attorney, he would have dismissed Aaron as a low-life species of punk. But now, ostensibly, they were pals, on the same team — a team that had just vanquished their opponents, the prosecutors.

They'd been making small talk for a few minutes when suddenly Aaron came forward to the edge of his chair, elbows on his knees and his hands clasped in front of him. "Anyway," he said. "It was awesome, and I can't believe you never even wanted to know if I'd actually done it or not." *It,* in this case, being a vicious assault on his roommate, who'd allegedly stiffed him for several hundred dollars' worth of cocaine.

Farrell dredged up a polite half-smile. "That's because it doesn't matter what actually happened, Aaron. What matters is what they could prove, and there just wasn't enough evidence that they could let in for the trial. As the judge agreed."

"Yeah, but you made her see it."

"Maybe." Farrell shrugged. "In reality, once she ruled the entry was illegal and suppressed the evidence inside, it was pretty much over."

The defense had found a video surveillance camera that clearly showed that the arresting officers hadn't followed the protocol mandating that in serving a warrant, before they broke down a door or other impediment to entrance, police had to "knock and announce" themselves as law enforcement. The cops had knocked all right — but then, in an excess of enthusiasm, had smashed open the door and entered before "announcing," i.e., identifying themselves as cops.

Therefore, the search was tainted and any evidence discovered in the raid was inadmissible. Which left no significant evidence for the prosecution to introduce to convict Aaron. Farrell had been surprised that the case had made it through the preliminary hearing to Superior Court without being dismissed, but stranger things had happened.

And, bottom line, Aaron had walked out of the courtroom a free man, saved by this technicality.

"Still," Aaron said, "it was way cool you never even wanted to know."

"Yeah, well, that keeps things from getting too complicated. If I'm fighting as hard as I can to get a client off, the old motivation takes a pretty good hit if I find out you're factually stone guilty."

Aaron broke a broad smile. "Which I was. You've got to know I was all along."

Farrell held up his hands. "Don't want to hear it. Even now."

"Come on, Wes. You had to have known."

He shook his head. "Didn't know as a matter of pure fact. Didn't want to know then. Don't want to know now." He patted his jacket pocket. "Though I'm grateful for the payment. Thank you very much."

He slid himself off the corner of the table, a sign that their meeting was over.

A sign that Aaron did not read. He settled back into his chair and put an ankle on his knee. "I'm just sorry," he said, "that Jackson" — the roommate — "is still walking around with my cocaine and my money. He needs to get taken care of. For good, I mean, this time."

"Shut up, would you?" Farrell said.

Aaron chortled. "What? You're going to turn me in? I don't think so. And don't we have privilege, too? Between us? You can't talk about me and what I might do. Or what I did, for that matter. Right?"

"Well, the argument could be made that you stopped being my client when you gave me this check. But you know, a lot of this stuff, I'd just rather not know, Aaron. It would be nice if you decided you wanted to take getting off on this last beef as an omen. Next time you might not get so lucky. I know your dad would like that."

A dismissive snort. "My dad's got no clue."

Farrell felt himself getting hot. "He's the reason you're walking around in the sunshine, dude, instead of getting used to your new cell and your new roommate. You might want to keep that in mind."

"Hey. What I'll keep in mind is you're my lawyer next time."

"Maybe, but it'd be way better all around if there just wasn't a next time, Aaron. That's what I'm saying."

"Well, sure, but shit happens." Cocking his head, he said, "You telling me you're not there if something comes down again? 'Cause I don't want to hear that."

A chill ran down Farrell's back. "Are you threatening me?"

"No. I just like my ducks in order in case

I need them."

"Yeah? And I'm saying it'd be better if you didn't need them at all."

"But if I do, I come to you. We're straight there, right?"

Farrell let out a heavy breath. "How about we take it a case at a time?"

Aaron seemed to find that funny. "Sure. And whatever it is I do, I'll say I didn't do it, so you won't have to worry about your motivation since you'd be standing up for an innocent man. How's that sound? Best of all worlds, huh?"

Farrell couldn't find a response.

After a semi-tense moment of silence, Aaron straightened up, slapped his thighs and got to his feet. "Well, hey, whatever," he said. "Just having some fun." He extended his hand, and Wes waited a beat and then took it.

"Till next time." Another chuckle and Aaron turned and was out the door.

Farrell got to his corner window and looked down onto Sutter Street. Suddenly dizzy, he reached up and gripped the siding, the light-headedness threatening to knock him to his knees.

He didn't have to wonder what his reaction was about. Thirty-some years before, when he was just trying to get himself established as a criminal lawyer, his best friend, Mark Dooher, had been arrested for the murder of his wife, Sheila. To Wes, the idea that Dooher could have played even the smallest role in his wife's murder had been ludicrous. Mark was charismatic and already wildly successful — the managing partner of his own large and profitable firm. He was the attorney for the Catholic Archdiocese of San Francisco, among many other high-profile clients. Beyond that, Wes knew him as a dedicated family man and father, a doting husband, a true and loyal friend.

Sheila's death was a tragedy, certainly, but to Wes it had been obvious that she had come upon a burglar in their Saint Francis Wood home and the intruder had panicked and strangled her.

The trial had captivated the city for weeks, and as he grew into his role as Dooher's defense attorney in the courtroom, Wes had found an eloquence and passion that he'd never before known or even suspected that he possessed. He had never been more motivated and never more committed. And by the time the trial drew to a close with Mark Dooher's acquittal and complete exoneration, Wes discovered that he himself had become something of a celebrity. In the immediate aftermath, his own career had taken off.

The only problem was that in the course of the trial, even as Wes was brilliantly reinterpreting the evidence, keeping swaths of it from being admitted on technicalities similar to the one in Aaron's case, he had grown to doubt that Mark was in fact innocent, until eventually that doubt had turned into a certainty. In fact, Wes learned that not only had Mark killed his wife, he had murdered another young attorney who was suing the archdiocese, and had also dispatched who knew how many more individuals with whom he'd sold drugs in Vietnam.

Finally, Wes, in another stupendous misreading of the character of his former friend, had brought these new certainties to Dooher's attention, which made Wes a threat to Dooher's new life — and, unbeknownst to Farrell, that threat had to be eliminated.

Under the guise that the guilt had gotten to him and that he now wanted to confess, Mark had played the gullible Farrell one last time. At Dooher's insistence, the two men had met in a neutral spot and then gone for a walk together to work out the legal details of Mark's surrender. The walk took them to a three-hundred-foot escarpment, a cliff overlooking Lake Merced.

Dooher's linebacker's charge at him had pitched Farrell over the railing and into nothing but air.

In the here and now, in his office, the long-suppressed memory of that moment took the last of the strength out of his legs and, all but unaware, he sank down until he was sitting cross-legged on the floor.

It was a miracle that Wes had survived the fall, saved by the bough of a cypress tree that had somehow found purchase to grow out of the wall of the cliff, breaking Wes's fall just enough. He still had suffered a concussion and a slew of broken bones — six ribs, both wrists, his right femur, and an ankle — and surely would have died there at the base of the cliff had he not in an excess of caution given his itinerary to a police lieutenant before he'd left to go meet Dooher, who had found Wes, unconscious but breathing, in just time enough to get him to the ER.

He shook his head, coming out of his reverie. "Lord," he said.

Dismas Hardy, the managing partner of Freeman, Farrell, Hardy & Roake, didn't have nearly Wes's repertoire of games set up in his ornate office, but he did have a dartboard hidden behind a pair of cherry cabinets, along with a cherry throw line in the hardwood floor. The cabinet doors were open now, revealing the board on its green cork backdrop.

Stuck in the 20 wedge were two custom darts, and Hardy was about to fire his third one after Wes had bet him twenty bucks that he wouldn't get all three.

"O ye of little faith." He let fly and the dart smacked exactly between the other two. "I should have warned you that I once shot a perfect game of three oh one."

"I knew that," Farrell said. "In fact, everybody knows about that, long ago in the vast reaches of time though it was."

"And yet you still bet against that last shot."

"You were due to miss."

"Not likely. Not when I'm in the zone like that." Hardy had moved forward and was pulling his darts out of the board. "You want to go? Take a shot? Double or nothing?"

"No thank you." Farrell had his wallet out and extracted a bill. "Don't spend that all at once," he said.

Hardy put the twenty in his pocket, set

the darts in their holder beneath the board, and turned around. "So, what up?"

Farrell made a face. "Well, the good news first: Aaron Ewing just dropped by with the final payment on his account. All of it."

"Good for him. What could be the bad news after that?"

"That would be if he threatened me."

Hardy cocked his head. "What kind of a threat?"

"Undefined, but the basic idea was clear enough. He's going to stay in the drug business and if he has the bad luck to get arrested again, he wants me running his defense."

"And you're not so inclined?"

"You've been reading my mail."

"Talking to Gina is more like it." Hardy paused. "She tells me you're getting a little burned out on the basic mission."

"Getting scumbags off, you mean?"

"Not the most elegant way to phrase it, but okay."

Farrell hesitated, then sighed. "It's more than a little burned out, I'm afraid, Diz. I think all those years as the DA putting bad people away, prosecuting instead of defending, I realized that's the side I want to be on. I don't want to defend these cretins. I want them to go to jail. And then I get threatened on top of it all? Why do I want to do this anymore? Bad guys ought to be punished, right?"

"If they did it."

Wes snorted. "Perfect answer for a defense guy. But guess what? They did do it. Ninety-nine times out of a hundred. At least. We all know this."

"Okay, but the one guy who didn't do it. What about him?"

"He probably did something else." Wes raised a palm. "I know, I know. Except it doesn't strike me as being as noble as it once did, after all. Not anymore."

Hardy leaned back against his desk, his arms crossed. "So, are you talking retirement?"

"The word's come up at home. Sam" — Wes's wife, Samantha Duncan — "doesn't have any problem with it. We're set up financially for a while, God bless our pensions."

Hardy made a face. "Well, I don't know what to tell you, Wes. We'd miss you here, of course, but it's really up to you."

"I know. And thanks for that. I don't know if I'm completely there yet, but I wanted to float the idea by you so there wouldn't be any large surprises."

"Surprises averted," Hardy said. "Check."

4

Late in the day on the twelfth anniversary of his daughter Dana's death, Douglas Rush stood in front of her grave in Colma. Lines of seemingly identical headstones stretched out in all directions, but his darling daughter's gravesite had drawn him to it inexorably.

Driving his Harley to the cemetery, in his earbud Doug had heard the report on the news about the murder of Paul Riley. The radio station had already gotten the spin worked out, painting his death as tragic, the senseless murder of an innocent man who'd only recently gotten out of prison after eleven years due to the efforts of the Exoneration Initiative. Paul Riley had spent the past few months getting his life together; he finally had a steady job and a newly renovated apartment behind his father's house.

Homicide inspectors declined to comment on any potential suspects or motives, citing only that the investigation was ongoing.

Doug didn't care at all about the progress of the investigation. It would be what it would be. To hell with the Exoneration Initiative and its politically driven, spurious conclusions, he thought. The bottom line was that twelve years to the day after Dana's death, Paul Riley, her convicted rapist and murderer, finally no longer walked upon the earth.

Nothing could make him happier.

Normally, given James Riley's unequivocal identification of his son's murderer as Doug Rush, Yamashiro and Waverly would have gone back to the office and tried to strengthen their case by getting search warrants for Rush's cell phone and Internet connections to see if there was anything incriminating that he'd left online. Normally, they might have interviewed the neighbors to see if anyone else had seen someone who fit Doug Rush's description running away; maybe they could check local security cameras to see if they could spot Rush or his car in the neighborhood.

But now Waverly wanted to move more quickly. Technically, without any more information, they could arrest Doug Rush on the strength of James Riley's positive ID.

So they decided to head over to the suspect's apartment to see if they could catch him unawares.

With still half an hour until sunset, Doug Rush pulled the Harley into its space on Green in front of his apartment building and locked it up. Taking off his helmet, he came around the bike and across the sidewalk as two men stepped out from under his recessed entryway.

One of them, a well-dressed Asian guy, held up his wallet and its badge. "Doug Rush?"

"Guilty," Doug said.

The other cop, a white guy, barked a one-note laugh. "No shit," he said.

Doug picked up some unspoken tension flashing between the two men as the Asian continued, "I'm Inspector Yamashiro from Homicide. This is my partner, Inspector Waverly. We'd like to take a few minutes of your time to answer some questions."

"Sure," Doug said. "Shoot."

Another laugh from Waverly. "This guy's a clown. Are you a clown, Doug?"

"I don't know what you're talking about," Doug said, "but I've got a minute."

The inspectors had meant to start out on

the murder of his daughter, Dana, and when Doug had begun to cooperate, they would slowly work into the subject of Paul Riley. That plan in the here and now went immediately into the dumpster.

"What's up?" Doug asked. "Is this about Paul Riley?"

"Why would it be about Paul Riley?" Yamashiro asked.

"Because he got shot. It's all over the news. You guys are Homicide. I did the math."

"Well, then, yes. This is about Paul Riley." Yamashiro reached into his pocket and surreptitiously turned on the tape recorder function on his cell phone.

"So, Mr. Rush, do you mind telling us where you were between two and three o'clock this afternoon?"

"Getting right to it, aren't you?"

"I just asked you about where you were."

Doug slapped his helmet impatiently against his thigh. "Well, you know, I'm not sure I want to answer that question. You're asking for my alibi and that means you consider me a suspect. Which means I don't say a word to you until I've got a lawyer on board."

Waverly, committed to his bad-cop role, took a half step in front of his partner. "Fine and dandy, but here's your other option. You're welcome to call your lawyer, of course, but if that's your decision, it's going to be your one and only call from a holding cell downtown."

"You've got to be kidding me. You're threatening to take me downtown?"

"It's not a threat. You don't talk to us here, you're coming with us. Simple as that."

"For what? Murder?"

"That'd do," Yamashiro said.

"That's total bullshit is what it is."

"No. Murder is what it is," Waverly said.

"Seriously. Not seriously?"

"As a heart attack," Yamashiro said. "Look," he added, "we're talking about where you've been over the past few hours. How hard could that be?"

"That is so not the point. What are you guys, the Gestapo? I'm a fucking good citizen with a clean record who doesn't have to tell you where I've been, today or any other day."

Waverly snorted. "Why wouldn't you, though?"

"Because I don't feel like it, how's that? You want to talk to me, say the word and I'll call a lawyer. Meanwhile, you've got no right to hassle me like this."

The two inspectors shared a flat stare.

"This is nothing like hassling you," Yamashiro said in his most reasonable voice. "We're asking you the simplest question on the planet. The fact that you're not cooperating —"

"Hey! This just in, cowboys, I don't need to cooperate. Last I heard, I'm innocent till proven guilty, and you got nothing to connect me to Paul Riley being dead, goddamn his soul. And you know why? 'Cause I never even been there."

"And where was that?" Waverly asked.

Doug Rush stuck out his chin. "Jesus, guys," he said. "I think I'm about all done here."

Yamashiro let out a long, frustrated breath. "Mr. Rush. Don't say we didn't warn you. Now, turn around and put your hands behind your back."

"Fuck you."

The interview getting out of hand, Waverly shot a look at his partner, got an affirmative nod, and in a second or less had his handcuffs out and had gotten hold of Rush's left arm, which he started to twist around behind his back.

Rush pulled away, coming up and around with his helmet in his right hand, and with a grunt of exertion, slammed it as hard as he could against Waverly's head, knocking him backward.

But the inspector didn't go down, didn't even let go of Rush's wrist. Yamashiro slammed into Rush at the waist, knocking him to the sidewalk.

But the force of the tackle also wrenched him out of Waverly's grip, and Rush again swung his helmet, although this time his angle kept him from putting too much power into the swing. Yamashiro had just enough time and good enough reflexes to block the blow with his forearm, and Waverly, with a knee now down on Rush's back, got one of his cuffs around a wrist behind his back; with a practiced move he then almost pulled Rush's other arm off and snapped the other cuff into place.

It was over.

Or should have been.

Yamashiro grabbed hold of Rush's arm. "Got him," he said.

Waverly picked himself up, shook his head, found his bearings, and took a beat, then kicked Rush in his side as hard as he could. "Dirtbag!"

Yamashiro reached for his partner to forestall another kick. "Hey, hey, hey. Enough of that. We got him. Enough!"

But the helmet, right there behind them on the low stoop, was still in play, and

Waverly picked it up and swung it with full extension down against Rush's head.

The suspect groaned in pain.

"Eric!" Yamashiro yelled. "Cut it out. Shit!" He'd gotten himself up and now was pulling his handcuffed captive to his feet, trying to push him, stumbling along, to where they'd parked in a driveway about thirty feet up the street.

But he hadn't gotten five steps when he was suddenly looking at three kids — two guys and a girl — all of them somewhere in their twenties from the look of them, advancing on him. The guy on the right was holding up his cell phone.

"I got it," he crowed. "I got it all. Did you see that shit? Can you guys believe that?"

"It wasn't . . ." Yamashiro began, then realized that anything he said by way of explanation would only make this bad situation much worse. So he kept it simple. "Get out of my way, please. We're homicide inspectors trying to arrest a murder suspect. Let us go by."

The kid with the cell phone was holding it up. "I'm still shooting. I got it all."

Waverly, who'd somehow managed to stagger up and join in on the forced march of Rush, now took it into his aching head to make a sudden and unexpected (and stupid) lunge for the young man's cell phone, but the boy was agile and spun away, shooting video all the while.

"Eric! Leave it. Leave them. Get the door. The door!"

Waverly stood touching his hairline, seemingly unable to focus. He turned back to his partner, and then suddenly seemed to put it all together. He snapped into action, double-timing it to their vehicle, getting the back door open.

Yamashiro was only a few steps behind him, both of his hands on the cuffs behind Rush's back, pushing as hard as he could.

Finally, at the car's open door, Yamashiro bent Rush over and pushed him into the backseat, banging his head hard against the door in the process, then stepping back to give his partner time and space to slam the door behind him.

They were rolling in under half a minute, a bloody and battered Doug Rush caged in the backseat, Waverly slumped in the passenger seat, his hand to his head and his eyes closed.

5

Farrell and his wife, Sam, had met twenty or so years ago at the Little Shamrock bar, just across the street from Golden Gate Park, on Lincoln Way between Ninth and Tenth Avenues. It was a decent though not exhausting walk from their house on Buena Vista, and the two of them made the trek every week or two.

The Shamrock had opened in 1893, making it the second oldest bar in San Francisco. In the small world department, Farrell's law partner Dismas Hardy had traded out his legal fees to his brother-in-law (the Shamrock's former owner) for shares in the bar and had become the majority owner a few years before. Sometimes Hardy himself would even come down and bartend, though this was apparently not one of those nights.

Wes brought two Irish coffees to the tiny table they'd claimed by the front window; as he set them down, he said, "Surely not *everybody* was kung fu fighting."

Sam made a long-suffering face. "No," she said.

Wes blithely went on. "Okay, what do you call a rabbit with fleas?"

With an exasperated shake of her head, Sam said, "No again. We're not —"

Wes cut her off. "Bugs Bunny." He beamed a sunny smile down at her. "I love that guy," he said. "Tee Rex, get it?"

"King of T-shirts. Not that hard to figure out, actually."

"Still, just when I think I'm going to run out of T-shirts —"

"Which, since you've got approximately a thousand of them, could never happen . . ."

"Yeah, but still." Wes lowered himself into his seat. "This guy — Tee Rex, I mean — he's got an endless supply of what I need if I don't want to double up on stuff I've already used."

"And you wouldn't want to do that."

Wes grimaced. "Many would be disappointed, Sam. You laugh, but client and foe alike expect me to show up on time and wearing a funny T-shirt under my dress shirt. If I didn't, I shudder to think what might happen. Chaos would ensue at the very least."

"Chaos. Scary to ponder."

"There you go," he said. "I knew you'd understand."

The strum of Wes's telephone intruded on the moment.

"Sorry," Wes said. "That's me. I should have muted it."

"Or just don't answer now."

"Let me just see who it is, then I'll mute."

"Or you could just not —"

But it was too late.

The caller was an inspector from the Fraud unit, Nick Halsey.

Wes said hello and asked him to wait a minute so he could go outside where he could hear better. With an apologetic gesture at Sam, he got up and went out to the sidewalk, then brought the phone to his ear. "Yo. What up?"

"Hey, Wes. Sorry to bother you at this hour, but a situation's come up. Do you remember Doug Rush? Right about when you first came on as DA?"

"Yeah. Sure. His daughter was killed. Dana?"

"That was her, and that's him."

"What about him?"

"Well, right now he's chained up in a bed down at SFGH." San Francisco General Hospital, also known as County General.

"He got in a beef with a couple of inspectors who were questioning him and now they've got him locked up. He got his one phone call. The only guy to call he could think of was me. We've kind of stayed in touch, on and off, since the trial."

"Okay." This wasn't all that unusual, Wes knew. Cops sometimes bonded with the families of victims and kept up some of these relationships long after the trial was over. "And he wants me on board," Wes said. It was not a question.

"You're the only lawyer he feels good about."

"I only met him a few times."

"Yeah, well, evidently you're his man. And he didn't just randomly beat up a couple of cops, I'll tell you that. They must have done something to start him off." Halsey paused, then went on, "Doug said it was an Asian guy and a white guy. I'm thinking it must have been Yamashiro and Waverly, which would fit with some other things I've heard about them lately."

"Does Doug know he doesn't need me? He'll get assigned a PD" — a public defender — "tomorrow?"

"I told him that. He said he'd rather be hooked up with someone he knew. He felt good about you, since you sent down the guy who killed his daughter —"

"Paul Robespierre Riley."

"Yeah, that was him. You've got a good memory."

"Some of them stick with you," Wes said. "So Doug wants me to defend him?"

"If you can spare the time."

"You got a number for him? He'll still be awake, wouldn't you think?"

"I just hung up with him ten minutes ago. Call County. They'll put you together."

"All right. But wait a minute — Waverly and Yamashiro are Homicide, right?"

"Last time I checked."

"So they were talking to Rush about a homicide. Do you know anything about that?"

"Nope. But you're right. If it was them, they weren't talking to him about shoplifting."

Wes walked back inside the Shamrock and pulled out his chair across from Sam, who was obviously on a low simmer. "I thought," she said, "that we had a deal about our phones."

"We did. I'm sorry. Force of habit. But when I see it's from a cop I know —"

"You know all the cops, Wes. So what you do when they call, and what we agreed to do, is let voicemail take it and then sometime later, when it's not interrupting our life together, you call them back. Do you have some vague memory of discussing this?"

Wes looked down at the table. "Yes. Of course. I said I was sorry. I'm sorry now all over again. Where'd my drink go, by the way?"

"This" — she pointed at the half-empty glass in front of her — "is what's left of your drink."

Wes nodded. "That seems a little harsh."

"Harsh happens," she said. "Acts have consequences. Was that call a new client?"

"I'm not sure. Maybe."

"Terrific," Sam said.

"So," she said when Wes returned to the table with his replenished drink. "Who's the client? Somebody you know?"

"Somebody we both know. Remember Dana Rush?"

For more than twenty years, Sam had been the executive director of the Haight-Ashbury Rape Crisis Counseling Center. Her memory about each of the women she'd helped and worked with was prodigious. Now, at Farrell's mention of Dana Rush, she straightened up in her chair. "Of course I remember her. Didn't I hear her killer just got released a while ago?"

Wes broke a small smile. "Her alleged killer, once convicted, now exonerated. Paul Riley. And now, today, they just arrested Dana's father."

"Jesus. The cycle never ends, does it? Dana's father? Doug, isn't it?"

Wes nodded. "Doug it is. He got himself arrested for mixing it up with a couple of cops. Now he's locked up at County General and they're not letting him take any calls. I know because I just tried." Wes tipped up his glass. "I'll try again in the morning if they're leaving him where he is, but unless he's really hurt, they'll bring him to the jail and we'll hook up down there."

"What do you think he did that he got beaten up?"

"I don't know. Maybe he was drunk, maybe he's on drugs. Maybe both. But I'm sure he wasn't just hanging out minding his own business."

"You're sure of that, are you?"

"Well, all other things being equal."

"Ah." Sam sat back, reached out and turned her glass.

"What do you mean, 'Ah'?" Wes asked.

"I mean this is one of those times you asked me to tell you about. When you're in

DA mode and refuse to believe that it's ever the cops doing something even a little bit wrong. It's always the suspect, who's drunk or stoned or otherwise brought things down on themselves."

"Well, in this case, that's what seems to make the most sense."

"It couldn't be the cops?"

"Not likely, is all I'm saying. Not who started it, anyway."

"Why not?"

"Because it usually isn't, Sam. Almost never."

"Powerful," she said. "Persuasive. I don't think you really want to defend this guy, Wes. You think that he's probably guilty and you'll walk him through the process and get him a plea or something, but down at the bottom of your soul, you think whatever it is he's charged with, he probably did it."

"Because he probably did, that's why. They don't arrest people who probably didn't."

"And how about that old 'innocent until proven guilty' thing?"

Farrell rolled his eyes.

Sam pointed a finger, then leaned in and spoke quietly. "You asked me to let you know when you reverted to sounding like a prosecutor and not a sensitive defense person. Well, consider yourself told."

Wes huffed out a breath. "I can still defend the guy, Sam. It's not like it matters if I believe him or not. I'll get him a fair deal, and that's the job."

"You could do that, sure. But maybe in your heart you just plain don't want to do the job anymore, Wes. If I remember right, Dana's dad was a good guy. Don't you think he deserves a lawyer who believes him?"

"That doesn't matter. He wants me. I'll psych myself up and do everything I can. How's that sound?"

"Honestly? Still. Unenthusiastic."

"Don't sugarcoat it," he said.

"I never do, and it's why you love me."

Wes let out another sigh. "I'll think about it," he said.

6

At 7:15 a.m. sharp, Farrell — who hadn't slept much — showed up at the jail's reception window wondering if his prospective client had been delivered yet.

The deputy sheriff behind the counter shook his head. "No."

"When I called, they told me they left SFGH at six thirty."

The deputy raised his eyes to meet Farrell's. "Traffic," he said.

"Any idea when they're expected?"

"No." Then, in a burst of oratory, he added, "When they get here. After they get him processed."

"And how long will that be?"

"When it is." The deputy turned away so he wouldn't have to deal with these ridiculous questions anymore.

Wes took a seat on one of the institutional fold-up chairs in the chilly waiting area across the lobby from the reception window.

The time ticked away while he pondered Doug Rush's situation. His arrest meant that Farrell's would-be client was hip-deep in a murder investigation. Farrell didn't need much more than that to consider himself suddenly in a compromised position. Everyone — Halsey, Sam, even Farrell to some degree — seemed to remember that Doug was a nice guy and a bereaved father. Halsey himself had befriended him back when he was — mostly — a victim, and the friendly relationship was apparently ongoing.

But now Wes wasn't so sure about the kind of guy Doug Rush really was. The prosecutor Wes had been for the past eight years had altered his DNA and he believed what he had told Gina: that once you got yourself all the way to arrested — he didn't care too much about the individual circumstances or even the crime itself — you were guilty.

In Doug Rush's case, guilty of murder. Or at least that is what Wes could assume, given the fact that he'd been arrested by homicide inspectors.

And as to Doug being a good guy, Wes knew for an absolute fact that nearly every con man in the world came across as "a good guy" — that was how they fooled people. They were believable and sympathetic, reasonable and articulate.

The clock on the wall of the jail reception center suddenly read 7:48 and the deputy was knocking on the window, even calling him by name. Had the guy known that he'd been talking to the former DA all along?

In what must have been record time, Doug Rush had arrived at the Hall of Justice and gotten himself processed into the jail and was now waiting for his lawyer with one of the deputies in the attorney visiting room just down the hall.

Light-headed, his eyes burning from lack of sleep, Wes grabbed his briefcase and went down to get reacquainted with Doug Rush. He knocked at the door to the visiting room and the deputy opened it.

The room, very familiar to Wes, was about two hundred square feet, furnished with a linoleum-topped steel table and two metal and plastic chairs, all bolted to the floor to prevent inmates from using them as weapons. Its curved outer wall was glass blocks from floor to ceiling.

Even though it had been the better part of a decade since they'd laid eyes on each other, Wes recognized Rush immediately. They'd not only gotten him processed into the jail but already had him suited up in his orange jumpsuit. He had a four-inch-square piece of blood-soaked gauze taped over his right ear. At a glance, Wes noticed there was obvious bruising on both wrists.

Suddenly impatient with the bureaucratic pace of things, Wes gestured at Doug's handcuffs and shackles. "We don't need the goddamn hardware, Deputy," he snapped in a commanding tone, then pointed at the door. "And I'll knock when we're finished. You're dismissed, thank you." In under a minute, the deputy had unlocked the offending gear and was gone.

Wes waited until the door closed behind the deputy before he turned and extended his hand. "So? Doug Rush. How you doing?"

Taking Wes's hand in an intimidatingly firm grip, Doug shook hands and let a bitter smile tighten his lips. "I've been better, to tell you the truth." Releasing the grip with a sigh of what might have been an apology, he continued, "But it's good to see you. Are you okay with Wes?"

Farrell nodded. "That's my name. It's fine."

"Nick Halsey said you might . . . anyway, it's good to have you aboard. I didn't know you'd be here. Nick said you'd try to call me last night, and when you didn't —"

"I did. They didn't put it through."

"Bastards."

Wes shrugged. "Cops. Maybe you've heard, they stick together. You hit a cop, other cops aren't going to do you any favors. Down at County, they got told to give you one call. So that's what they're going to do. End of story."

"Yeah, I get it."

Wes sat, laid his briefcase on the table, and clicked it open. Doug lowered himself gingerly onto his own chair.

"So. How bad are you hurting?" Wes asked.

"I'm all right. They didn't kill me and they could have if they'd put their minds to it. The guy, the white guy —"

"Waverly?"

"If you say so, yeah. He just went off on me. Grabbed my arm and tried to break it off. So I'm supposed to let him twist my arm off so he could cuff me? And look what they did to me." He pointed to the bandage on his head. "I was already down and the bastard kicked me, then slammed me with my helmet."

"You just reminded me." Wes retrieved his phone from the briefcase on the table and put it in front of him. "Let me get a few shots of this damage while I'm thinking about it."

"Be my guest."

When Wes finished with the head and wrist shots, Rush said, "You don't want to forget this, either." Pulling open the top of his jumpsuit, showing off the massive black-and-blue swelling over his lower ribs, he said, "This was the bad one. He kicked me when I was down with handcuffs on. So he's allowed to kick an unarmed guy who's curled up on the ground?"

"No. I want to get a picture of that, too. Hold that top open."

"I got it."

After a few more shots to make sure that he had gotten everything he wanted, Wes sat back. "So, how'd all this come down, Doug? From the beginning, I mean."

"I don't have any idea." He went on, "No, really. I pulled up in front of my place down on Green. I'm riding a Harley now, and I'd been down in Colma going to pray at Dana's grave. Which I do every year on the anniversary of the day she died.

"So anyway, when I get back home I'm crossing the sidewalk and these two guys come out from where they've been hiding by my entry and flash some badges and say they want to ask some questions. I ask them what about and is it Paul Riley? And this gets them all stoked up. 'What do you know about Paul Riley?' And I say something like, 'Well, I know somebody killed him, and good riddance.' Other than that, I don't know nothing."

Wes fought against the tightening in his gut. In all that had been going on, he hadn't yet heard about the simple fact that one of the latest Exoneration Initiative poster children, Paul Riley, had been the homicide Yamashiro and Waverly were investigating. "So bear with me here, Doug," Wes said. "I'm a little behind the curve. Why did they want to talk to you about Paul Riley's death?"

"They were trying to set me up as his killer, which I'm not. Glad though I am that the bastard is dead. The world's a better place for it."

Wanting to keep Doug on point, Farrell prompted him: "The inspectors . . . ? What made you think they were trying to set you up?"

"Well, they started off by asking for my alibi when the guy got shot. As soon as I heard that, I knew that they were considering me a suspect, so I said I wasn't going to answer any questions. I learned something about how the system works from Paul's trial way back when. So I knew I needed to talk to a lawyer."

"Why would they think you were a suspect?" Wes asked. "Did they say they were arresting you for murder?"

"Yeah. But things went south before they said anything about why." Doug came forward, elbows on the table. "Listen, Wes. This guy Waverly got all up in my face and next thing I knew he twisted my arm back and things went to hell in a hurry. Now here we are."

"Yes we are." Wes scratched at the table. "Let me ask you this, Doug. Have you had any trouble with the law between the last time we saw each other and now?"

"No. Why?"

"Just trying to predict what's going to happen next. You've still never been arrested?"

"No. I haven't even had a parking ticket."

"Just checking. It would make a difference if you had some kind of history. But still, they've got you charged with murder, so there's likely to be an issue with bail. But I'll be trying to get you out of here soon."

"Thank God for that. And thanks to you, too, Wes. I know you didn't have to do this."

Farrell waved that away, faked his own smile. "Wait till you get my bill. We'll see how you feel about me then. You do know that you could request a public defender, right? There would be a hearing at the end of the trial to see how much you could afford to pay. It might not be anything at all, and these guys are very good."

"The difference being that I don't know any of them, Wes. And I do know you. I saw how you fought so hard to get Paul Riley convicted. I figured you'd fight the same getting somebody off. And I'm going to need a fighter. And now" — he touched his bandage, showed off his wrists — "with all this drama . . . anyway, if you're up for this, I'd appreciate it."

"No worries," Wes said. He sat all the way back in his chair. "Just to clear the air, Doug, do you mind if I ask you a few more questions?"

"Not at all."

"All right." Wes drew a breath. "Why do you think the homicide guys came to talk to you, of all people?"

"They told me. They wanted to know if I had an alibi for when Riley got shot."

"Which was when?"

"When Riley got shot? I didn't know. I don't know. First I heard about it was on the radio yesterday. But the inspectors asked me where I'd been between two and three, so I gathered it must have been near then.

But I didn't know. It could have been yesterday morning. Or the night before." At Wes's skeptical look, Rush asked, "What?"

Wes said, "That's the wrong answer. Now's the time you're supposed to tell me that on the day and hour Riley got killed, you were at a convention in Monterey with a hundred people around you and you were never out of their sight."

Doug said, "How do I get an alibi if I don't even know what time I'd be going for? I didn't shoot the guy, Wes. Really."

"Okay, we'll live with that for now. But just between us, for the record, the bigger question is why would the inspectors even have gotten the idea to talk to you so soon after the murder if they didn't think you were somehow involved?"

"Because they're idiots, that's why."

But Farrell was passing familiar with both Waverly and Yamashiro, and he knew that neither of them was stupid. They must have come up with something to pick Doug out of a universe of suspects. He said the same to his client.

And Doug replied, "Well, the obvious, of course, is they let Paul Riley out of prison and that was such a gross injustice to Dana's . . . well, to Dana. So I had a motive. A hell of a good motive at that."

"Let's not say that, even between ourselves, Doug. But go on."

"Hey. I hated the guy, and I don't care what the EI" — the Exoneration Initiative — "found. I'll believe to my grave that he's the one who raped and killed my baby. You believed it, too, when you were the DA. You damn well got him convicted."

"Yes, I did. But with Deacon Moore's confession —"

Doug held up a hand. "Don't go there, Wes. Don't get confused. Paul Riley did it. The EI cut some prison deal with Deacon Moore in exchange for his helping to get their client — Paul Riley — out. And Deacon, remember, is not the sharpest tool in the shed. But whatever the EI offered him, he got persuaded to confess to a crime he didn't commit."

"Why would he do that?"

Rush shook his head. "I don't know. Maybe the EI told him they'd work on his case next. In exchange for him helping out on Riley now. You know how that works. But we don't have to talk about that and try to figure some new stuff out. I mean, whether Deacon really killed Dana or not. I'm betting he didn't, but it doesn't matter. Just 'cause the EI got Riley out doesn't change the basic fact. You know that, too."

Wes nodded. He did know that. He'd read enough EI case files, including Paul Robespierre Riley's, to know that the bar to win release of an inmate — even one convicted of murder — was far lower than most of the public ever realized.

Wes also believed that the EI was good at reinterpreting evidence — and even in some cases providing new evidence — indicating that some serious technical error had sullied the inmate's trial such that the guilty verdict was clearly tainted; some of the EI-released prisoners had in fact done the crimes they'd been convicted of. It was no stretch at all for Wes to believe that Paul had been released as a result of some kind of prison deal with Deacon Moore and that, factually, Paul remained guilty as hell.

Paul Riley had, in fact, killed Dana Rush.

And if Dana's father, Doug, believed the same thing, he had plenty of motive to have shot Paul Riley. "So in a general sense," Wes said, "can you give me any idea of what you had been doing at any time before the inspectors came to question you?"

Showing now a bit of frustration, Doug grimaced. "I already told you I had been down in Colma. The last couple of days, actually. Well, I've already told you about that."

"Wait." Wes held up a hand. "So you went down to Colma two days in a row?"

Doug took a moment to consider the question, looked up and met Farrell's eyes.

Here comes a lie, Wes thought.

"Yeah. Both Monday and Tuesday. Yesterday and the day before."

"And did you stay awhile at the gravesite either day? An hour? More? Less?"

"So now you're coming at me, too."

"Not at all, Doug. I'm trying to establish a timeline that eliminates you from suspicion as to when Paul got shot."

"I didn't kill him, Wes."

"Yeah, you mentioned that and I heard you. But if there were just a few hours we can prove you weren't physically present where and when the murder took place, well, there's your ball game." Straightening up in his chair, Farrell said, "Come on, Doug. We're talking two full days here. What were you doing?"

"I still don't know exactly when he was killed, Wes. Or even where. I don't know anything about it."

"All right, but what were you doing for the last couple of days?"

Doug sighed. "All right. On Monday, after I paid my respects to Dana's bones, I drove down the coast to Half Moon Bay where I walked around on the breakwater. I probably hung there for a couple of hours, but I don't know if anybody saw me. I was inside my head about Dana — which, you know, happens — and I wanted to be alone, and that's a good place to do that. Nobody bothers you. I didn't talk to anybody; nobody talked to me. Then I came home, ate alone, watched some tube, went to bed."

Wes nodded. "So . . . Tuesday?"

"Basically the same thing. I felt like I hadn't given my baby's bones enough time, so I went down again to pay them my respects again. I stayed down there longer, touching base with her. Then I rode around a bit, down the coast again, clearing my head as much as I could. I got back to the city around dinnertime, when the inspectors were there." He paused. "Now do you want to know what I was planning to have for dinner?"

If his client thought he was joking, Farrell didn't appreciate it. He shook his head. "You think this is funny, Doug?"

"More like absurd, Wes. I didn't do this killing and nobody's going to prove I did."

"But you can't tell me where you were when Paul got shot?"

"I can't? I thought I just did."

"Did you? I must have missed it."

"Maybe you want to pay a little more attention."

Biting his tongue, Wes wanted to say, "Maybe you want to go fuck yourself and get a new lawyer." But instead he took a long beat with a flat stare, then reached for his briefcase. "Maybe it'll all become clearer to you when we get closer to the arraignment."

"I don't see how that's going to happen."

"Well, that'll be your homework between now and then. Give it a little thought."

Farrell closed his briefcase, stood up, and went to knock on the door to call the deputy and let him know that the attorney and his client were done for now.

7

Dismas Hardy broke a third egg into the black cast-iron pan in which he was cooking breakfast for himself and Frannie. The shower had stopped upstairs and he knew that she'd come down in about a minute and a half wearing her nightgown, her graying reddish hair still wet. He'd already cooked up six thick slices of bacon in the microwave and buttered the two English muffins he'd taken from the toaster. The coffee machine had started up automatically at the same time as their bedroom alarm — eight o'clock — and he'd already poured himself his first cup.

Bankers' hours, he knew, but he felt that he'd earned them.

Hardy the domestic hero, he thought, somewhat bemused.

The eggs popped gently in the buttered pan. He slipped the spatula under them one at a time, appreciating as he always did the perfectly smooth, naturally nonstick, dark-sheened surface that he'd somehow managed to maintain over the nearly fifty years since he'd claimed that pan from his parents' house in the wake of their deaths in a plane crash when he was nineteen. It was really the only thing that could be called a memento from his childhood home.

This same pan had also survived the fire that had all but destroyed this house twenty-some-odd years before. In some ways, he considered it his magic talisman, protecting him and Frannie and their kids, although he would never tempt the fates by mentioning that aloud.

When the eggs were done, he would slide them onto their respective plates with the bacon and muffins. Then he'd turn off the heat and rub down the pan's surface with some paper towels — no soap ever. When it had cooled, he'd hang it from the marlin hook he'd mounted in the wall at the side of the stove.

Taking another sip of his coffee, he heard her footsteps. Intent on watching the eggs so they'd be perfect, he felt her come up behind him and put her arms around him. He was wearing his workout sweats, and she hugged herself against him.

"Ten seconds," he said.

"I'll just stay here while the clock's running."

"That would work," he said.

They sat at the dining room table with sections of the paper spread out in front of them, the empty plates too, talking about Wes.

"Do you think he means it?" Frannie asked. "He might really quit the firm?"

"Not impossible."

"Why? What's different?"

"Well." Hardy put his mug down. "Having been a prosecutor now for all those years, he's kind of bought into the ethic on that side of things."

"Which is . . . ?"

"Everybody's guilty. Anybody who gets charged actually did it. The cops are always right and they never overreact or misread anything. I remember it well from when I started out. Especially after having been a cop myself. It was all totally unambiguous. We were the good guys and the bad guys were the bad guys. Period. Since then I've tried to take a more . . . let's say balanced approach, maybe because I've had actual, bona fide innocent clients, which I admit is not the norm. But it's also not the point."

"And the point is?"

"Making sure the system works."

"Simple as that?"

"Pretty much, yeah." He saw something in her expression. "What?"

"I could be wrong, but I think I've heard you bemoan the state of the system a time or two. Or was that somebody else I was married to?"

"No. That was probably me. Sometimes, many times, maybe most of the time it's true, the system doesn't work — but if somebody doesn't keep trying to make it work the way it should, then it all falls apart. And that would truly be not good."

"But maybe Wes just doesn't want to do that job anymore."

"And I can see that."

She hesitated. "You know, I'm not sure that he's all wrong, either."

Hardy took a breath. They'd had elements of this discussion before, and it had not always ended amicably. "Well, we need some good guys on the right side," he said, hating the defensiveness that had crept into his response.

"Except if it isn't the right side, Dismas. And you're defending somebody who really did what they charged him with. Shouldn't those people get convicted and then put in jail? I mean if they really did whatever it is?"

"Well . . ."

"And then on top of that, maybe it's just not a risk Wes wants to take. Given the actual danger of dealing with murderers."

"Both sides deal with murderers, Fran."

But she shook her head. "You know exactly what I mean. You've told me yourself that killers don't blame prosecutors who are trying to put them away half as much as they blame their own defense lawyers who couldn't get them off. Which, might I point out, is exactly what's happened to you, Mr. Lawyer Shot Three Times. They all figure if they had money, they could hire Johnnie Cochran and walk like OJ did. And while we're on the topic, if you never take on another murder case in your life, it'll be too soon for me."

Hardy picked up his mug to calm down. In some ways, Frannie was right. And it was undeniably true that he had been shot three times — well, four, if you counted Vietnam, but he didn't for these purposes. But criminal defense attorney was his job, his career, in some ways his vocation now, although it had not always been so.

"I mean," Frannie went on, "I think if I were you and I was his friend, I'd tell Wes he ought to try to get hired back into the DA's office. You don't need him in your office anymore. And think how you'd feel if he took somebody on over all these objections and he winds up getting himself killed."

"Fran —"

She held up a hand. "Okay, okay, we've been through this a hundred times."

"More like a thousand," he said.

"Not funny. Not if something really does go wrong with a supposedly innocent client and Wes winds up in the hospital, or worse, in the ground."

Hardy shook his head. "That's just so unlikely —"

"It is? You want to talk to David Freeman about that?"

Freeman was Hardy's former partner. "It wasn't a client who killed him, Frannie."

"I know who it was. It was just all around the defense work you were handling, and don't say you didn't know that. And maybe that's also why Wes wants to get out while he still can. And you shouldn't stand in his way. In fact," she said, pushing back from the table, "this whole thing, every time we talk about it, it's awful."

Hardy pushed back his own chair. "Fran . . ."

But she was already out of the room, on her way up the stairs.

8

It was pure luck of the draw, but Wes would take it. Doug was going to be the fourth "line," or case, called for his arraignment in Department 12 that morning (in San Francisco, courtrooms are referred to as "departments"). This meant, practically speaking, that he'd probably be arraigned by about eleven or so. Bail in a homicide was problematic, even in notoriously liberal San Francisco. But if the gods smiled on Doug and the judge set a bail he could make, it was conceivable he could be back out in the world by around noon.

With any more luck, Doug might even get his bandages cleaned up and himself dressed back in his street clothes, if they weren't too trashed from the beating and arrest. Wes could take Doug out for lunch before sending his client on his way home where he could take a much-needed nap.

And after that, so could Wes.

When he came through the bar rail from the first row in the gallery, where he'd been waiting for the better part of a half hour, Wes realized that he'd become subliminally aware of a low humming behind him. Turning back to look at what was causing the ruckus as he got to the defense table, he was somewhat surprised to see that every seat in the courtroom was taken.

The room had been half-empty when he'd arrived, but now he recognized at least a dozen reporters, a small posse of uniformed police officers scattered about, a slightly larger crop of what he took to be young attorneys with pending business here, and several assistant DAs, nearly every one of whom had been working under him less than a year ago and who now reported to the new DA, Amanda Jenkins. There was a mixed bag of maybe twenty regular citizens whom he couldn't identify, except that they were mostly young and seemed angry, even just sitting there, restive and whispering. Most of the remaining seats were occupied by the trial junkies who drifted from department to department hoping to get their free daily fixes of courtroom drama.

Something unusual was going on here, but he had no idea what it was.

For the moment, these people were not

much more than an unexpected presence in the gallery. And then, suddenly another wave of energy seemed to pulse in the room.

Turning back, Wes was just short of stunned to see his former chief assistant, Amanda Jenkins — now the district attorney — come through the back door of the courtroom with two of her acolytes in tow. Without so much as a moment's pause, she led the way up the center aisle to and through the bar rail. Nodding amicably to Wes, she wasted no time in getting herself set up at the prosecution table, removing some yellow legal pads and a couple of manila files from her briefcase.

Wes watched her, wondering about her sudden appearance here. In his own eight years as district attorney, he had come down to the courtroom to appear in person on the business side of the rail perhaps four times. It could be that Amanda felt his eyes boring into her, because she half-turned to him with a shrug, a tense smile, and another nod.

Ready to go.

The court reporter obviously took some kind of signal from her; without further ado, he cleared his throat, being a little more formal because of the number of people in the audience. "All rise. Department Twelve of the Superior Court of the city and county of San Francisco is now in session, Judge Marian Braun presiding. Please be seated and come to order."

Farrell, already on his feet, turned to face the judge as he heard the gallery getting to its feet behind him. Braun in her robes took the bench on her elevated podium without any fanfare. Looking out across her courtroom, frowning at something she saw, she ran a hand through her helmet of short gray hair. Raising her eyes to the gallery, she intoned, "Please be seated."

Then, to the clerk: "Call the fourth line, please."

Wes was not shocked that they had called his line out of order. This was the case attracting all the attention, after all, and the sooner the judge got through it, the sooner her court could go back to business as usual.

But no sooner had the clerk called his line and the bailiff escorted Doug in his jumpsuit from the holding cell behind the courtroom up to the defense table than Farrell heard a voice boom out from near the back door: "No justice!"

And a chorus in reply, another fifteen or twenty voices joining in: "No peace!"

Farrell shot a glance at his suddenly smiling client, then whirled in time to see the relatively familiar face — although he hadn't recognized it initially on his way in — of one of the city's professional rabble-rousers, Michael Rawley, in the back row leading his gang of protestors in getting to their feet, keeping up the chant: "No justice! No peace!"

Thirty years a judge, Braun had no intention of letting her courtroom get away from her. She had her gavel in her hand and slammed it down again and again. "Order. Order. There will be order."

Bam bam BAM!

"Order. I will have order or I will instruct the bailiffs to clear this courtroom." She pounded her gavel again. And again.

"No justice! No peace!"

Five gavels later, Braun found herself standing up to her full height behind the lectern. "All right. I am leaving the bench until the courtroom is cleared. Bailiffs!"

It took a while.

A full forty-five minutes later, when once again Farrell and Doug Rush sat at the defense table in the mostly empty courtroom, Wes had given up on the idea of a nice lunch after his client's release on bail.

And he didn't yet know the half of it.

Judge Braun wasted no more time before

she pulled some paper over in front of her. She didn't wait for the clerk. "Mr. Rush," she said. "The charge is murder."

"Waive instruction and arraignment," Farrell said. "The plea is not guilty."

Braun paused, then said, "Mr. Rush, I need to hear it from you. What is your plea?"

"Not guilty, Your Honor. I didn't kill anybody."

Farrell cut to the chase. "Your Honor, on the subject of bail —"

Jenkins shot up from her chair. "Your Honor, this was a cold-blooded, premeditated murder. The defendant waited for the victim and shot him dead in his own home. The crime is vicious, the defendant is a danger to the community, and there should be no bail."

Farrell let himself show a little heat. "I'm actually reading the complaint, Your Honor, and I don't see an allegation of lying in wait, which would be a special circumstance, making the defendant ineligible for bail. So either Ms. Jenkins has misspoken, or she's trying to mislead the court. This defendant is eligible for bail, and in this case, it ought to be a reasonable bail that he can make. Everybody in this courtroom knows that this case has been charged on the thinnest of evidence because the cops beat the hell out of my client, and now they're trying to manufacture some justification for it by calling him a dangerous guy. They have no physical evidence. After his arrest, they got a warrant and ransacked his apartment and found nothing. Their entire case is one shaky ID from a witness with a grudge against my client."

Jenkins responded. "Your Honor, we have a strong motive here. In fact, the defendant had previously attacked the victim, and we got an ID from somebody who knows him. The defendant is asking for bail? Fine. The People are asking for ten million dollars."

Braun, uncharacteristically, raised her voice. "Enough!" she said. "Counsel needs to calm down right now. I'm going to take a fifteen-minute break, and when I come back, we're going to discuss this with the decorum such a serious case deserves."

She slapped her gavel once, stood up, and, turning on her heel, left the courtroom.

Jenkins and Farrell stood there in silence. Neither of them had ever seen Braun come that close to actually losing her cool.

Braun had barely gone when Jenkins, obviously chastened by the judge's comments, picked up one of her manila folders and dropped it in front of Wes on his table. "Professional courtesy," she said.

"Thank you." He flipped it open to the top page, the next few. The police report on the arrest. "What do you know about this, Amanda? I can't believe you filed a case this thin."

"No comment," she said, then lowered her voice. "But you might check out the witness. Paul's father. Positive ID, close range. That ought to do it."

"But I wasn't there," Doug butted in. "Wherever there even was."

Farrell put his hand on his client's shoulder to keep him quiet. Nothing a defendant ever said in this setting helped the case. Jenkins gave Doug a quick, dismissive look, then came right back to Farrell. "For the record, we'll entertain a plea to manslaughter, eleven years quick and dirty."

Doug suddenly leaned in, across from Wes, his voice high-pitched with ill-disguised panic. "Are you out of your mind? Eleven years? Prison for eleven years?"

Wes put a hand on Rush's forearm while Jenkins pointedly ignored him. "The clock's ticking lots of ways," she said to Wes. "Nature calls, and I've got to take advantage of this break. See you back in" — she checked her own watch — "eight. I've got to hustle." She tapped her finger on the folder. "Meanwhile, good luck with that."

"She can't be serious," Doug said as soon as she was out of earshot. "Eleven years."

"Shut up, please. I'm reading here."

"I'm not going to shut up. I didn't kill him, Wes. We both know I didn't kill him. How can somebody say they identified me? That's just bullshit. And even if I do admit it, their offer is eleven years? That's ridiculous. I'm supposed to accept that as some kind of a real deal that I could live with?"

Looking up from his pages, Farrell kept his voice low. "I thought you didn't do it, so why would you plead to anything? But if you did, this might be your best shot."

"It's all bullshit. They don't have anything."

"It might be bullshit," Wes said, "but it's also eyewitness testimony, which was obviously enough to get to charge you with murder."

"One guy says it was me and that's enough?"

"Maybe. Sometimes. Depends on how close he was when he saw you and what he says exactly. Depends on what the jury hears." He met his client's eyes again. "But generally speaking, first-person eyewitness testimony from somebody who knows you is considered more or less the gold standard. At some point, we'll have to talk about the eleven years, Doug. That's a hell of an offer on a case like this. Are you still completely sure you didn't kill him?"

Rush shot Farrell a flat eye. "I didn't kill anybody. Are you hearing me?"

"Yeah. Sure."

"But you don't believe me?"

"Not the point."

"Seems to me it ought to be."

"Well, thanks for your input. I'll take it into consideration."

"And meanwhile, I'm not pleading to any eleven years for manslaughter or anything else."

"Well, thanks. That makes my decision so much easier."

"I don't care about your decision. This is my life I'm talking about."

"Hey," Wes said with another trace of heat. "This just in, dude. It's mine, too."

"Bullshit. Your life?" Rush said sarcastically. "Bullshit. If I lose, I go to prison. If you lose, you go to lunch."

When Braun next ascended to the bench, she wasted no time with amenities. "On the matter of bail —" she said.

Farrell did not try very hard to hide his exasperation. "Your Honor, my client has owned his own condominium in the city for over thirty years. Calling him a flight risk is nothing short of absurd. He has no prior criminal record, and in fact, he looks forward to proving his innocence at trial. He has pleaded not guilty. In fact, so anxious is Mr. Rush to prove his innocence at trial that he will not waive time. He wants to get back in this courtroom and prove his innocence to a jury of his peers . . ."

Not waiving time on this case wasn't as crazy as it sounded, even though it was a murder.

Barring the testimony of Paul Riley's father, James, Farrell had seen nothing in the discovery folder that even remotely looked like more, or damning, physical evidence. The prosecution apparently had only the one witness. Farrell didn't want to give them time to assemble an airtight case, or even a marginally stronger one.

What they had now wasn't much. And without more, he thought, the People weren't likely to convince an always-liberal San Francisco jury that Doug was guilty of anything, much less murder beyond a reasonable doubt.

He also believed that Jenkins was not holding back on the discovery that she'd given him. He could be wrong, of course, but he had worked closely with her for most of a decade, and he believed that he knew her character; she wanted to win, as did all good trial attorneys, but she was incapable of cheating. If she'd had other evidence regarding the murder, it would already be in the discovery folder.

But there was nothing.

Farrell met the judge's eyes and wrapped it up. ". . . And so, Your Honor, we request that bail be set at fifty thousand dollars. Greater bail is both unnecessary and punitive."

Braun had clearly run out of patience. Including the time lost to the demonstration in the courtroom, this simple arraignment had taken almost two hours out of her busy day and made her afternoon look very dismal indeed. She glanced over at the courtroom's wall clock, double-checked her wrist, and said, "I will set bail at one million dollars. Court is adjourned for the lunch hour."

"Well, first," Hardy said, "I want to thank you for ruining my breakfast this morning."

"You're welcome," Wes said, "but how did I do that? I don't recall being with you for breakfast. In fact, from the crack of dawn on, I was down at the jail."

They were in Wes's office. Hardy had shot

a few random Nerf balls as soon as he'd come in, and now he sat on one of the library tables. "What were you doing there?"

"Chatting with a new client."

"Up for what?"

"One-eight-seven."

Hardy took a beat.

"Plus, they beat the shit out of him making the arrest," Wes said. "He, of course, did nothing to provoke them. But again, how did I ruin your breakfast?"

"I was talking to Frannie about how you were quitting defense work and not taking any more cases, which I'm guessing from what I just heard is no longer the song you're singing. But we went a couple of rounds around it. She thinks you ought to quit, and she wouldn't mind if I followed in your footsteps. Who's your defendant?"

"Doug Rush. He's a dad who shot the latest Exoneration Initiative guy. Paul Riley. Who'd raped and killed his daughter, Dana."

"I think you meant to say 'allegedly raped and killed.' "

Wes gave him a dead stare. "Maybe not so alleged as you might think. Back in the day when I was DA, I prosecuted Paul and he got LWOP" — life without parole — "but they let him out last December on some

Exoneration Initiative bullshit. Doug Rush, my client — the dead girl's father — seemed to think this was unjust, so he went over and shot him."

"And you're taking on the case?"

"For now anyway."

"And Mr. Rush is pleading what?"

"His story is he's pretty sure he didn't do it. But the dead kid's dad, James Riley, begs to differ. And James apparently saw Doug coming out of the scene right after the shot and recognized him from Paul's trial long ago. That's why they arrested him."

"But he says he didn't do it?"

"More or less. But he sure had every reason in the world, doesn't have an alibi, and hated Paul, so I'm keeping an open mind."

"But you think he's guilty?"

Farrell rolled his eyes. "He did it, Diz. Take it to the bank."

"But you're still taking the case?"

Farrell tightened his lips. "Paul Riley raped his daughter and came back later and killed her in cold blood because she was going to testify against him. He goes on to get righteously convicted by me and sent away for the rest of his life, but the Exoneration Initiative gets a tip and takes on his case, finds a loophole around missing DNA evidence or some such crap, and they let him out. So my guy Doug decides he just can't live with the injustice of that. Paul Riley has got to die — *he needs to die* — and that's all there is to it. If anybody in the whole world ever had a better reason to kill anybody, I haven't heard about it."

Hardy scratched at his jaw. "But still, Wes, what if he didn't?"

"Didn't what?"

"Actually do it. Kill Paul, I mean."

Wes smiled. "Well, as Gina has repeatedly instructed me lately, that shouldn't matter."

"And yet," replied Hardy, "I sense that it does."

9

Devin Juhle was back in his job as head of the city's homicide detail.

An administrative review for mismanagement only a month before had cleared him of any wrongdoing in the assignment of his inspectors to various investigations not expressly approved of by the DA.

But the accusation of this alleged misconduct had affected his tolerance of the personality foibles of his troops. Particularly Yamashiro and Waverly. Whatever was going on with those two, it had reached a critical juncture with this apparent beating of the murder suspect in the Riley homicide.

Juhle had no sooner arrived at his office than he got the not-so-gracious note — *See me now!* — from his boss, the chief of police, Vi Lapeer. Juhle's relationship with Lapeer was tenuous at best, since she was the one, after all, who'd initiated the investigation into his purported mismanagement three months and six paychecks ago.

When he'd gone to her office, Chief Lapeer had shared with him the newly released YouTube video of this beating, and she wanted action *now* on these irresponsible inspectors, who as it turned out had not yet come into work.

So now Juhle sat behind his big desk in his office on the fourth floor of the Hall of Justice and looked across at the two uncomfortable folding chairs that he'd put out underneath the whiteboard that listed active homicide assignments. He checked his watch, gave it a shake, flicked a finger on its face. It was a few minutes after noon and time didn't seem to be moving.

Where were those clowns?

Glaring off to his left, he tried to will his office door to open. At last he opened his middle drawer and took out a deck of cards, shuffled, and dealt out a hand of solitaire.

Four aces up and playable. About as good a deal as it got. Shifting in his chair, Juhle made himself comfortable and with the aces faceup on top, started turning cards over. The way he played, he "bought" the deck for fifty dollars, then got five imaginary bucks back for every card he played on his aces one time through the deck. So breaking even was ten cards up. Today, he'd already moved sixteen cards up, on his way to a winning hand, something he hadn't seen in a while, when of course someone knocked on the door and ruined everything.

Swearing silently, he shoveled his cards into his desk drawer and called out, "It's open."

Yamashiro led the way in, followed by a hangdog, perhaps hungover, Waverly. Juhle watched them without a word as they each took a seat. After what he took to be an appropriate silence, he surprised himself with the anger in his voice. "Nice of you guys to check in before we close. I really appreciate the courtesy."

Yamashiro straightened in his chair. He was obviously planning to confront his lieutenant and brazen it out, whatever was coming. "We got hung up, sir. Sorry."

"I'm glad it was something then, and not you both just deciding to take half a sick day. Eric, now that I mention it, and if you don't mind my saying so, you don't look so good. Is everything all right?"

"Fine," Waverly said. "Everything's fine."

"Is that how you read it? Really? Everything's fine? Maybe you boys haven't seen the YouTube that you're starring in? Could that be it?"

Yamashiro said, "They took that thing out

of context. It wasn't near as bad as it looked."

"That's good to hear, Ken, because to me and to your chief of police, it looked pretty damn bad. Unconscionably bad. Like 'what were those idiots thinking?' bad."

Waverly sat up a little straighter. "The guy hit me in the head with his bike helmet. What was I supposed to do?"

Juhle leaned forward in his chair. "I'm not talking about how it started, Eric. I'm talking about when he's down on the ground and handcuffed. Traditionally, that ought to pretty much be the end of the fight. Wouldn't you say? And instead, it looks a whole lot like you kicked him in the ribs when he was just lying there, fully restrained. And then, as if that wasn't enough, you whacked him upside the head with his helmet."

"The guy's a stone killer, sir. I didn't know what he was going to do next."

"*He was handcuffed on the ground,* Eric. He wasn't going to do a goddamn thing. And while we're on this, you, Ken, that was a pretty good slam getting him into your cruiser. What were you trying to do, knock him out? Maybe even kill him?"

"He never ceased resisting, sir. I had to get him locked into the backseat for our own safety and even the people around us. That's all I was thinking about. The guy's a righteous suspect for murder and he's fighting us all the way."

"Well, then you better goddamn hope that he is a rock-solid, no-bullshit, guilty murderer, not that what you did is acceptable whoever it was aimed at. All right." He took a deep breath and let it out. "Where things stand now, I'm putting you both on admin leave until we can do an investigation into your behavior — and frankly, I can't tell you what conclusions it's going to come to. The video is pretty damning. And I don't know if you guys have noticed, but there's a little sensitivity lately around police brutality in this town. You guys just did a primer on what we're *not* supposed to do, and now it's all on tape."

"He started it," Waverly said.

"Oh, really," Juhle replied. "Tell it to somebody who gives a damn."

An hour later, torn by indecision, Eric Waverly sat in his city-issued vehicle in the Riley driveway. The fog was thick outside his windows. He was still hungover and in a vile humor, having left Homicide a half hour ago. Ken, too, along with Juhle, was being an asshole, picking the moment after leaving Juhle's office to tell Waverly that, regardless of how this investigation turned out, they would be splitting up as a team. He wasn't going to cover for Waverly anymore.

He also couldn't believe that Juhle was actually putting him — well, both of them — on administrative leave. That was just a crock to cover his own ass with Chief Lapeer. But no matter what about the politics of it, one thing was now crystal clear: especially with Yamashiro out of the picture, Eric had to make sure that the case against Doug Rush was solid. Because it was one thing to restrain a murderer and another to lay into an innocent suspect. That kind of thing didn't just get you fired; it got you sued for enormous bucks. And with that in mind — to hell with Yamashiro — he had called James Riley to make an appointment to get his eyewitness testimony on tape.

They probably should have taken James down to the Hall of Justice for a formal statement, or at least taped him at the scene; but when everything had gone to shit and they'd decided to go after Doug Rush right away, that hadn't happened. So as Waverly sat there now in the driveway, they didn't actually have a memorialization of James Riley's identification of Doug Rush. That was a problem he was going to fix right now.

Because what Juhle had said was a fundamental truth: it would make a huge difference to the administrative investigation if James Riley's testimony, particularly his eyewitness testimony identifying Doug Rush as his son's killer, got squishy in any way.

He suddenly remembered that he had an actual appointment here. Glancing at his watch, he saw that he was on the verge of being late. And tardy was something he could just not afford to be. Not now. He was technically on leave; he had no business doing an interview with a witness. But James Riley wouldn't know that, and Waverly felt he had no choice.

He sighed, opened his car door, and stepped out into the fog.

James opened up before he'd even rung the doorbell. He was wearing the exact same clothes as he had yesterday when they'd first come by here — worn jeans, plaid shirt, hiking boots. Beyond that, he looked quite a bit the worse for wear; understandably, Waverly thought, given that his son was a homicide victim.

After he'd come inside and James had closed the door, the two of them stood awkwardly for a moment in the mini-foyer that led to a stairway ahead of them and the living room off to the left. "So what are we here for again?" James finally asked. "I'm sorry, I haven't been sleeping. The funeral's got to get planned, you know. I had to call his work and tell them he wouldn't be in. I don't know when I'm going to get his place cleaned up."

Even through the pain of Waverly's hangover, dulled somewhat by the two shots he'd taken from his pocket flask on the way over, the non sequiturs spoke volumes about the man's state of mind. The greedy and mostly uncooperative witness from yesterday was nowhere to be seen. This man, today, looked and acted beaten down and hollowed out.

Waverly gave him a shrug that he hoped conveyed some sympathy. They'd gotten off on the wrong foot with each other before. Waverly's bad-cop role wouldn't help him this time around, so he forced a smile and said, "Ready then?"

"Okay." James led the way into the living room and then through it into the kitchen, where he pulled out a chair at the linoleum table and sat down. Eric followed, noticing the sink filled with unwashed dishes.

Pulling back another chair, he sat straight across from his witness.

James met Eric's eyes. "So . . . ?"

"So I was hoping we could go over again your identification of the man you saw leaving your son's place yesterday."

"You mean Doug Rush. That's who it was."

"Well, all right. But give me a second. I'm going to be taping our conversation, and I've also got some pictures I'd like you to see."

James had nothing to say to that, and Waverly thought he might as well be talking to a stone. Nevertheless, he took out his cell phone and set it to record. "One, two, three," he began. "This is Inspector Eric Waverly. Today's date is . . ." He went on with his introduction, substituting yesterday's date when he and Ken had been here before, while they were both still on active duty. When he was finished, he sighed in relief that James hadn't noticed the change.

Satisfied, he looked across the table. "I know this is painful, but I wonder if you could go over the way you remember things happening in the minutes before you heard the gunshots."

"It wasn't gunshots," James said. "There was only the one."

"All right. Just the one."

"I was watching TV in the other room we just walked through —"

"The living room?"

"Whatever you call it."

"Were you watching a particular show?"

"Yeah. Of course. Streaming, you know. *Deadliest Catch.*"

"And what time was that?"

"I don't know. Two, maybe closer to three, somewhere in there. I saw Paul out the side window there, beside the TV, getting home from work, I guess. That's when he usually got home, about then. Anyway, he didn't stop or anything, just went up the stairs."

"Out by the garage?"

"Yeah. I thought he'd come down and have a beer after he got into something more comfortable, so I didn't think anything of it. That was what he'd do a lot of days."

"You just kept watching TV?"

"Right. Waiting for him to come by."

"Did you see anybody else coming up the driveway with him? Or after him?"

"No. I'm pretty sure he was alone. Also, he must have had, you know, all that stuff with him. I mean, he probably didn't go to work with it."

"All right. So how long was it, just an estimate is fine, before you heard the gunshot?"

"I'm going to say ten minutes. The show was still on."

"So you were watching TV, but didn't see anybody go up the driveway?"

"Not so it registered. I was watching the show."

"But you didn't see anybody coming up the driveway?"

"I already said that. What does it matter? We know he got up there."

"But you didn't see anyone earlier? That you could have had a good look at before."

"That never happened."

"Okay. So . . . ten minutes?"

"Ten minutes. I had the TV muted for commercials, which I always do. That I remember. I'm sitting in my chair in there and *bam.* And I'm all, 'Shit. What the fuck is that?' But then I realize it's from up at Paul's place and I jump up and come in here."

" 'Here' being the kitchen?"

"Right." He turned and pointed. "Going for this door, but before I could get to it, I see somebody out on the stairs, coming down. So I lean in here over this table, checking out who it is, and there's this fucking guy hauling ass down, couple of steps at a time."

"You saw him clearly from in here?"

"Yeah, you can see. It's only like twenty feet. I was standing just where you're sitting, and" — he turned farther around — "right there's the steps."

"Now, when you saw the guy, did you recognize him?"

"Yes. It was Doug Rush."

"Where did you recognize him from?"

"From my son's trial. The motherfucker attacked Paul in the courtroom back then."

"How sure are you that it was Doug Rush?"

"I'm pretty sure. Who else would have done it?"

Waverly felt his brain go haywire. It had never occurred to him — as certain as James Riley had been yesterday in identifying Doug Rush — that he wouldn't come across as positive on the tape. But he had just introduced an element of doubt. Eric wasted no time trying to repair the damage. "Now, by 'pretty sure,' " he said, "you mean it was him, right? Doug Rush."

"Yeah, that's what I meant."

This wasn't going the way Waverly had expected. He decided to leave it and move on.

"So what did you do next?"

"I yelled, 'Hey,' or something, and he looks right at me. But now I'm going for the door."

"Wait a second. So he looks at you. Does he stop?"

"No. He's flying out of here."

"Did you see any gun? Did he aim at you?"

"No. But I know damn well there's a gun, since I just heard it."

"All right, so you're at the door now?"

"I'm outside and the door to Paul's is still open. Rush is at the bottom of the steps, and he stops, taking a look back up at me. But then he takes off to the left and he's out of my sight."

"And so what did you do then?"

"I stand there a second, trying to decide. But what am I gonna do, chase down a guy with a gun? Dumb move. And besides, there's still Paul. I gotta see if he's all right, so I turn and go up the stairs and . . ." Stopping his narrative, James let out a heavy breath. ". . . and Paul's . . ."

"It's all right."

"No. No, it's not really." He looked across at Waverly. "You know, we were getting where we were working things out — living in the same place again. I mean, Paul hadn't been around for eleven years. You lose track, even if you visit him in prison. It's not the same. And there wasn't much of seeing him inside anyway after the first few years, especially after his mom died. I didn't really care about the rent. I didn't really need it."

His brow furrowed in sudden confusion,

Eric asked, "What about the rent?"

"We were working it out. How much, I mean, he was going to pay me. It was going to be okay. I should have just let that go. It was all working out."

Waverly wasn't sure there was a thread to follow as James tried to deal with the inarticulate agony of his grief. He knew he had to clean up the earlier uncertainty of James's ID. He figured that he could do that by showing him some photos.

He thought about turning off his tape recorder so that he could clean it up if the ID remained uncertain. But he didn't know how he would be able to explain a big, fat pause in the middle of the recording. He decided to go for it. Giving the silence one last long beat, he reached into his jacket pocket. "I've got a thing we call a six-pack, James, that I'd like to show you." He pulled out a sheet of laminated photographs labeled one through six, taken from California driver's license photos that he'd pulled up after Ken had left the homicide detail to go do what he was going to do.

Eric had assembled the six-pack himself. One of the pictures, number three, was of their suspect, Doug Rush, and the five others were white males who more or less fit the same age and description. Given James's certainty about his identification of the man who'd shot his son, Waverly more than halfway expected this exercise to be a mere formality.

He handed the six-pack across the table. "Take your time," he said, "and look at these photos. Then please tell me if you see the man that you told us you'd recognized on the day of your son's shooting. I must tell you that it may not be any of these six, either. We'd like you to be one hundred percent certain before you make your pick. And again, take your time."

Riley laid the pictures on the table in front of him with an air almost of enthusiasm. Clearly, he shared Waverly's view that this formal identification would be a piece of cake. But as he perused the pictures one after another, by the time he'd gotten to the sixth photo, his expression had clouded. And then everything went south.

James Riley looked up, blinked, shot a quick glance across the table to Eric, then went back to the pictures. "You're saying it might not be one of these guys?" he asked.

"You tell me, James."

His frown deepening, Riley went back to photo number one. Then, painfully slowly, he moved to the next picture, then the next — Doug Rush. A pause. Then he resumed at number four . . .

Stop.

Five . . .

Stop.

Six . . .

His eyes down, he drew in a labored breath and let it out.

"James?"

Frustrated, Riley held up a hand. "You told me to take my time." His voice shimmered with anger.

"All the time you need." Waverly sat back and waited.

Riley returned to the six-pack one more time. "It's definitely not one, and it's not five or six," he said, adding aloud, almost to himself, "Not two. Gotta be three or four. Three or four." Keeping his eyes on the photos, he finally made up his mind, then looked up at Eric in relief or satisfaction. "It's three. No question. Three."

"All right," Waverly said. "Nice job."

"It's him, right? Number three?"

"You got it."

"It's funny. It's tougher than you think. I could have easily gone with four."

Riley needed to shut up right away lest he undo everything he'd done. Albeit in a tortured way, he'd finally correctly identified their murder suspect.

Trying to derail his witness's train of thought, Eric said, "Well, listen. This is what we needed and you did a fine job on it. Now I'm afraid I've got another couple of appointments. You good here?"

A shrug. "No place much else to go."

"Well, hang in there." He gathered up his stuff. "We're going to need you to testify at the trial, so you take care of yourself."

"Sure," James said. "You bet."

On the way back to his car, Waverly wondered how a solid ID had become such a clusterfuck so soon. He thought seriously about dumping the tape entirely, but in the end he figured he would be better off with the ID that Riley eventually had made than with trying to explain what had happened to the recorded statement that Riley would certainly remember he had made.

Part Two

10

Abraham Glitsky had gone to the police academy after graduating from San Jose State, where he'd majored in history and been a standout tight end, though not standout enough to get drafted by the NFL. In the San Francisco Police Department, he started out, like everybody else, as a patrolman. Two years into that rotation, he got teamed up with a new guy named Dismas Hardy, who'd been shoulder-wounded in Vietnam before coming home to San Francisco and entering the academy and then, while still a patrolman, going to law school at night.

While Glitsky steadily progressed in the SFPD, Hardy graduated from law school and quit being a cop but stayed with criminal law, getting himself hired by the city and county district attorney's office. So the two men had remained on the same side, the prosecution side — Glitsky making his arrests and Hardy prosecuting the bad guys in a variety of cases, learning the ropes on misdemeanors and then felonies in the courtroom.

They'd stayed in relative contact through Hardy's first eighteen months or so as an assistant DA, through both of their marriages, the first kids for both. But the connection ended in the aftermath of Hardy's world collapsing around him. His seven-month-old son, Michael, had gotten to his feet for perhaps the first time in his crib, then somehow managed to flip himself over the side and onto the hardwood floor.

Hardy had tucked Michael in that night, leaving the sides lowered just exactly as they had always been. It had never occurred to him that the boy could stand up yet. None of the books warned him that it was even possible at that age. But the books were wrong. Michael died the next day.

And Hardy's marriage came off the rails, and so did the law career. His friendships, hobbies, interests. Everything.

And then, from nowhere really, although actually from his hideaway behind the bar at the Little Shamrock, Hardy — now married to Frannie, with a couple of their own children — had reappeared in Glitsky's life. Though Hardy's reentry into criminal law took him on a short sojourn back with the DA, the politics of that office hadn't worked out very well for him, and he'd eventually punted on prosecuting people and hung out his shingle on the defense side.

Meanwhile, Glitsky had continued to raise his own three boys, then lost his wife, Flo, to cancer. Professionally, he became an inspector — vice, burglary, robbery, and finally homicide, which was the top of the heap. He'd married Treya Ghent and adopted her teenage daughter, Raney, and the two of them had produced two kids of their own, Rachel and Zachary.

The two guys — Glitsky, a half-Jewish, half-Black hard-ass inspector, the boss of the homicide detail and a cop down to his bones; and Hardy, the good if fallen away Irish Catholic defense guy — wound up befriending each other for a second time.

They couldn't have been more different, more unaligned. Glitsky's potion of choice was tea, he only rarely drank alcohol, and he never swore. It would be fair to say that none of those things could be said about Hardy.

But the friendship had endured for thirty-plus years now, and none of that seemed to matter.

■ ■ ■ ■

Glitsky was closing in on sixty-five years old. He'd retired with a full pension three years ago and frittered away about four months doing crossword puzzles and playing sudoku before he realized he didn't want to be retired and so began the process of becoming a private investigator. For someone with his background, this took him, figuratively, about fifteen minutes, and when he got his license, it meant that he was at least nominally back in the game. Dismas Hardy's regular private investigator, Wyatt Hunt, had offered Abe a cubicle in the offices out of which he ran his shop, the Hunt Club. Now every day Glitsky came into the nicest environment he'd ever worked in and looked out his window over his desk at the Bay Bridge and the Ferry Building just across the street. Life was good.

Today, a cold Wednesday in May, he was in his cubicle, on his second cup of Earl Grey, playing some computerized chess, when his cell phone rang. Seeing who it was, Abe punched him up and said hello.

"How busy are you?" Hardy asked him without preamble.

"Pretty much overwhelmed. You?"

"Barely keeping up with the load. Which is why I was hoping to pass some of it along to you. But if you're too swamped, I'll leave you alone and call Wyatt."

"No. I can take it."

"I thought you were busy."

"I lied. I'm currently getting whupped at computer chess. My opponent here is smart, I'll tell you. Serve him right if I just end the game. In fact . . ." Abe did some magic on his keyboard and his monitor cleared, then came back to the wallpaper shot of Treya. "He's meat now. That ought to show him." Changing his tone, he asked, "So what do you got?"

"Have I mentioned our client, Doug Rush?"

"I think so. I know Treya has. The Paul Riley homicide? Isn't he Farrell's client?"

"Yeah, but we share. If you haven't heard, we're a highly evolved firm."

"That must be it. But what about him, Rush?"

"Well, he's been out on a million dollars bail for the past month. Put up his condo for collateral and took a personal loan to pay the bondsman a hundred K and gave Wes a retainer of another hundred K. So he does all that and — I don't know what the boy is thinking — then he doesn't show up this morning for his prelim, which as I'm sure you know is traditionally a fairly weak strategy if you want to stay out free on bail."

"I've heard that."

"Believe it. It's the truth."

"He ran out on a million dollars?"

"If he ran, yep."

"You think he did?"

"Ran? I don't know. Either that or somebody kidnapped or killed him. Or he killed himself, in which case he might have given Wes the courtesy of telling him that's what he had in mind. But as of last night, he was still planning on coming in."

"Last night?"

"He and Wes talked at around nine. Everything seemed fine."

"So what's Wes doing now?"

"He's still down at the Hall in case Rush shows up with some kind of excuse, but that's probably not going to happen."

"So what do you want me to do?"

"Well, I'd start by going by his place and seeing if he's there, dead or alive. After that, if nothing turns up, then he's a bona fide missing person and you take it from there the way you do. But I'd start where he lives, out on Green, a couple of blocks in from Van Ness. You could be there in twenty minutes, even stopping by my office to pick me up on your way over."

"And what role exactly would you be playing if you came along?"

"Basically, just keeping you in line in case you're tempted to go rogue."

"I probably won't, you know."

"Maybe, but you can't be too careful."

"Sure you can. You, for example, are too careful all the time. But whatever, I'll see you in ten."

The manager of the Green Street building, Julia Bedford, was number one on the mailbox, and she buzzed the foyer door open almost before Hardy had let up on the button. She came across as friendly and competent, an ex-hippie two or three years on either side of sixty, with striking ice-blue eyes and thick gray hair halfway down her back. She sported a fisherman's sweater, blue jeans with a multitude of tears down both legs, and Birkenstock sandals.

"Did you try ringing six?" she asked after the introductions and explanations. "Doug's apartment?"

"We rang a minute ago before we tried you," Hardy said. "No answer."

"So how can I help you?"

"Well, first off, we wanted to make sure he was all right and were hoping you could let us check the apartment."

"Of course. Let me just get my keys. Oh, but before that . . ." Excusing her way around the two men, she went out the front door, to the sidewalk, where she looked up and down the street. Turning, she came back inside and shook her head. "His bike's still here, which usually would mean that he is, too. But I don't see how it could hurt to check and make sure." She pushed the doorbell for Rush's apartment, waited a moment, then shrugged. "Let me get the key and we'll check it out."

"Has he been here the last few days?" Glitsky asked.

"In and out, but he was definitely around some of the time," she said, then added by way of apology, "I usually just automatically notice who's in and who's out. Not that I try to be nosy. It's just become a habit, I suppose."

"Did you see or hear him leave?" Hardy asked. "Last night, for example?"

"No. But I'm a pretty good sleeper. I doubt I would have. Well" — bringing her hands together and rubbing them — "give me a second."

When she came back out, they took the elevator to the third floor and headed to the right down a wide and well-lit hallway at the end of which was a door with the numeral 6 in brass just below the peephole. Hardy knocked, got no answer, and then stepped aside to let Julia use her key.

"This feels a little weird," she said. "Are you guys sure it's okay? I mean, legal and everything? I don't know. What if he's — ?"

"We're not going to disrupt anything," Hardy said. "If we see something that doesn't look right, we'll make some calls. If he's unconscious or worse, we call an ambulance or the police." This did not answer or even address the question, but Julia seemed to accept it. She nodded, inserted the key, turned it, and pushed to open the door. "I'll just wait out here if you don't mind."

"We'll only be a few minutes," Glitsky said.

The few minutes turned out to be about forty, but they left thinking that they could have taken an hour or even half a day and come up with the same results. Doug Rush was gone and probably had been for at least one night — he'd made up the bed, and both the shower and the bathroom sink showed no signs of use anytime in the recent past. His toiletries were still there. The coffeepot on the kitchen counter held a room-temp half a cup, and two other cups sat upside down where they'd been left to dry on the rack next to the sink. There were no clothes obviously missing from his closet or drawers, nor any sign of forced entry.

At last, Julia knocked and asked if they were about done and they took it as their cue to finish up.

"Anything interesting?" she asked when they came back to where she'd been waiting by the door.

"He keeps the place up pretty well," Glitsky said.

"Yes. He does. I wish everybody who lives here was more like him. But that, I'm afraid, is wishful thinking."

One of the perks of working directly above the restaurant Boulevard was that by now all the staff knew Glitsky and he could usually score a table faster than the rest of humanity. Now he and Hardy occupied one of the prime window booths, which comfortably sat four. While they waited for Farrell, who had given up on his client at the Hall of Justice, they passed the time talking about the Giants, who were in the midst of a dismal season.

"You realize," Hardy said, "that I've been to four games this year and they haven't won one of them. And this on top of last year, when I went to twelve games and they lost every one of them, too. That's oh and sixteen, for those of you keeping score."

Glitsky chewed some ice. "If I owned the team, I wouldn't let you come into the park. There's obviously a clear connection between you going to the game and them losing."

Hardy sipped his white wine. "As we lawyers like to say, Abe, don't confuse a connection with a causation."

"Thanks. I'll try to remember that. But first" — he chinned toward the door — "here comes Mr. Smiley Face."

He flagged Farrell with a wave, and in half a minute Wes was settling into the booth, pointing at Hardy's wine. "Did either of you think to order me a drink, knowing about the morning I've had? Guy walks out on a million bucks. Are you kidding me?" He turned his head and raised a hand in a vague attempt to get a waiter's attention. "I need a lot of gin and I need it now. But I'll take half your wine, Diz, while I'm waiting."

He held out the empty wineglass from his place setting, and Hardy dutifully splashed him a few ounces that Farrell immediately drank off. "Better," he said. "Thank you."

"So what do you think?" Glitsky asked.

Farrell's face was haggard. He shook his head. "I am rendered thoughtless, Abe. No shit. Never did I consider him not showing in court. I can't imagine what it gets him walking out on his bail. To say nothing of my retainer, a mere drop in the bucket of a hundred K, which I'm not going to be tempted to refund to him if he ever does show up again. Ah, Steven."

The waiter nodded. "Mr. Farrell. How are you doing today?"

"I'm so glad you asked. I have a thirst in dire need of slaking. How about a double Hendrick's on the rocks? And another half glass of whatever Mr. Hardy's drinking."

"Half glass?"

"He shared his wine with me just a minute ago. I don't want to be in his debt."

"Might as well make it a whole glass, Steven," Hardy said. "Put it on Wes's portion of the bill."

Wes began to remonstrate. "I don't really think —"

"Guys, enough already," Glitsky piped in. "Give Steven a break here and let him do his job."

"One double Hendrick's, one Pinot Gris," the waiter said crisply, threw a grateful glance at Glitsky, then turned and went to place the order.

Wes took in a breath, then huffed it out. "I'm really pissed off," he said.

"We guessed," Hardy said. "So where are we at now?"

"Nowhere. Back before we started, more or less. I can't *believe* he didn't show. What the hell is he thinking?"

"Probably that he didn't want to go to prison," Glitsky said. "When he knew that his own lawyer believed he did it, what chance was he going to have with a jury?"

"A hell of a good chance," Wes said. "I've gotten off dozens of guys who actually did what they were charged with. So has Diz."

"That's why we make the big bucks," Hardy said. "Not exactly dozens, though."

"But still," Abe went on, "you can't really blame the guy if he didn't want to take the chance."

"Sure you can," Wes all but exploded. "You can blame the absolute shit out of him. This is San Francisco, where juries don't want to convict anybody ever. And he had the greatest motive in the world. His daughter's rapist and killer let out on some technicality? They could have had him shooting Paul Fucking Riley on video and I still would have had a better than even chance at getting him off. Plus, you throw in the way the cops treated him when he got arrested, he's the most sympathetic defendant on the planet. And with all that going for him, he gives up a million dollars and leaves me holding the bag. I hate that guy. I really do."

Hardy said, "You've got to learn to say what you really feel, Wes."

"I'm working on it."

The drinks arrived and they drank and ordered, and then Farrell asked, "You guys find anything at his apartment?"

"Half a cup of room-temp coffee," Glitsky said. "If that counts."

"Not for much. Diz?"

Hardy shook his head. "What time did you talk to him, Wes? Last night, I mean."

"Nine thirty, quarter to ten."

"And you thought he was home then?"

"That was my impression, but I could be wrong. I didn't hear any background noise, so he wasn't, like, in a bar or someplace obvious, I don't think."

"Well, wherever he went, he didn't take his chopper," Glitsky said.

"He always rode his bike," Farrell said. "Why wouldn't he have taken it this time?"

"Well, for whatever reason, he didn't." Hardy nodded. "Which leaves Uber or a cab or somebody picks him up or he's on foot."

Farrell snorted. "Narrowing it right on down."

"Uber or cab," Glitsky said, "there'd be a record. I could look into that if you think it would be worthwhile."

"I just don't know," Farrell replied. "This whole thing doesn't make any sense." Suddenly, his eyebrows went up in a sign of hope. "You think somebody kidnapped him?"

Hardy tipped up his wine, swallowed, and then shook his head. "No sign of struggle at the apartment."

"Well," Glitsky said, "somebody points a gun at you, you don't necessarily struggle."

"True. All too true," Hardy agreed. "But if he's been kidnapped, he's in serious trouble."

"Or dead," Glitsky said. "Either way, not so good."

Steven arrived with their food, and the men stopped talking while he set them up.

Finally, Steven finished and Wes let out a sigh. "Maybe you want to follow up on the Uber/cab angle, Abe. See if he's left any record on his way from his apartment to wherever he went."

"I can do that."

Hardy put in, "But say we find him, Wes. What are you going to do about it? If he's even alive?"

"I don't know. But you're right. Maybe I should just let it go and leave it to Amanda" — the DA — "to try to find him. After which he can get himself a public defender and rot in jail while he waits for his trial, for all I care."

"I might as well look, though," Abe said. "He paid your retainer, didn't he?"

"Don't remind me," Wes said.

"What about me?" Hardy said.

"What about you?" Farrell asked.

"Well, I'm not here just because I'm so good-looking. Perhaps, since Mr. Rush has retained one of my partners, I could contribute something."

Wes pondered a moment. "I don't know," he said. "You can always read over the case file and see if I've missed something. But don't get your hopes up. I'm betting he lit out. He's had plenty of time to get himself a bogus passport and might be in Mexico by now. Or Europe. Or Argentina. Or anywhere, really."

"Or dead," Glitsky said. "Let's not forget dead."

"No," Farrell said. "Let's not forget that. But probably not, and there's your wages of sin for you."

"Except, of course," Hardy said, "if he

didn't do it to begin with."

Farrell leveled a gaze at him. "Well, yeah, sure, of course. That."

After lunch, the three men returned to the firm's Sutter Street offices.

When Farrell had gone upstairs to his playroom and Hardy had disappeared into his office, Glitsky made his way to his wife's workstation, little more than a couple of ergonomic chairs, a desk, and a computer monitor stuffed into a cubicle off the main hallway. Treya was in her chair at that desk, facing away from him, working intently on something, her fingers flying over her keyboard.

He hesitated for a few seconds, not wanting to interrupt her. But suddenly she straightened up, hit a few more keys, sending her monitor to its screen saver — her three children — and then was pushing out her chair, standing and turning around. "And as if on cue," she said, "my favorite man appears." She stepped over and gave him a quick kiss.

"That was a pretty good trick," Abe said. "How'd you know I was here?"

"Fantastic sensitivity to sympathetic pheromones." She touched the side of her nose. "Nothing escapes."

"I'll say. It's a little scary."

"It would be, I admit, but I only use my superpowers in the cause of truth and justice, so you're in no danger."

"Good to know. And now that you mention it, Sympathetic Pheromones would be a great name for a band, wouldn't it?"

"I can't believe nobody's used it yet. But in the meantime, what are you doing here?" She motioned to the chair that abutted her desk. "You want to sit?"

"I don't see how it could hurt." While he got comfortable, he gave her a quick recap of the morning's adventures — no sign of the client at his place on Green Street, Farrell's suggestion that Glitsky try to find some cab or Uber record of how he'd made his getaway. "Anyway," he concluded, "bottom line is I'll do some digging on that stuff."

"But isn't the DA going to be looking at all this, too? Plus his credit cards or other bank activity. Plus his cell phone. Plus whatever else they do."

"Right. And bringing a lot more juice to the investigation than I can. They can get search warrants on all this stuff, which I can't. But all of this will probably be a waste of time anyway."

"Why do you say that?"

"Because my gut tells me he's dead."

Treya's hand went to her mouth. "Why would you think that?"

"The short answer: a million dollars."

"His bail?"

Glitsky nodded. "You don't walk out on a million dollars, Trey, I don't care who you are. And Wes says Rush didn't have much more than that. Between the bail and the loans, he was damn near broke. He's not letting that money go."

"But he couldn't use the money, I mean, if he were in prison."

"True. But really not the point."

"And the point is?"

"He's not willingly going to forfeit that money. That's human nature. I think it's more likely that he would kill himself first, before that alternative would even occur to him."

"So he's dead?"

Glitsky nodded solemnly. "That's my bet."

"He didn't kill himself?"

Glitsky shook his head. "He would have done it where we could have found him, and possibly, probably, even written a note."

"That's really going to upset Wes."

"Why do you say that?"

"Because he's believed all along that Doug actually killed Paul Riley. It fit so neatly into his worldview. Now, from what you're saying, someone else might have killed Doug. And if that's the case, in all probability that means Doug didn't kill Paul Riley after all, doesn't it? Somebody else did, and then that same person killed Doug last night."

"But why?"

"I don't know. Maybe Doug knew something he didn't know he knew, and it might come out in the trial?"

"Hmm." A shrug. "That's a good theory, but there's no way to know. Not yet, at least." Clapping his hands gently, Abe got to his feet and said, "But first things first. Let me get a lead on where Mr. Rush has gone to and eliminate some possibilities of how he got there, if I can. If he's moving, he's not dead, and that would be all to the good. But I don't have high hopes."

Treya put her hand on Glitsky's forearm. "You be careful."

"Always."

"This is a lot like when you were in Homicide, isn't it?"

Glitsky's face cracked in a grotesque facsimile of a smile. "A little bit. Yeah, it is."

11

For a murder case, the file was surprisingly small.

Hardy had worked many murder cases in the past that had as many as fifty binders and/or bank boxes with transcripts of witness interrogations, police reports, forensic analysis, physical original tapes of testimony, lab results, memos to file, motions to the court, and responses to those memos. In the thick of things, the huge conference room table in the office that they called the Solarium would be stacked high with evidence binders and boxes filled with everything that might be, or soon would become, the official record of the trial.

This was what happened when your client waived time or, much more often, deliberately stalled. The vast majority of defendants were in no hurry to get to trial. Most murder trials ended in conviction. On the other hand, if you could stall the case for months or even years, evidence could get lost or a key witness could recant or get run over by a bus. "A continuance is half an acquittal" was an expression in common currency at the Hall of Justice.

When your client did not waive time — Doug Rush's situation — and demanded that his trial begin within sixty working days of his arraignment in Superior Court, there might still be a few binders, but often nothing like the glut of material that choked trial preparation in the normal course of events.

Hardy got his hands on the entire case file — one banker's moving box with four binders and some loose paper — at a bit before five o'clock and had read and skimmed through the salient material within an hour and a half.

When he finished, he had come away with four areas that seemed incomplete, to say the least, if not downright provocative.

On the pro–Doug Rush side — in other words, arguing that he was innocent of killing Paul Riley — James Riley's eyewitness testimony about the day of the shooting and his "positive" identification of Rush were, to put it kindly, squirrelly.

On the opposite side, most damningly, the cops had found a record that at one time Doug Rush had purchased a Glock 40.

Rush said that the gun had been stolen in a burglary, and there was a report on file that his condo had in fact been burglarized after the date he purchased the gun. But that report didn't list the gun as a stolen item. Rush claimed he'd forgotten to include it when he listed the items stolen in the burglary. In his own mind, Hardy filed that under, "Oh yeah, sure."

So the fact that it appeared to be a Glock 40 that the killer had used to shoot Paul Riley was not exactly in Rush's favor; next, Rush's story about what he'd been up to on the day before and the day of Paul's murder left a gaping hole in his alibi; and finally — on the Rush-did-it side — there was the trove of heretofore unseen (at least by Hardy) news articles in the *Chronicle,* the *Bay Guardian,* the *Courier, Newsweek, Time,* the *New Yorker,* and *Mother Jones.* The police had discovered these at Rush's apartment and they collectively proved beyond a reasonable doubt (at least to Hardy) that, rather than being casually attentive to the progress of the Exoneration Initiative in getting Paul Riley out of prison, Rush had in fact been nearly obsessed by it. His comments on social media alone betrayed anger and outrage, to put it mildly.

In the weeks before and after Paul Riley's

release from Avenal, Doug had cut out and saved twenty-seven different articles about the situation and the new findings of the EI case in general. Their client was a guy, Hardy was starting to think, who couldn't wait to right this egregious wrong by killing Paul Riley. He wouldn't even feel bad about it.

Hardy called Frannie and told her that he'd be home for dinner by eight.

An hour before that, he found himself ringing the bell at the front door of James Riley's house. The May fog was in, heavy enough to carry a smear of drizzle on the gusting breezes. The wind chill brought the real-feel temperature down to the low fifties and Hardy, standing there shivering in his coat and tie, almost gave up before he heard footsteps inside, then saw an eye in the peephole. The chain rattled, the dead bolt got thrown, the door opened.

James Riley sported three or more days of whiskers, some uncombed gray hair over his ears. He carried thirty extra pounds and wore baggy jeans and a San Francisco Giants sweatshirt.

Quickly looking Hardy up and down, he said, "Are you guys ever going to give this up?"

"I'm sorry," Hardy said. "James Riley?"

"Yeah. But really? Again?"

Hardy cocked his head, perplexed. "Again what?"

"Again with you cops. How many times do we have to do this?"

Hardy took a beat. "I'm with Doug Rush's defense team. My name is Dismas Hardy."

"Dismas? What kind of name is that?"

"He was the good thief on Calvary, next to Jesus."

"Well, good for him. And you're not a cop?"

"No, sir."

" 'Cause the cops have been around three times now, asking the same damn questions. I'm getting tired of it, tell the truth. How many times do I have to hear them ask if I was sure it was Rush who killed my boy? Jesus. Who else would it be? I saw him, that's who it was. That's my story and I'm sticking to it."

"Right. I understand."

"So why are you here, then? And if you're with Rush, why do I want to talk to you?"

"Well, Mr. Rush has gone missing. He didn't show up for his court appearance this morning for the beginning of his trial. We're trying to run him down."

"And what? You think I know something

about that?"

"You're the main witness against him, sir. It's not impossible he might seek you out to keep you from testifying."

With a grim little chortle, James said, "I'd like to see him try. And you've come by to warn me? Is that it? 'Cause I don't need it." Reaching around behind himself, he brought out a handgun. "Let him try. If he was standing out here on this step instead of you, he'd be a dead man right now."

Palms out, suddenly truly shaken, Hardy backed up a step. "I get your point." Keeping his hands far apart, he said, "I won't take much of your time."

With a dismissive chuckle, Riley shook his head and tucked the gun back into his belt. "We might as well go on in. It's ball-freezing out here." Pulling open the door, he stepped aside to let Hardy pass, then gestured left toward the small living room. Hardy sat in a wing chair across from the television, which was wall-mounted above the fireplace. Riley lowered himself onto one end of the couch. "All right," he said. "So why do you think I'd be interested in helping you with Rush's defense?"

"I don't. But I do wonder why the cops have come to talk to you three times."

"Well, the first was right after I called

nine-one-one, so I get that. Then they brung along that six-pack, they called it — head-shot pictures — and told me to pick Rush out of five other guys. That was the white cop coming back for that the day after the shooting."

"Waverly," Hardy said. He'd been surprised to see Waverly's name on the police report for Riley's six-pack testimony, because he knew that he'd been put on admin leave the day after Rush's arrest and in theory shouldn't have been doing any official police business, such as interrogating a witness. "Are you sure that this was the day before the funeral?" Hardy asked.

"Yeah. Absolutely. Waverly. The guy's crazy, by the way."

Hardy shrugged. "So what was the third visit?"

"Last week sometime. Another homicide guy."

"Bracco," Hardy said.

"Yeah. I think so."

"What did he want?"

"Same as Waverly. Another six-pack. Different people."

"And how'd that one go?"

"Better than the first one, which is probably why they wanted me to do it again."

"How's that?"

"Politics, I figure. I been around cops before, you know, when they were building the case to bust Paul, my boy. They didn't have squat on him, but once they made up their minds, they wouldn't even look at anybody else. They just charged ahead and built the case against Paul out of nothing. Which is pretty much what they're doing with Rush, not that they shouldn't with that scumbag, but they get a guy on their radar and stop looking. It's screwed up, is what it is."

Hardy had him talking and wanted the conversation to continue. "So what's the political part?" he asked.

"That was Waverly. He beats the shit out of Rush when they arrest him? So how's it look if Rush isn't the right guy? Not saying he isn't. There's no doubt about that, but here comes these homicide inspectors whaling on him. It's one thing to beat up a no-doubt stone murderer, but not so good if he turns out to be just some sorry-ass innocent citizen. Again, not saying it was that this time with Rush. But Waverly wanted to nail it down as soon as they could so there wouldn't be any hassles about police brutality and all that shit."

Hardy sat back in his chair. "I read your statement to Waverly," he said. He phrased his words carefully. "It seemed like it took you a while to identify Mr. Rush."

"He told me to take my time."

"Okay, but if you were so sure . . ."

An edge of impatience crept into his tone. "A couple of the other six-pack guys, there were similarities with how they looked, that's all. Compared to Rush, I mean. I wanted to be solid sure before I made the call. I got it right, don't forget. Both times. And the last time, with Bracco, that was right down the pipe."

"And you don't have any doubts now that the person you saw running away after your son was shot was, in fact, Doug Rush?"

"None. None at all."

"It couldn't have been any of the other six-pack people? Or anybody else entirely?"

"Why would anybody else have wanted to kill Paul?"

"I don't know, James," Hardy said. "Why don't you tell me?"

As James and Hardy talked, it turned out that James's degree of certitude about the identity of his son's killer was actually quite a bit lower than even the discounted version in Waverly's six-pack exercise.

Driving home, Hardy could think of several scenarios off the top of his head why someone would have wanted to kill Paul Riley:

- An enemy from his time in prison with a score to settle or an ax to grind;
- An ex-convict or new business acquaintance whom he had cheated or provoked;
- A woman he'd dumped or mistreated;
- That woman's jealous boyfriend.

None of these would have had anything to do with Paul's release due to the Exoneration Initiative. In fact, the whole EI connection might never have surfaced at all had not James dubiously "recognized" Doug Rush as he made his escape down the steps from Paul's apartment. And without that identification, it seemed to Hardy that there was no case at all — no evidence, no motive, no narrative, no suspect.

By the middle of the night, Hardy had given up on sleep.

It made no sense. Now that there was little likelihood that a jury would ever sit in judgment over Doug Rush, the case should have had little meaning for Hardy.

But it rankled.

Rush wasn't even his client, yet Hardy's

brain would not shut off. He tossed in bed until after 2 a.m., then finally gave up and went downstairs to commune with his fifteen tropical fish. Sitting half-buried in the depths of the dark leather chair across the family room behind their kitchen, he allowed himself to be lulled by the gurgling bubbles and the dim bluish light until finally the frenetic pulsing in his head eased into the more regular rhythm of his heart.

He sighed, considering and then rejecting going back upstairs and trying again to sleep. Instead, he hunkered down farther in his chair, fingers templed in front of his mouth.

James Riley's identification of Doug Rush was the first of the discrepancies that Hardy had uncovered in the case file, and was in many ways the most damning for the prosecution. If they put James on the stand as their chief witness — an all-but-foregone conclusion — his testimony wasn't going to do much to convince a jury that the person he'd seen after his son got shot was Doug Rush.

On his cross-examination, Wes would have him eat his testimony for lunch. Hardy could all but hear the interrogation:

"Well, Mr. Riley, the man you saw running down the steps to your son's apartment

looked a lot like Mr. Rush. Correct?"

"Yes."

"And it certainly could have been Mr. Rush. Correct?"

"Yes."

"Those were the words you used: 'looked a lot like Mr. Rush.' Correct?"

"Yes."

"But you must agree that looking a lot like something isn't the same as being identical to something. Correct?"

"Well, but —"

"Let me ask it this way. You didn't say it was Mr. Rush, did you?"

"Well, no."

"You didn't say it was exactly like Mr. Rush, did you?"

"No."

"Now, some of the photos you were shown by police looked like the shooter, correct?"

"Yes."

"And they looked like Mr. Rush, correct?"

"Yes."

"But the other photos you saw were not the shooter, were they?"

"No."

"But just like Mr. Rush, they looked a lot like the shooter. But they weren't the shooter, correct?"

And on and on and on until the prosecution and the judge put a halt to it.

A smile twitched at Hardy's mouth.

God, he loved the law!

Next, Doug's insistence on his two separate trips to Colma (and one to Half Moon Bay) didn't really provide him with an alibi for the date and hour of Paul Riley's murder so much as call into question what Doug had really been doing. Who knew? Maybe he had in fact gone to his daughter's cemetery plot in Colma. Maybe he'd actually gone down there twice in two days, and rode his bike to Half Moon Bay in the interim. And hung out for a few hours exploring the breakwater, speaking to no one. Sure, he could have done that. Possibly.

But that didn't explain why his phone had been basically turned off for two days. Not a single phone call where the defense could use the cell tower records to prove he'd been somewhere besides San Francisco killing Paul Riley. The answer, memorialized in Wes Farrell's notes, was simple enough, though somewhat difficult to believe: Doug Rush only rarely used his cell phone at all! He'd told Wes that he refused to be chained by what he called the tyranny of the telephone and, although he used it for social media, most of the time his cell phone remained turned off on the bed table in his condo, waiting to be charged.

Finally, the news articles on Riley's release from prison that Doug had meticulously cut out and saved in their own little scrapbook and his obsessive social media posts offered compelling evidence of Doug's ongoing fascination with Paul Riley and the Exoneration Initiative mechanisms that had brought about his release. Then again, maybe it was just a scrapbook that he'd kept up with as a memorial to his daughter. Maybe.

And maybe, Hardy thought, maybe I'm the king of Ethiopia.

Two minutes later, having reached no conclusions, Hardy was asleep in his leather armchair.

12

First thing the next morning, Thursday, Glitsky was sitting across from Devin Juhle's desk trying to exert leverage that he didn't have. He was reminding Juhle that they shared a history as head of Homicide. Glitsky had run the detail several years before, but still . . .

Also, Juhle's best friend was Wyatt Hunt, and Glitsky worked in Hunt's offices every day. They should all be cooperative pals.

Glitsky had been trying since yesterday to get his hands on taxi and Uber records in the city, but this turned out to be far easier said than done, especially without subpoena power. "Come on, Dev," he was saying. "You know there's some bureaucrat out there who can just press a button or two and, bingo, we've got those records — which, by the way, you guys can use as well. You want to find Doug Rush as much as I do. That's all I'm trying to find out, is where and when did he go. Whatever I get, I promise I'll give whatever we find right back to you. We're not trying to locate him so we can hide him away. If we can get him to turn himself in, we just hope that we still might have some shot at having his bail reinstated."

Juhle waved that off. "I'm not concerned about that, Abe. You know as well as me, we're going to hunt him down ourselves if we can, and then he goes back into custody. We're not about to give you a head start while we get up to speed. That's just not happening. I expect I'll have somebody on this in the next day or so, and then maybe —"

Interrupted by his desk telephone, Juhle held up a finger and grabbed the headpiece. "Just a minute," he said to Abe, then spoke into the phone. "Juhle, Homicide. Yes." Listening, his brow furrowed, he pulled a notepad in front of him and started making notes. "How old? . . . Roughly is good. . . . And where? Any ID? . . . Okay. All right, I hear you. Who's nearest out there in the field? . . . Good, they'll be good. . . . All right. Let's get them rolling. Thanks."

Hanging up, he looked across at Glitsky and seemed to be considering something for a long moment. "Somebody's wedding day just got ruined," he said. At Glitsky's quizzical look, he went on. "The Shakespeare Garden in the park. Most popular wedding venue in the city. They just found a body under the gazebo there. White male, fifty or sixty, no ID. Maybe homeless, but maybe . . ." He paused.

"Maybe Doug Rush," Glitsky said.

Juhle nodded. "Maybe."

Glitsky hadn't been to a homicide scene in a while. By the time he made it out to the Shakespeare Garden in Golden Gate Park, the usual apparatus of a murder investigation had kicked in, lining up along Martin Luther King Jr. Drive — the coroner's van, four black-and-white patrol cars, several more of what Glitsky assumed were unmarked city vehicles used by homicide detectives, and the crime scene van. He parked at the back of the line and stepped out into a fog that today did not feel like it would burn off early.

When he got up to the line of yellow crime tape that delineated the actual scene, one of the several patrol officers standing guard gave him a salute and said, "Good morning, Lieutenant," and Glitsky, enjoying the moment of misidentification and chuckling to himself, saluted back at him, lifted the tape, and let himself under it.

Fleetingly, he wondered how long it would take for the word of his status as a private investigator to reach down to the street cop level. Maybe forever.

It wasn't a long walk down to the gazebo, where another knot of five folks, two of them in uniform, stood around chatting. Glitsky recognized two homicide inspectors in plain clothes — Jack Royce and Jill Gomez — and decided not to make the usual tired joke about their names. Instead, he nodded all around. He knew neither of the uniformed cops, but guessed they were from Park Station.

The last of the group was Lennard Faro, the as-always nattily dressed head of the Crime Scene unit, whom Glitsky knew well. "Hey, Abe." He extended his hand. "Long time no. What brings you out on this fine morning?" He chinned at the area behind the gazebo. "You know our dude who remains deceased?"

"I'm hoping not. I was talking with Devin this morning when the call came in. He thought I might want to get on down here and talk to you guys. You got an ID yet?"

"Tentative, but decent. It looks like somebody lifted his wallet, took whatever money or credit cards he found in it, and threw it into the bushes right over behind us. Our vic down there looks like the same guy on his DL."

"Doug Rush?" Glitsky asked.

"You knew him?"

"Enough to tell you if it's him."

"Let's go take a look."

"I'm right behind you."

Glitsky, Hardy, Farrell, and Gina Roake sat around the enormous round conference table in the Solarium, a large circular room under a glass dome that was otherwise the habitat for about fifty plants, including a couple of redwoods, several rubber trees, some citrus, gardenias, camellias, and a few dozen other exotic ferns and flowers.

"Okay, but all that said," Hardy continued, running the show, getting them back on point, "what are the odds that he killed himself?"

"Does anybody really think he did that?" Gina asked.

"Not sure," Glitsky said. "Len Faro thinks it's not impossible —"

"Very strong," Hardy said.

Glitsky shook his head. "Actually, coming from Faro, that means it's still something to consider. Len is not a flake. If he says it's not impossible as a suicide, it's possible."

"Even with no gun?" Hardy asked.

Glitsky said, "The gun disappears when the guy takes the wallet that was sitting there on the ground next to a dead person. That guy —"

"What guy are we talking about again?" Gina asked.

"The guy who takes the wallet sees the gun," Glitsky said. "No way he doesn't take it."

"So what's that theory leave us with?" Hardy asked. "Rush talks to you, Wes, at about nine thirty two nights ago. Everything's fine. He's going to be in the courtroom the next morning. Then, out of the blue, he leaves his apartment and somehow doesn't take his Harley, but winds up out in Golden Gate Park, where he shoots himself in the head. And by the way, where'd he get that gun? The one that killed him? Either it was really well hidden or it wasn't in his apartment when Homicide searched the place. So maybe he went out and bought a new one on the street. But when he's out on bail? Hard to believe." Hardy looked around the table. "It's a long shot that he killed himself. To say nothing about why."

"Why," Wes said, "is because he's going to prison for the rest of his life. He's done his vengeance number and killed Paul Riley. All of his family is dead. What's he got to live for?"

"Stretching it," Gina said, "that he wouldn't have taken his bike. Guys and their bikes. They don't use other transportation. It's automatic — he's going out on any kind of personal errand or meeting, he takes his hog."

In the gathering silence, they heard the phones ringing out in the reception area.

Finally, Hardy spoke up. "So what does that leave," he asked, "besides the fact that we don't have a client anymore?"

"Well," Gina said, "going back to his bike, let's say I'm right. No matter what, he would have taken it, but we know he didn't."

Glitsky asked, "So you think somebody he knew came and picked him up?"

"If he didn't kill himself," Farrell said.

Gina shot Wes an impatient look. "He would have taken the bike. But more than that, if he was going to kill himself and even had this phantom gun hidden away somewhere, why not just do it in his apartment? But he didn't. This means he didn't kill himself at all. Abe called it. Somebody he knew came and picked him up, drove them both around, and then killed him."

"Had to be the same person," Hardy said, "who killed Paul Riley."

"No," Gina said. "It might have been James, Paul's father, out for his own revenge."

"That's a tough sell," Hardy said. "Possible, okay, but I can't say James works for me."

Farrell pushed back from the table. "Guys, how many times do I have to tell you this? Doug's the one who actually did kill Paul and next he did himself. He had every reason in the world. He'd run out of time. He was going to get convicted. He killed himself."

Glitsky, the ex-cop and only nonlawyer in the group, cleared his throat. "All this is fine theorizing, gang, but maybe we'd be better off cooling our jets until the autopsy and forensics stuff rolls in. Get a little evidence on the table."

Hardy threw a sardonic glance around the table. "Who invited this guy?" he asked.

13

The bottom line was that they no longer had a client.

This left Glitsky with an empty plate, which, in turn, made him uncomfortable. After the meeting in the Solarium had broken up with nothing essential having been decided, Abe stayed on a few minutes in Hardy's office, reviewing the trifling litany of evidence from Doug's case file. This, too, turned out to be mostly unproductive, although Hardy told him that he'd keep an eye out for the minute something came in.

Glitsky's next stop was his wife's station down the main hallway, to see if she'd like to go out and grab a bite with him, but she was just leaving for her own lunch with Carly Kayson, one of her book club pals who was, frankly, not one of Abe's favorite persons. So he turned down his wife's offer to join them and soon enough found himself out on Sutter Street, walking toward his office in the fog with his hands in his pockets and his collar up against the cold.

When he got to Maiden Lane, a block-long pedestrian walkway of high-end retail space that abutted Union Square, he stopped, figuratively sniffing at the site for karma. This was where his unacknowledged biological daughter, Elaine Wager, had been murdered almost twenty years before, and he suddenly realized that he had all but subconsciously been avoiding the spot almost since the day it had happened.

Now, after a lifetime of investigating homicides, he knew all about murder, how it sullied everything it touched, the entire physical and emotional landscape. He believed this to the very core of his being. It was undoubtedly why — long before Elaine, and even more so afterward — he had found such satisfaction in his work. And still did. Identifying and bringing killers to justice was one of the world's most important jobs, and he'd been born to do it.

He suddenly realized that Doug Rush's death was likely going to gnaw at him until he got to the truth of the matter. Because he already knew it was not just Rush. The cycle of violence and retribution around Doug Rush's death had begun with the rape and murder of Rush's daughter, Dana, twelve years before, and the question of who was guilty of that murder, at least to some people, still hung in the air. Evidently, another man named Deacon Moore had been Dana's rapist and perhaps killer, although Paul Riley had been the man originally charged and convicted, and Paul Riley had ultimately paid the price.

A gust of wind whistled up Maiden Lane, throwing some grit up into Glitsky's face. Squinting, he half-turned to get away from it. And now, since he was facing in that direction, he decided that he knew where he wanted to go.

Twenty minutes later, he was behind the Hall of Justice in the coroner's office, shaking hands with San Francisco's medical examiner, Amit Patel. "Thanks for seeing me on such short notice," he said.

"No worries. How can I help you?"

"The short version, Doctor, is maybe you can tell me if Doug Rush was a suicide or a murder."

"Doug Rush. This morning's client, if I'm not mistaken?"

Glitsky's lips twitched, holding back the tic of a smile. "That would have been him, yes. Although I can't say I've ever heard them called 'clients' before."

Patel shrugged. "Gotta call them something besides 'stiff' or 'dead guy' or 'cadaver,' and people get sensitive. 'Client' has got a nice, respectful ring to it, don't you think?"

"You put it that way, I guess I do. And I guess that 'bill-paying customer' is out of the question."

"I'd guess so. People don't think enough about these death protocols," Patel went on. "They matter. They really do. You can't be too careful. When I first came on here, I debated with myself for — I don't know, it must have been a few weeks — about whether or not to call them 'patients,' but there's an unfortunate connotation where people somehow unconsciously think that if they're a patient, then they might somehow get better, which is really never the case here. So I finally settled on 'client.' "

"Good call," Glitsky said. "So . . . about Mr. Rush."

"Yes, well. I'm afraid I do go on sometimes." He broke an apologetic smile. "That's what happens when the people you're working with, your clients, tend not to talk back to you. You prattle sometimes. Sorry."

"No worries." Glitsky waved that off. "But

Mr. Rush . . ."

"Of course. I haven't even begun the full autopsy yet, but if you'd like to come back to the cool room with me, there's a chance we can answer some of your questions."

"That'd be good. Thanks."

They walked out the back door of his office, down a short hallway, and through another door into the lab. There were several bed stations covered with the silvery kind of runner's blanket commonly found near the finish lines of marathons. Patel walked over and switched on the light over one of those stations, then pulled the sheet down to expose Doug Rush's head and chest.

Glitsky, in the sudden chill, looking at the lifeless head, felt an unexpected surge of nausea and brought his right hand up to his cheek.

Patel didn't miss the reaction. "Are you all right?" he asked.

"Fine. I guess I haven't spent enough time down here in a while. I'm out of the habit."

"That's probably a good thing."

"Maybe it is."

"If you need it, there's a bathroom just behind you there."

Glitsky shook his head. "Got it. But I'm good. Thanks."

"Okay. Let's see what Mr. Rush has to tell us."

Quietly and perhaps unconsciously humming the melody to "The Battle Hymn of the Republic," Patel leaned over and brought the overhead light down lower to get a better look. He took some kind of caliper or measuring tool from his coat pocket and turned the head to more clearly expose the entry wound. Turning the head in the other direction, he performed the same measurement on the exit wound. Back on the entry side again, he frowned and stopped humming. "Well," he said, straightening up.

Glitsky, swallowing against his physical reaction, still hung back away from the table. "What's that?" he asked. "Did you find something?"

"Always," Patel replied. "I would say that, subject to a complete autopsy of course, there is only a very small chance, if any, that this wound was self-inflicted. In fact, I would almost say no chance at all."

"Based on . . . ?"

"Well, primarily, there are no signs of powder burn, which means that the muzzle of the weapon wasn't anywhere near his head when the shot was fired; certainly it was farther than an arm's length. Assuming, of course, that he wasn't wearing a hat or hoodie, and there's no sign of that. As I said, I will have to run some further tests as part of the full autopsy to make sure that there isn't some microscopic residue or other explanation — maybe it will turn out he was wearing a hat or a cowl, I don't know — but from what I see here with the naked eye, I'd have to say it would be very unlikely that he was holding the gun."

"That's what I needed to know."

But Patel raised his palm, stopping him. "Beyond that," he said, "as you can see, the entry wound is above the left ear. I don't know if Mr. Rush was left- or right-handed, although we will determine that shortly, but if the latter, then there's about an eighty percent chance that he didn't shoot himself with his off hand. And beyond even that, the entry wound — probably our old friend the Glock, by the way, forty-caliber is my guess — is way toward the back of his head and above his left ear." Patel put his finger against his own head up behind his ear. "So, a little bit awkward, do you see? Not what I'd expect in a self-inflicted wound."

"So you're saying this doesn't look like a suicide?"

"Informally, and off the record, I would pretty much bet the ranch on it. Somebody shot him. It might not even have been at particularly close range."

14

Figuring he could always use the exercise, Glitsky headed back up toward Sutter and closed the circle he'd walked in since leaving the Freeman Building an hour before. Glitsky was a big believer in the element of surprise and so didn't want to call first and make an appointment. Of course, the downside was that sometimes nobody would be free to see him.

But he was willing to take the chance.

Phyllis — Hardy's receptionist, secretary, and above all gatekeeper — greeted him cordially enough from where she sat at her station in the lobby, but her face clouded over when he mentioned that he needed to see her boss right away. It was relatively urgent and no, he did not have an appointment. He could wait down at Treya's cubicle if Hardy needed some time to clear his schedule, he said.

Phyllis sighed in exasperation, pushed a

button on her intercom, and spoke quietly into the mouthpiece. Her shoulders sagged in disappointment as she nodded, then told Glitsky, "He says he can spare ten minutes if it's really urgent. His door is unlocked. I believe you know the way."

Since "the way" was about twenty feet across the open lobby and Glitsky did in fact know it well, he thanked Phyllis and was moving before she changed her mind. In ten steps he was there, knocked once, and pushed the door open.

Hardy was sitting, poring over pages at his atypically cluttered desk.

Glitsky came all the way into the office and closed the door behind him. "I would have bet you'd be throwing darts," he said.

"No." Hardy gestured to his desk. "As a matter of fact, I'm working. Believe it or not, I have an actual practice here with real clients and everything. So I can give you six minutes."

"Phyllis said ten."

"She was being generous. Six is the billing unit. Ten units per hour. And your first half minute is gone, so talk fast."

"All right. I just went and had a talk with Amit Patel, whose latest client, speaking of clients, is Doug Rush."

Hardy put his pen down, straightened up,

and pushed back a few inches from his desk. "What did he know?"

"He wouldn't swear to it, but he pretty much eliminated the idea that Rush killed himself. No powder burns, trajectory of the shot, probably no GSR" — gunshot residue — "on the hands, although he'll have to wait for the lab results on some of that. But the bottom line is he's got all he needs now. Rush didn't kill himself."

"Wes is going to be disappointed, isn't he?" Hardy said. "This increases by a lot the odds that Rush didn't do it after all, doesn't it? I mean killed the kid, Paul."

"I'd say it makes it about a thousand times less likely."

Hardy looked around at the corners of his ceiling, then let out a breath and came back to Abe. "Well, shit. So whoever did kill Paul, I think we've got to believe that they went after Doug, too."

Glitsky picked up on Hardy's chain of thought. ". . . to keep Doug from saying something at his trial that would incriminate Paul's real killer."

"Right."

". . . who Wes has never really looked for because he always believed in his heart that it was Doug all along."

"Right again."

Glitsky nodded. "And don't forget that Homicide hasn't really looked for this new guy, either. Not yet anyway."

"You're thinking the same guy shot both Paul and Doug?"

"The easy answer," Glitsky said, "is yes, but . . ."

"You're frowning."

"That's because the one guy we know of with a good motive for killing Doug is James. Paul's own dad. I have a hard time getting myself to believe that he killed his only son. For whatever reason. And then tried to lay it on Doug. That's a heck of a reach."

"No," Hardy agreed. "That didn't happen."

"So . . ." Glitsky sat for a few seconds with his thoughts. "Where's that leave us?"

Hardy pondered for a moment, chewing at the side of his cheek. Then, brightening, he pulled himself back up to his desk, checked his watch, and favored Glitsky with a smile. "Mostly," he said, "it leaves us out of time and out of clients. So now there's an unsolved murder or two out there, but the good news is that they're not our problem anymore. We can just let them go. There's a lot of killers in the world, and when you come down to it we don't know most of them. I guess we'll just have to live with this guy and hope he doesn't wreak too much more havoc than he already has." Hardy checked his watch again. "And on that cheerful note," he said, motioning at the pile of paper on his desk, "the real world awaits."

"Easy for you to say."

"Reality," Hardy said. "Something to believe in. That ought to be one of Wes's T-shirts."

"Yeah," Glitsky said. "That would be a laugh riot."

Unlike Hardy, Farrell didn't have a backlog of billable hours that he had to catch up on. Nor did he have a gatekeeper/receptionist stationed outside his door to impede access. So less than a minute after leaving Hardy, Glitsky was knocking on Farrell's door on the third floor, and five minutes after that, after he'd admired Wes's T-shirt — *Where there's a will . . . there's a relative* — he'd brought him up to date on his visit with the medical examiner.

The news seemed to take a toll. Farrell's shoulders sagged into the couch; his jaw went slack. Letting out a labored breath, he brought his hand up and took a slow swipe at first one cheek, then the other. "Man," he said.

Glitsky nodded in agreement. "Yeah," he said.

"Just when you think you've got things figured out. In spite of all his denials, it honestly never occurred to me that Doug didn't kill Paul."

"And you think that this rules him out now on that score?"

"I'm sorely tempted to believe that." Farrell cocked his head. "You're not?"

"No. I agree with you. At least it ought to be among the presumptions moving ahead, that whoever killed Paul also killed Doug."

"Well, yes, if we were somehow involved in moving ahead. But, if I recall, we cut off that avenue of endeavor this morning."

"Sure, but that was before this new information about real evidence that I got straight from the mouth of Dr. Patel."

"So you're suggesting that we . . . what? There's no client here anymore, Abe. There's no nothing, really, except perhaps another murder victim."

With the scar through his lips top to bottom, the hooded brow and hawklike nose, Glitsky's bad-cop look was a formidable weapon, rumored to have coerced confessions from dozens of miscreants without him having to say a threatening word. Now, having trotted out that look for Wes, he came forward in his chair, elbows on his knees. When he spoke, it was with an exaggerated calm. "Diz just sang me the same song, but it's not singing for me."

"So what else is there?"

"Pay attention, because lest you forget, here's how the criminal justice system worked for Doug Rush." Abe drew a breath. "His only daughter is killed. The man who was convicted of murdering her — Paul Riley — gets out of prison early. When Paul winds up dead, Rush is first beaten by homicide cops, then arrested for killing Paul. Last, when he's out on bail, Doug himself is murdered."

"Okay. So . . . ?"

"So do you hear what I'm saying, Wes? At every turn, this poor guy, most probably just a law-abiding joe in all ways, the system has screwed him. Look what it's put him through, and now as his reward he's a stiff at the morgue while his killer is walking around on the streets. And you know what? I don't get the sense that anybody over in Homicide is going to be super motivated to find out who Doug's killer is — they're not going to want to revisit the botched and sloppy arrest, and besides, it was just one bad guy taking out another one. The circle's closed, right?" Glitsky paused. "Or it will be, if we just drop it where it lays."

Farrell's face had gone dark. With a bit of effort, he forced himself up from his spot on the couch and picked up one of the Nerf basketballs from the library table that held his working papers and folders. He pegged it at the basket protruding from one of his bookshelves, missing by a wide margin. His second shot went in. He sighed and came back to Glitsky. "The firm's still holding on to his hundred grand," Farrell said. "And, just in case you were wondering if the guilt hadn't kicked in sufficiently for me yet, don't kid yourself. If I'd believed him, I realize that I might have been able to change something."

"Like what?"

"I don't know. Maybe pushed Juhle over at Homicide a little more. Hell, who am I kidding? A lot more. To keep at least a couple of inspectors looking for whoever really killed Paul. Or talked Doug out of making bail so he wouldn't have been out on the street. But the real truth is that he could deny it all he wanted and I just flat didn't believe him."

"Yeah. I gathered that."

His shoulders sagging farther, Farrell met

Glitsky's gaze. "But that horse is out of the barn, Abe. What am I supposed to do now? Nothing's going to bring Doug back."

"I never said anything would."

"So?"

"So I guess I'm just venting. But Doug's just gotten such a raw deal on so many levels it's stuck in my craw."

"And you want to do something about it?"

"I think I do, yeah."

"And you're talking to me about this because . . . ?"

"Mostly because I'd just want somebody to know what I'm working on."

"In case something happens?"

"Maybe a little of that. Not to sound dramatic."

"No. God forbid. None of that."

The two of them double-teamed Phyllis and with an absolute minimum of fanfare found themselves in Hardy's office. As luck would have it, Gina with her secretary — Abe's wife, Treya — in tow had already breached the sacred gates for a meeting on other business, so it was a bit of a reprise of their earlier meeting in the Solarium: Hardy behind his big desk, Gina and Treya seated at either end of the clients' couch, Farrell and Glitsky standing and hovering.

"To what do we owe — ?" Hardy began.

But Farrell cut him off. "We won't take a minute of your precious time, Diz. Abe just needs to get his hands on the Rush file and then we're out of here. He thought you wouldn't give it to him unless I told you it was okay."

"And he's not all wrong. But just out of curiosity, can I ask what he's planning to do with it, with Mr. Rush dead and all?" He turned to Glitsky. "Has something changed in the last twenty minutes since we last talked about this?"

Glitsky made a face. "Apparently," he said. "Wes and I just got to talking about the raw deal Rush got . . ."

"Mostly," Farrell picked up the thread, "because I never really considered the possibility that he was actually innocent. And if I had, maybe he would still be alive."

"That might be a bit of a stretch," Hardy said.

"Maybe," Farrell said. "But it might also be a bit of the truth."

Gina joined in. "Even so, and I'm not saying it is so, what can we do about that now? Mr. Rush didn't kill himself because you didn't believe him, Wes."

"He didn't kill himself at all, Gina. Sorry to leave you behind the curve on that, but

Abe went and talked to Patel this morning and he's ruled that out. So somebody killed him."

"And you're proposing we investigate that?" Gina asked. "Why do we need to be involved? Just asking: What about the homicide detail?"

Glitsky answered. "I talked to Devin Juhle this morning, and I had the distinct feeling that they're not going to be too motivated. Mr. Rush's arrest was an embarrassment to the detail and they're going to want to put it behind them about as fast as they can. Bottom line is that nobody cares."

Treya finally found her voice. "Except you," she said.

Glitsky looked across to her and shrugged. "And Wes, too, I believe."

"True enough," Farrell said. "This guy was my client and to say I let him down is a major understatement. I should have seen this coming. Or something like it. But I didn't, and I feel like I owe him. Not that anybody in this room has to agree with me. But the more I talk about it, the more it seems like I ought to be doing something if I can. Putting Abe on it is at least a start."

"Okay, Wes," Hardy said, "I take your point. But you're right, this guy wasn't just your client. He was our client, the firm's client. The argument could be made that we've got a duty to him even if he's dead. Gina? What do you think?"

"That's how I see it, too. If Abe's going to do anything on this, we back him up. Financially, at least. Logistically if other stuff comes up."

Treya spoke up. "And on the home front, while we're at it."

Glitsky gave her a tight smile and a nod of appreciation. "There's my last hurdle," he said.

15

As a lifelong cop, Glitsky wasn't exactly an enthusiastic supporter of the Exoneration Initiative. Like many police officers, he remained deeply cynical about the organization's mission and tactics. After all, his job while on the force had been to apprehend murderers and establish their guilt beyond a reasonable doubt. The idea that the EI existed to undermine those efforts struck him as difficult to defend, although he admitted — in fact, it couldn't be denied — that attorneys, judges, and police made mistakes and worse on the prosecution side and sometimes sent the wrong people to jail. Glitsky believed that these errors, if proven, should be corrected, even when it meant releasing prisoners. Everyone had to play by the rule of law, and sometimes that rule demanded that exonerated prisoners be released.

But that still didn't mean that the prisoner

was factually innocent.

That said, Glitsky knew that there were at least five levels of appeal in every case. After a defendant has been found guilty, the case then goes to one of the California Courts of Appeal, where technical, procedural, and factual errors are addressed and adjudicated. If that appeal is denied — i.e., the conviction is upheld — the case then moves to the California Supreme Court, with the same issues ruled upon. If the defendant still does not prevail, the next steps are the US District Court, followed by the federal Courts of Appeals (the Circuit Courts), and finally the US Supreme Court. The cliché in law enforcement is that any convicted defendant is only "one idiot judge away from the street."

In essence, any conviction goes through six levels of review, if you include the jury finding in the initial trial. And after all that, the Exoneration Initiative might then step in to allege another issue of fact or law.

At some point, one might argue, it got a little ridiculous. Worth the exercise, undeniably, if it allowed a truly innocent person to go free; but one would think, and Glitsky did think, they could arrive at the factual truth a bit earlier in the process.

In spite of this, Glitsky would admit —

and he'd gotten into more than one heated debate on the subject — that the EI served an essential purpose in the cause of justice, especially in cases where there was something genuinely new, such as an advance in DNA science, that cast doubt on the earlier conviction. But usually all they offered was a rehash of what had been gone over before. And all too often, Glitsky thought, they would find a judge who, years later, simply disagreed with the conclusion of all the previous courts and tossed out the conviction. And by then, far too much time had passed for the case to be retried, and the defendant walked out loudly proclaiming his innocence from the front steps of the courthouse.

Nevertheless, the real world among those who practiced criminal justice tended to be tremendously, sometimes viciously, adversarial. And sometimes — no doubt — a conviction represented a real injustice, and it was important to review and correct those injustices.

Glitsky now sat at his desk in the Audiffred Building looking down through the fog at the Embarcadero, where the late-afternoon traffic had come to a stop; he was trying to gear himself up into talking to someone at the Exoneration Initiative, whose headquarters were down the Peninsula.

"This is Martin Dozier. How can I help you?"

"Mr. Dozier. My name is Abe Glitsky and I'm a private investigator up in San Francisco. I understand you worked on the Paul Riley case."

"That's correct. Terrible situation. That poor guy. What do you want to know?"

"Well, that's kind of an issue. I'm not exactly sure. I don't know if you've heard yet, but the man who'd been arrested for Paul's murder — Dana Rush's father, Doug — was shot to death a couple of days ago."

After a brief pause, Dozier said, "I hadn't heard that. Wasn't that trial about to get going pretty soon?"

"Yesterday. But Mr. Rush never showed up at the courtroom."

Another hesitation; when he spoke again, Dozier's tone had shifted and hardened. "Mr. . . . Glitsky, is it?"

"Glitsky. Yes, sir. Abe Glitsky."

"You wouldn't be related to the guy who used to run Homicide in the city?"

"That would be me. But it's been a while and I've gone private since then."

"And who did you say you were working for?"

"Wes Farrell."

"The DA?"

"Ex. But yeah, that's him. Although as I said, his client, Mr. Rush, is dead."

"So who is he representing?"

"That's still a little ambiguous. He'd only recently come around to the idea that Mr. Rush didn't kill Paul Riley and my feeling is that he still wants to prove that, even if there's not going to be a trial."

"Because he cares so much about justice?"

Glitsky had been expecting a gradual descent into overt hostility, so when it showed up as it did now, he was ready and didn't rise to the bait.

Instead, he waited, letting the question air out in silence until Dozier sighed and with a tone of resignation asked, "So what's he got you doing?"

"Well, one thing is we're treating Paul Riley's case as though it's open again. Mr. Farrell thinks, and I agree with him, that it's pretty likely that whoever killed Mr. Rush also shot Paul. So that means the motive we've been looking at for Mr. Rush isn't in play anymore."

"And what was that? That purported motive?"

"Paul getting out of prison unjustly."

"That's not what happened. What happened was he got put *into* prison unjustly and served eleven long years."

Glitsky took a beat. "I don't think we have to argue about that, sir. The point is that if Mr. Rush shot Paul, then that was why he did it. But if he didn't shoot him, then that wasn't why Paul got shot at all, so we're looking for a whole new motive, which is what I called to talk to you about. Nobody's trying to undo or undercut your work. I'd just like to have a conversation about Paul Riley."

Another hesitation, until finally Dozier said, "All right. What about him?"

"Well, did you or someone else out of your shop get a chance to interact with him in prison, maybe find out what kind of inmate he was?"

"And why would that be relevant?"

"It would be relevant if he was the kind of guy who made enemies in the population. Or got something cooking in the outside world — drugs, weapons, fencing something — while he was behind bars, but then got out and started messing around with that operation, with people who didn't appreciate the input."

"And you think something like that was

going on?"

"We don't know. We know that when he was shot, he had a lot of jewelry and cash in his apartment. Could be these were the fruits of a robbery. Also, they might be nothing. But it would be helpful to know what kind of guy he was. Did you have any sense of that?"

Dozier sighed into the telephone. His voice took on a weary tone, but the hostility was gone, mostly. "I don't think anybody here knew him too well. If there is one, that's the problem with our program. It's not like we get to know these guys as people. Ninety percent of what we do here is strictly on the legal and technical side. We're looking for arguments or evidence that somehow judges or juries missed in the appeals process. We usually don't get to go out and have lunch with our clients, find out if they're fun to hang with, or what else they're doing in their lives. Besides time. And most of them are bitter about that, as they should be. Although more bitter with the system, I would suppose, than with the other inmates."

"So what about the jewelry?"

"I don't know. Maybe, as you say, he stole it from some citizen. Nothing to do with jail or who he knew there." Another sigh. "One of the tragedies in this whole scenario — besides when our clients get out and get themselves killed in the first couple of months or even weeks — is that the state isn't always prompt at getting these guys their money, which can be pretty substantial, once it actually gets around to cutting the check. Paul was looking at a little over a half a million dollars, but I know he never saw any of that by the time he got shot."

"Half a million dollars?"

"Fifty K per year for every year served. Do the math."

"So he probably wasn't hard up for money."

"Well, depends on your perspective. He hadn't received any of it yet. So he might have been. It's a cash-flow world out there, and these guys don't necessarily have sophisticated skill sets for getting legitimate work once they get out. They usually need some gap money, and where do you think that's coming from?"

"I hear you."

"But didn't you say that this jewelry and cash was still with him when he got shot?"

"Yep."

"So whoever it was didn't shoot him, gather up the loot, and run."

"Right," Glitsky said. "And it wasn't like

he went to rob him and panicked after he shot him. Paul was killed execution-style when he opened the door." He shifted in his chair. "So let's talk about the half mil. If he had that coming, why was he stealing from people? If things got tight, he could borrow against that."

Dozier actually laughed. "Right. In your dreams. The banks are dying to make loans to unemployed ex-convicts. You could check it out."

Glitsky sat back. "Maybe not, huh?"

"No maybe about it," Dozier went on, "which is not to say that you're all wrong looking for different motives that might have developed in or out of prison. But as I said, nobody here really knew Paul at all as a person. That's just not what we do. He might have had a shrink there — I mean in prison — somebody he saw, who might have some ideas, but I think we're talking long shot. Real tough guys, especially young ones, don't go to shrinks and talk about their problems."

"Well, thanks for your time. If you think of something — anything at all — would you mind taking my number and getting back to me?"

"Not at all. And hey, Lieutenant —"

"I'm not a lieutenant anymore."

"Well, still. You don't mind my saying so, I'm impressed that you and Farrell are keeping the fire burning under this. I would expect you law enforcement guys to ignore the exoneration and just figure he was another dirtbag who got what was coming to him. When in fact, if you really look at the case, Paul got a raw deal."

"So did Dana's father. I just wonder if they're connected."

"What? The murders?"

"You never know about these things," Glitsky said. "People start getting killed and the world comes apart."

Dozier sighed one last time. "And on that cheery note . . ." He paused, perhaps changing his mind about what he originally wanted to say. "You were going to give me your number."

16

Julia Bedford, Doug Rush's downstairs neighbor on Green Street, had invited Glitsky into her apartment, and now that she'd delivered their respective teas, she plopped down on one of the living room's upholstered chairs just across from him. To Glitsky, everything about her demeanor seemed somehow more fragile than the confident and cheerful woman they'd interviewed only yesterday; following his instinct, he picked up his teacup, took a sip, and decided to run with it. "How are you holding up?"

She put down her own untouched teacup and met his eyes with a wan smile. "Last time I saw you, I didn't want to let myself think that it was possible he was dead. I thought that maybe he'd just gone out for the night somewhere, or even decided to run off or take a road trip, although of course he would have taken his bike and he hadn't, so that was unlikely. Still, anything but that he . . ." She stopped and blew out a sigh. "I'm sorry. This was so unexpected." Tears welled up and overflowed onto her cheeks and she wiped them away one side at a time. "I'm sorry," she said again.

"Were you two close?" he asked.

Gathering herself, she looked up at the ceiling, at the corners of the room. Trying a smile that didn't take, she nodded and said, "I guess you'd say we were intermittently intimate. He was a wonderful man. And so tortured by what had happened to his daughter, and to him. Having to deal with all of that over so much time. I can't believe he's just gone. That somebody could just shoot him. It doesn't make any sense. He was such a good guy. I mean, really."

"Did he have any enemies?"

"No."

"Just no?"

"Well, I mean, 'enemies' is a strong word. He had a real life, so he had people he probably disagreed with sometimes. But the only guy I ever heard him say anything truly bad about was Paul Riley. You could say he probably hated him."

"Do you think he shot him?"

She shook her head. "No. No chance."

"No chance? Why not? The police report

says he had a gun —"

"No. Well, I mean, yes he did, but that got stolen a long time ago when somebody broke into his place."

"I know that's what he said to the police. But really, what if he kept it? Until he needed it after Paul got out?"

She chewed on that thought for a second, then shook her head. "I see what you're saying, but in his heart he wasn't really any kind of a gun guy. You know, he and I talked about this when he first bought that gun. He actually told me that it was for when or if Paul Riley ever got out of prison. He was going to blow him away. We had some arguments about that, but then when Paul actually did get out, he told me he couldn't do it. He didn't have the gun anymore; he was just going to leave it all alone."

"So Doug no doubt hated Paul Riley and still you're sure he didn't kill him?"

"Right. Absolutely. After all these many years of believing Paul was guilty, and Doug read all the articles about his release — I mean like every single one — he finally got convinced that it could actually have been the other guy —"

"Deacon Moore."

"Yeah, I think that was it. That it had been this guy Deacon — who confessed and everything — and that maybe Paul hadn't killed Dana after all. Doug still believed that whoever did kill his daughter deserved to die, but he wasn't going to kill Paul when he wasn't a hundred percent certain it was him. He just wouldn't do that."

"All right."

"Not just 'all right.' And I mean, look, Paul Riley was out of prison for like four months before whoever it was shot him. Why would Doug have waited all that time? If he was going to kill him, why wouldn't he have done it right away? I'll tell you why — he got persuaded by all those articles that it wasn't Paul who'd killed Dana after all. And Doug wasn't going to shoot an innocent man." She picked up her teacup, then put it down untouched on the coffee table between them. "So am I sure Doug didn't kill him? I'm totally positive."

Glitsky, nodding, set his cup down. He knew it could easily have taken Rush four months to find out where Riley was living, then stalk him and make his plan, and eventually get up the nerve to carry it out. But he wasn't about to argue with this woman now. "I believe you," he said. "In fact, how did we get on that? I didn't come here thinking that Doug had shot Paul; I came here wanting to know if you have any suspicions about who shot Doug."

"Not really. Didn't the *Chronicle* say that they — the police, I mean — suspected it was some homeless guy in the park?"

"Yeah. Well, I hate to say it, but the police don't seem to be at the top of their game on this investigation. And why would Doug have been out there alone in the park in the middle of the night? Does that make any sense?"

"It doesn't really."

"I don't think it does, either. So it must have been someone he knew. And the problem is, I don't even know where to start. I thought you might have an idea or two."

"I can give it some thought. But right now I'm thinking not so much."

"Well, thank you. You've been a help."

"I hope so."

Treya and Abe were in their kitchen. A large pot of salted water boiled on the stove and the steam had humidified the small room and condensed on the kitchen windows just above the sink. Treya was stirring the clam spaghetti sauce when what Abe had told her rendered her all but apoplectic. She nearly spit out her wine before she could get out a word. "Fifty thousand dollars a year! You have got to be kidding me. You're talking about half a million dollars?"

"And then some, but basically that's the number. And a great deal at that, since it costs us good taxpayers seventy K a year if we want to keep him behind bars. So if we let him out, we're actually making a net of twenty grand a year, plus opening up another bed in the prison."

She gave her sauce another good stir, looked over at her husband. "Just what we need."

"Don't kid yourself. We do need every one of those beds. And then some."

"But Paul Riley never saw any of that money? The half million?"

"Nope. He got himself killed before they got around to writing him his first check."

"So what did he live on while he was waiting for the money to arrive?"

"He got a job with one of the Delancey Street restaurants. Possibly augmented with some breaking-and-entering income, which would explain the cash and jewels in his apartment."

"You're saying he went back to stealing?"

"Sure looks like, yeah."

"Why would he do that and risk going back to jail again, after he'd just gotten out?"

Glitsky clucked. "Maybe he didn't think the odds were very good he'd get caught, and I don't think he was all wrong."

"So he's exonerated for rape and murder but he's still a thief."

Glitsky shrugged. "Evidently it's a tough transition."

"You hear about a guy who's cleared by the Exoneration Initiative, you tend to think he's not guilty, don't you?"

"Maybe you tend to think that. I, on the other hand, being a cop down to my bone marrow, tend to think he's still more likely guilty than not. And that doesn't talk about anything else he might have done. Most of these guys had long records before their convictions, and they've been in prison, not visiting Lourdes. So the idea that Paul would get out and go back to breaking into people's houses doesn't startle me."

"And that's what Paul did?"

"Most probably."

"That sure takes away from the uplifting quality of his story."

Glitsky nodded. "Doesn't it, though?" he said.

Hoping he wasn't treading too heavily upon the good nature of a grieving Julia Bedford, Glitsky called her after his dinner at home and asked if he could come by again to take another look around Doug's flat. He wasn't sure exactly why he felt he should go there or what, if anything, he hoped to see, but he had no other leads and no better ideas, so when she said he was welcome, he told her he could be there in half an hour.

He and Hardy had given the apartment a perfunctory toss yesterday, but at that point they hadn't been certain that Doug had been murdered. This time, as he closed the door from the hallway, his plan was to be a lot more thorough.

Turning on all the lights in the place, he started in the bathroom, just to the left by the front door as he entered. There weren't any surprises behind the mirror in the medicine cabinet — Lipitor, Viagra, low-dose aspirin, Airborne, Robitussin, shaving stuff. A basket next to the toilet held a relatively large selection of reading material, including several back copies of magazines — *AARP, Costco Connection, Sports Illustrated, American Iron* (for his Harley-Davidson updates), and a somewhat anomalous *New Yorker.*

Doug's bed was still made as it had been when Glitsky was last there. The small closet in the bedroom was neat and well organized. Glitsky paused to realize that Doug owned two business suits and four Italian sport coats.

Where and when, he wondered, did he have occasion to wear them? He also had a dozen dress shirts and as many ties to go with them.

He'd have to ask Wes about what his client had done for a living. Glitsky had assumed that he was probably retired, but suddenly this no longer seemed a certainty; and if he had a community of coworkers or partners at his job, maybe someone there would have wanted him dead. A chest of drawers, sideways to the bed under the windows, held the rest of his clothes — T-shirts, underwear, sweaters, socks.

Slowing himself down at every opportunity, Glitsky next went to the living room, which was almost exactly the same size as the bedroom. Over by the large windows through which he could make out the spires of the Golden Gate Bridge, Doug kept his computer on his desk. Glitsky turned it on but didn't know the password to get him beyond the home page. Doug's wallpaper on the computer screen featured himself as a much younger man, smiling between, and with his arms around, a woman and a teenage girl — undoubtedly his wife and Dana.

Glitsky settled into the chair and stared at the picture. More questions for Wes came to the surface of his consciousness: Was the wife still alive? If so, what was her relationship with Doug? And if not, how had she died?

Shutting the computer down, he started in on the file drawers — three on either side of the desk. Again, Doug's penchant for organization was on display: all six of the side drawers were filled with files in alphabetical order. By far the thickest file had a tab that read *Exoneration Initiative.*

Glitsky was more than a little surprised to see that this file was in such good condition, with the EI articles from various sources carefully copied and easily accessed, especially since the police had searched this place right after Doug's arrest, and they usually made a mess that they did not bother to clean up. But then Glitsky realized that Doug had been out on bail for nearly a month, and he would have had plenty of time to put everything back in order.

Another quick glance around the living room — a couch, two wing chairs, three lamps, a coffee table, a cupboard/bookshelf with some plants on the top that separated this room from the kitchen, which was as neat and organized as the rest of the apartment.

Having come around again to the front door, he took a last look around, then retraced his steps. He realized that he hadn't really checked out the hall closet between the bathroom and the bedroom. Here he found a vacuum cleaner, linens and blankets on the side shelves, some bad-weather gear including a couple of umbrellas, three heavy leather jackets, and two helmets — one black and one orange — for when Doug took out his hog.

In short, nothing helpful to his investigation.

Glitsky stood with the closet door still open, hands on his hips. "Come on, Doug," he said aloud. "How about a little help here."

Waiting another ten seconds or so for lightning to strike, he let out a frustrated sigh, then reached out and closed the closet door. Crossing over to the main light switch hard by the front door, he stopped again, his head cocked to one side.

He didn't throw the off switch, but stood still for another beat or two, then stepped into the bathroom, over to the basket that held the magazines next to the toilet. The first one up was the *New Yorker* that had struck him as somewhat out of place on his earlier pass. He picked it up and saw that it was three weeks old — in other words, it couldn't have been here when the police had first searched the place. His pulse beginning to race, Abe opened the magazine to the table of contents, where the article entitled "The Exoneration Initiative: A Report Card" all but screamed out at him. He flipped to it.

1989: Year of first DNA exoneration
365: DNA exonerees to date
37: States where exonerations have been won
14: Average number of years served
5,065.5: Total number of years served
26.6: Average age at the time of wrongful conviction
43: Average age at exoneration
20 of 365: Exonerees who served time on death row
41 of 365: Those who pled guilty to crimes they did not commit
69%: Cases involving eyewitness misidentification
42%: Cases based on a cross-racial misidentification
44%: Cases involving misapplication of forensic science
28%: Cases involving false confessions
49%: Exonerees who were 21 years old or younger at the time of arrest
33%: Exonerees who were 18 years old

or younger at the time of arrest

10%: Exonerees with mental health issues

17%: Cases involving informants

264: Exonerees compensated

160: Actual assailants identified

Glitsky sat on the toilet seat. He understood that this was the way the Exoneration Initiative characterized the outcome of these cases. And he'd be willing to bet that they'd get a strong argument from some of the cops and prosecutors involved that these characterizations didn't accurately describe what had really happened in the cases at all. But even allowing for spin, the numbers were pretty impressive — out of 160 assailants identified, the true perpetrators went on to be convicted of 152 violent crimes, including 82 sexual assaults, 35 murders, and 35 others.

He wondered how this article might have affected Doug Rush's state of mind. Not that it could have altered his feelings for Paul Riley. But the ambiguity of all of this must have ripped at Doug's guts as, in fact, it did Abe's. He didn't like to contemplate the possibility — hell, admit it, *the fact* — that prosecutors, cops, and juries sometimes got it wrong. Therefore the actual perpetrators of these violent crimes had gotten away with them.

Sitting for another moment with the magazine now closed on his lap, he finally got up and walked back to the desk in the living room. Laying the *New Yorker* on the surface of the desk, he opened the drawer that held the EI file and took it out. He thumbed through it quickly, took another pass at it with the same result — for whatever reason, Doug hadn't copied this article. Maybe with Paul Riley dead, the whole question had become moot for him.

Glitsky pulled the magazine back to him again, opened it, closed it. It had a fantastic cover, as the *New Yorker* often did — this one a bird's-eye view of a baseball diamond, with all the players and umpires in some kind of motion. It looked generic enough, change of seasons and all that, but Glitsky couldn't make much sense of what was really going on in the drawing until he went to the table of contents and checked the title of the piece. It was "Double Play" by Mark Ulriksen, so with that hint Glitsky turned back to the cover and there it was, suddenly obvious: everybody was caught in the moment after the batter hit an infield grounder that had already nipped the runner going into second base, and the second baseman had just pivoted and thrown to first, where the ball clearly would arrive just in time to get the runner by a step. Everyone on the field — infielders and outfielders backing up the play, umpires on the run to make the call — was in his perfect position, caught in that exact moment.

Fantastic.

Glitsky was tempted to tear the cover off and bring it into work — people needed to see how cool this was. Or maybe he should bring the whole magazine, and they could talk about exoneration instead, and the complexities that sometimes seemed so mind-boggling.

But in the end, even though Doug Rush was dead, the magazine was his property and Glitsky couldn't bring himself to take it with him.

Casting it a last appreciative look, though, his eyes fell upon another anomaly, the address label stuck to the bottom corner of the cover: the magazine hadn't been mailed to Doug Rush at this address in San Francisco, but to someone named Bridget Forbes, at 1441 Avenue Portola, Miramar, CA.

Miramar was an unincorporated neighborhood about four miles north of Half Moon Bay, where Rush had spent the day Paul Riley was killed, just hanging out.

Or maybe not.

Part Three

17

On Friday morning at a little after nine o'clock, Glitsky was at the wheel of his Subaru. He and Farrell were leaving the city, driving south on Highway 1. The fog that perennially clung to the shoreline over the spring months was nowhere to be seen, and after Glitsky had checked in at Farrell's office, the two of them, with a helpful nudge from Treya, had more or less spontaneously decided to go out together on the road trip. There was every possibility, she had told them, that they might never again get such perfect weather. Wes had no clients scheduled, and Abe could just plain use some company on his errands down along the coast; what the heck were they waiting for?

So here the two of them were, Wes finishing his Java Chip, slurping at the dregs.

Glitsky glanced over at him. "I hope that tastes as good as it sounds."

Farrell gave it another slurp to be sure,

then nodded. "It's possibly the single best fast-food item on the planet. Although admittedly you have to have the whipped cream for the peak experience, and that does add roughly seven thousand calories, which are completely worth it. You've really never tried one of these Java Chip things? Not even once?"

Glitsky shook his head. "I'm not a coffee guy, Wes. I'm all about the tea. It's my Asian heritage showing up when I least expect it."

Farrell threw a skeptical glance across the seat. "Since when do you have any Asian heritage?"

"I've had it for a while. I just don't like to make too big a deal about it."

"But they have tea at the Starbucks we just stopped at and you didn't want any."

"Right. I'm trying to cut down on drinks in general."

"I'm not sure I believe you."

"What part is not to believe?"

"Pretty much all of it, but mostly the Asian heritage part."

Glitsky shrugged. "Suit yourself." After a pause, he added, "Treya, you know, is one-eighth or something like that Filipino."

"I hate to mention this, but you're not related to Treya."

"Of course I am. She's my wife."

"That's still not a blood relation, Abe. She could be all the way to a hundred percent Filipino and it doesn't make you any part of that."

"Really. When did that start? It seems unfair. But then again, so much of life is. Unfair, I mean."

"When not downright weird," Farrell said.

"Yeah. That too."

They were just arriving at Devil's Slide, once one of the most treacherous stretches of road in the state; but the tenuous thrill of driving along a narrow, two-lane cliff edge that might at any time collapse into the Pacific Ocean a few hundred feet down (as it had several times) had given way nearly a decade ago to two modern, well-engineered tunnels, one in each direction.

As they emerged from the south end of the tunnel, Glitsky said, "I'm sure it's safer and all that, but this road used to be a lot more fun."

"This just in," Farrell replied. "Everything used to be a lot more fun."

Glitsky didn't have any response to that, but after a mile or two in silence, he said, "So before we follow up with our barely possible clue down in Miramar, maybe you can tell me something about Doug Rush that might put things in a little bit of context?"

The rogue blast of negativity behind him, Farrell nodded with what seemed to be sincere enthusiasm. "Sure. What do you want to know?"

"Basically, everything that might matter. Somebody killed him, almost definitely for a personal reason. So what did he have going on in his life before he got arrested? Or something that changed since? But we can start with the fundamentals. Was he married?"

"Widowed. His wife — Cindy — had cancer. She died a little over a year before Dana was killed. When she died, Cindy I mean, Doug quit the day job — some office work with Parks and Rec in the city — to take care of Dana full-time. Cindy evidently had good life insurance."

"Okay. Then?"

"Then what? He and Dana tried to pull their lives together. Which didn't work out so well when she got killed. After that, he went a little crazy around Paul Riley's trial, even had to be restrained a couple of times in the courtroom, going after Paul and even Paul's dad in the gallery. If I remember right, the only reason he didn't get himself charged with assault and contempt is because the judge felt sorry for him. But he was a mess. Not that I blamed him. Who wouldn't be? Even so, if it wasn't for Nick Halsey pleading with the judge, he might have done some jail time himself for contempt." Farrell let out a sigh. "But when Paul got sent down, Doug more or less disappeared, at least until he got arrested. That's about all we know of his life. My heart went out to the guy. Still does, if you want to know the truth."

"And how'd he get hooked up with Halsey?"

"Nick was the guy who arrested Paul Riley. He was in Homicide back then, before he went over to Fraud. Anyway, no question he saw Doug as another victim of the same crime. Nick took him under his wing to help him get through the trial."

"Did he ever go back to work?" Glitsky asked.

"Doug? No. Not full-time anyway. As I said, he had a lot of insurance money. He had no apparent trouble with my retainer."

"Hmm."

"What?"

"Nothing," Glitsky said. "Just trying to get a handle on the guy."

"I've got one if you want to hear it."

"Sure."

"Wife dies. Daughter gets killed. He's done, dude. Who wouldn't be?"

Bridget Forbes lived a couple of blocks steeply uphill to the east of Highway 1. The house was a converted dark-brown bungalow surrounded by cypress with a few eucalyptus thrown in at the property line in the back. The unseasonable weather was holding up even here right on the coast, warm and sunny.

Glitsky had his window open. Avoiding the driveway that led down to Bridget's garage, he pulled into a spot at the side of the road across the street; there was no curb. The two men let themselves out and stood for a second looking down.

Farrell whispered, "Well, here we are."

Glitsky nodded. "Pretty secluded."

"It is." Farrell hesitated. "Do you want to remind me again why we didn't call first and make an appointment?"

"The element of surprise really can't be overestimated. Besides, it was a beautiful day for a drive."

"Okay, then."

Glitsky shrugged. "Let's go."

Bridget Forbes could have been keeping L.L.Bean in business. Either that, or she actually modeled the clothes she wore. God knows, she could have pulled it off in the boots and the matching light-green shorts and shirt. Close up, Glitsky put her age as early forties, although at first glance he would have guessed younger — her artfully disheveled blond hair cascaded halfway down her back. The tiny gap between her front teeth did not in any way diminish the general effect of a distractingly beautiful woman.

She kept up a brave, lovely, impassive face when Abe identified himself as a private investigator, but as soon as Farrell said his own name, her shoulders sagged and she blinked a few times before she said, "Sure. Doug's lawyer." She unlocked the chain link that held the front door. "I suppose you were bound to show up sometime. How'd you find out about me? In connection to Doug, I mean."

Glitsky glanced at Farrell and got a nod to go ahead. "Your name and address were on a magazine at Doug's apartment. It was the only lead I had, so we decided to come down here and see where it led."

She stood for a few seconds absorbing this information, then came back to them. "I'm sorry. Do you guys mind? Why don't we go in?" Backing up, she opened the door all the way and led them into a large living room furnished in maroon leather and dark woods. A redwood burl table squatted between two couches, and the entire back wall was glass with a view to the shaded backyard.

When they were seated, Abe asked, "So can I ask you, why did you think we were bound to show up sometime?"

"I guess because just as a general rule, it's impossible to keep secrets. They have a way of coming out."

Next to Abe, Farrell came forward, elbows on knees. "You and Doug had a secret then?"

After a moment, she nodded. "Well. Us. You know. When Doug was supposedly going out to kill Paul Riley. He couldn't have been there because he'd been here."

"You're saying you were his alibi?" Glitsky asked.

"Or would have been. But he couldn't say that either because . . . well, mostly because he didn't think he really needed it. They weren't going to convict him — he didn't think — on what they had, just one ID that was evidently pretty questionable. Plus, he always thought that even without the alibi, you" — she turned to Farrell — "you'd get him off because that's what you did, and

Doug really didn't do it. Even though he wasn't exactly unhappy when Paul was shot."

"What was the other reason?" Glitsky asked.

"The other reason what?"

"You said Doug couldn't say anything about the alibi *mostly* because he didn't need it at the trial — so there was also another reason he didn't want to mention the alibi thing."

"Really? I thought that was obvious. My husband. Theo? He's a pilot and he's gone a lot. There was no reason to feel like I had to tell him — Theo, I mean — about Doug. Or that he had to know at all. Although now I guess that's all going to come out in the wash."

"Not because of us," Farrell said. "We can keep secrets."

"But getting back to the alibi," Glitsky said, "you're saying that Doug was with you the whole day, or afternoon anyway, when Paul was killed?"

"Yes. I'm positive when it was because I know Theo was in France. But I couldn't even mention that to the police, or anybody else really —"

"No," Farrell said, "we understand that. You wanted to keep it from your husband.

And it doesn't make any difference now since there isn't going to be any trial for Doug. We don't have any reason to bring it up. And it doesn't have to go anywhere beyond the three of us."

"And where is Theo now?" Abe asked.

"Paris again."

"Do you know when he left?"

"Sure. Of course. Yesterday morning. But why do you need to know that?"

"Just more alibi stuff. This time about Theo, I'm afraid."

"What about him?

Glitsky drew a breath. "Do you have any reason to believe that he had found out about you and Doug?"

"No chance. I'm a hundred percent positive. He doesn't know. What are you getting at?"

"Just that if he knew and was jealous enough . . ."

"I can't imagine that he could have known about me and Doug, and even if he did find out somehow, he's not a violent guy. And Doug is one of his . . . I mean, he's a little older than Theo, but still, he's probably Theo's best friend. Are you actually implying that Theo might have shot him? Over me? That's just ridiculous, even if he did know about us, which he didn't."

Farrell broke a conciliatory smile. "Mr. Glitsky's not saying he did, ma'am. He's asking if he ought to be eliminated from the pool of Doug's possible assailants. Which is easily done, if you could just bear with us for a few more questions."

Bridget sighed heavily. "All right. All right. Go ahead."

"Well, first," Glitsky said. "Do you remember what he might have been doing, or both of you were doing, on Tuesday night?"

A sudden anger animating her face, she snapped, "Why do you need to know that? What was Tuesday night?"

"That's when Doug got shot."

"Tuesday?"

"Yes, ma'am."

Some of the starch seemed to go out of her shoulders. She directed a flat gaze at Farrell, brought it over to Abe. "Theo and I went to dinner down at the Inn. It's just walking distance across the road. Tuesday is date night when Theo's home and we almost always go there."

"The Inn?" Farrell asked.

She nodded. "The Miramar Beach Inn. It's right down from here, on the water."

"And both of you were there all night on Tuesday?"

Bridget hesitated again, this time for a

couple of beats. Glitsky wondered if she was about to fabricate something. Either that or throw them both out. In the end, she did neither.

"We were both there until about nine o'clock. That's when the music started. And that's when I left and came home. I've got tinnitus and can't handle that kind of noise. Or any kind, really. But Theo really likes these guys who play down there on Tuesdays, so he stayed."

"Until when?" Farrell asked in a gentle tone.

"I don't know exactly. I really don't. What does it matter? I know that I came home, watched some TV, and went to bed. Theo was there with me when I woke up in the morning."

"You didn't hear him come in?" Glitsky asked.

"Didn't I just say that? No, I didn't hear him come in. He probably stayed down there until the music stopped, which is usually one-ish, I gather. Though I'm not usually around for that. I don't know if you know, but pilots have to take their recreation — especially if they like to drink a little — where they can find it. There's a limited window. So I give him however much time he needs. Do you guys really think this is worth talking about?"

"It's worth trying to eliminate Theo as Doug's killer," Farrell said.

"He's not. I promise."

"Let me ask you one more," Glitsky said. "Does Theo own a gun?"

Her jaw dropped in apparent disbelief. "You guys really think Theo did it, don't you?"

Glitsky shook his head. "No, ma'am. I'd like nothing better than to rule him out. But right now we've got Theo maybe finding out that his best friend is having an affair with his wife, and we don't know where he was when Doug got shot. The natural next question is, did he, or does he, have a gun?"

Closing her eyes, she sighed again. "Guys," she said, "there's no way he's finding out that I'm cheating with his best friend. That did not happen. I would have known. He would have brought it home to me."

"All right," Farrell said. Then asked again: "Does he own a gun?"

She finally gave it up. "Two of them. One in the headboard by his side of the bed."

"And," Glitsky kept pressing, "is that one there now?"

"I don't know. I assume so. I haven't

looked. But really?"

Farrell nodded. "Really, if you wouldn't mind."

With yet another sigh and a huff, Bridget was on her feet, disappearing down a hallway. Farrell and Glitsky exchanged a silent glance and a couple of shrugs, and then she was back holding the gun on a T-shirt folded in her hand. "Okay, this is the one he always keeps back there. I don't know if he's ever fired it."

She held it out and Glitsky took it, checked that it wasn't loaded, smelled it, turned it around. Handing it back to Bridget, including Farrell with a look, he said, "Well, this is a Beretta twenty-two, and Doug was hit with a forty-caliber slug. And also, either Theo's cleaned this thing recently or it hasn't been fired in a while."

"But even if it had," Farrell said, "it sounds to me like this couldn't have been the gun that shot Doug."

"I told you," Bridget said.

"Yes, ma'am." Glitsky gave her a reassuring nod. "Yes, you did. And we hear you. So where is the second gun?"

Farrell closed his door by the passenger seat and let out a breath. "That," he said, "is one dangerous woman."

"I picked that up. It also looks like our friend Doug had a lot more going on in his personal life than I would have thought. And I'll tell you what . . ."

"What's that?"

Glitsky got the car rolling. "If I still worked with Homicide," he said, "I'd get a search warrant and come back here and tear the place apart. In fact, I've got half a mind to call Devin Juhle and give him a tip so he could do just that. Except that it's not his jurisdiction either and he probably wouldn't do it in any event."

"Looking for what, though?"

"Theo's other gun, for starters. Check out the caliber, if nothing else. And I'd want to check the database to see if he bought the second gun legally, and what kind of weapon it was."

"Yeah," Farrell said. "I noticed that you kind of let that one go."

"She said she didn't know where it was. I didn't want to push her. He's probably got some secret hiding place." Glitsky threw a glance across the seat. "And besides that, being a trained investigator I could tell that she was pretty much done cooperating with us. Anything else and I'm thinking she would have kicked us out and never let us in again. This way, maybe we can come back later when we've got some leverage. If that ever happens. Meanwhile, on the plus side, it was nice to get some actual corroboration about Doug's alibi. If he was with Bridget, he wasn't out shooting Paul."

"She gave that up easily, though, wouldn't you say? Her thing with Doug."

"I get the feeling it wasn't the first time she's run around on poor Theo."

"Not to sound like a shallow pig," Farrell said, "but I'm pretty sure I wouldn't mind so much if she ran around on me, too, if she was waiting for me when I got home."

"Didn't work," Glitsky said. "The shallow pig part."

"Don't tell Sam."

"I won't. But you'll owe me."

Ten minutes into the drive back to the city, Glitsky slapped the steering wheel. "Dang."

Farrell started in his seat. "What?"

"Talk about getting stuck in our sexist stereotypes, Wes. It just occurred to me that the jealous party, if that's who killed Doug, might not have been Theo at all. It could just as well have been your dangerous woman, Bridget. We never even asked her if she had her own gun, and she was only too ready to show us Theo's, which she knew was the wrong caliber."

"So who was she jealous of?"

"You're going to love this. How about Julia Bedford, with whom Doug was, in her exact phrase, 'intermittently intimate'? Maybe that just started recently and Doug was down here at Miramar with Bridget on the day Paul was killed, all right, but he was breaking up with her, or at least Bridget was finding out about his thing with Julia. So she — Bridget — she's not as cool with the idea of sharing her men as she lets on. So she lives for a month with the idea that Doug's been unfaithful to her and then finally decides on Tuesday that she can't live with it anymore, so she has an early dinner with Theo, leaves him with his music at the Miramar, then drives up to the city where she picks up Doug at his apartment and then they stop for a walk in the park, where she kills him. She's back home in Miramar by one o'clock. Which makes it a pretty darned good, if not perfect, crime."

Farrell chewed at his cheek for a moment. "Not saying it couldn't have happened that way," he said, "but —"

"Wait, listen. Did you see a sign that Bridget was in any kind of mourning about her boyfriend who, after all, just died three days ago?"

"You put it that way, no."

"Maybe she is more dangerous than you think, and you already thought she was pretty far along that road. That's all I'm saying."

Farrell sat in silence for a long moment to let that idea settle. Finally, he said, "I guess I'm having trouble getting my arms around the idea that this whole thing is really about some love affairs gone bad. And nothing to do with Paul Riley or Dana Rush or the Exoneration Initiative. While we're at that, whistling in the wind for a suspect, we might as well add Julia Bedford, for the same reasons as Bridget, more or less, right? Jealousy runs both ways, and maybe Julia's sad about Doug's death because she's just not as good an actress as Bridget. Or a better one. And what was she doing Tuesday night? Julia, I mean."

Glitsky looked over at Wes. "Or all of the above," he said.

18

Glitsky dropped Farrell off at his Sutter Street office at four fifteen, then drove north a few blocks and pulled into a parking lot on Bryant, across the street from the Hall of Justice. As he passed through the metal detector at the front door, for a disarming moment he almost felt that he was going back to his regular old job. As usual, he got a couple of familiar hellos and salutes from some of the police staff hanging out in the lobby who quite possibly thought that he still had an office upstairs. After all, he'd worked out of this building for the better part of the last forty years.

And he did keep showing up.

But he wasn't here to reminisce as he walked over to the elevators, his terrifying frown in place to discourage anyone who might be inclined to have some idle chitchat with him. It must have worked, because he continued unmolested to the fourth floor, then past the admin station outside the main entrance to the homicide detail, and finally to Juhle's door, which yawned open.

He knocked and entered at the same time.

Wearing his own "don't bother me" frown — maybe it came with the position — Juhle looked up and over from his desk. "Not a good time, Abe," he said. "I'm out of here in ten and all this needs to get done before the weekend."

Glitsky kept walking over to the folding chairs in front of Juhle's desk, where he turned one around and sat on it backward. "I won't take more than five. Promise."

"That's what they all say." With a show of reluctance, Juhle closed the folder he'd been perusing. "Isn't anybody guarding the gate out there?"

"Apparently not. Getting a jump on Friday night."

Juhle rolled his eyes. "All right. What?"

"I'm making some progress on Doug Rush and I thought you might be able to use a little heads-up on things."

Glitsky would have thought it was impossible, but Juhle's frown deepened. "What do you mean, you're working on Doug Rush? Under whose jurisdiction? And who's your client?"

"No client, except if you count Doug."

"Doug? Doug is dead, Abe." He brought his hands up, then down over his eyes, the picture of end-of-week fatigue. "Okay, then, I don't get it. What the hell are you doing?"

"Helping build a case."

"You got a suspect? Is that what you're saying?"

"No. But I've got leads I'm betting you won't catch up with."

"Jesus, Abe. I wouldn't think I'd need to tell you of all people that we're not out there soliciting civilians to help with our investigations."

"If civilians had information I didn't have, I'd take it in a hot second. And so would you, Dev. You know you would."

"Not if it's going to screw up our evidence."

"Right. Sure. You got any of that yet? Evidence, I mean. Anywhere on the planet."

"We just started out, Abe. I haven't even checked with my team yet. I don't have any idea where they are, but I guarantee they're on it."

"Who'd you hand it off to?"

"Jack and Jill. The A team, as you know. Stone pros."

"Agreed. And I promise you that they're not going to care where my information comes from."

"That may well be, but I care. I don't understand what you're doing around this. You don't have a client and you're undoubtedly stepping into our shit even if you don't know you're doing it."

"How about this: you put me on to Jack and Jill and let them decide if they want to talk to me."

"They're not going to like it."

"Then they'll boot me out of here, but at least my conscience will be clear."

Juhle folded his hands on the desk in front of him. His eyes met Glitsky's. "Abe. Give me a break, would you. You know how the bureaucracy works up here. I'm just over my own administrative hassles, barely exonerated, while two of my troops are still out for the mess they made of Mr. Rush's arrest. Put that together with Rush not showing up in court, then winding up dead, and the general clusterfuck that this investigation has been all along just goes on and on. If I pull Jack and Jill off what they're doing right now, it's another arrow in Lapeer's quiver to shoot me down. Maybe for good next time. She's going to notice that here's yet another moment where I'm not doing things by the book."

"I'm not saying pull them off what they're doing. I'm saying let me talk to them."

Glitsky understood exactly what Juhle was saying, but he didn't really care — the lieutenant's trouble with the chief and other higher-ups came with the territory. If he couldn't handle the heat, he needed to get out of the kitchen. Meanwhile, Glitsky went on, "If they follow my leads and it gets them to a suspect, all will be forgiven, even by Lapeer. You know that. Rather than leaving you with a failure on a case that's been all over the news. You tell me what's better?"

Juhle hesitated, pursed his lips, finally shook his head. "Shit."

"There you go," Glitsky said.

"Keep it short."

"Will do."

Royce and Gomez — Jack and Jill — shared none of Juhle's reluctance to talk to Glitsky. After all, Glitsky had been visible at the Doug Rush murder scene as at least a person of authority; he had actually identified the body; he was on speaking terms with the CSI sergeant, Lennard Faro, and known to several of the other officers. And, of course, they could not be unaware that he had once been not only a homicide inspector but the head of the department. Besides that, no one had warned them off talking to him, and he apparently had made some relevant discoveries of his own that he was more than willing to share.

The two inspectors were at their face-to-face desks catching up on paperwork near the front windows in the wide-open bullpen room that housed the detail. It wasn't much of a hardship listening to the former assistant chief of inspectors. When Glitsky finished, Gomez asked, "So what about the murder of Paul Riley? How does that fit in?"

"Maybe not at all."

Sharing a skeptical glance with his partner, Jack Royce said, "You're saying he's no part of this Paul Riley thing?"

"No. I'm saying Doug Rush had other stuff going on. Personal stuff. And, P.S., we finally got pretty rock-solid corroboration on his alibi for the time Paul was getting himself killed. So he really didn't do that, in spite of getting himself arrested for it."

"Wait a minute. Wait," Royce said. "So you're saying he didn't in fact kill Paul?"

"Right. Way unlikely."

"Then who did?"

"No idea. I suggest that you talk to Devin about that sometime soon. Get out from under it. Like it or not, my man Rush is the case you're on now, and I'm betting that looking at Paul Riley isn't going to get you anywhere. Not with Doug anyway."

Royce looked over to his partner, then back to Glitsky. "Jeez."

"I hear you," Abe said. "And I'm sorry. Is that all you have up till now? Doug and Paul Riley?"

Gomez nodded through her chagrin. "But no wonder the evidence is so light. We've apparently been on the wrong track from the git-go here."

"Well, the good news," Glitsky said, "is it's still early in the game. And this stuff I've got at least leads back to Doug. He was definitely having affairs with both of these women, one of them married and the other a threat to the first one. Anyway, rich hunting grounds. If you can get yourself a couple of warrants, maybe a forty-caliber gun, do some interviews, you'll be off and running. Rather than barking up the Paul Riley tree."

"Thank you, sir," Royce said. "This might be worthwhile."

"Let's hope so." Glitsky hesitated for a beat. "Meanwhile, let me ask you something. Have you guys had any luck with transportation options — taxis, Ubers, Lyfts — picking up or dropping off at Rush's place on Green Street? Have you even had a chance to look?"

The two inspectors shared a glance, and Gomez said, "We've served the warrants and expect to hear back anytime now."

"Anything on Rush's phone?"

"Same story. They're getting back to us."

This, Glitsky knew, meant that in all likelihood they wouldn't have any useful information from those sources, if at all, until at least the upcoming Monday.

No wonder, he thought, that Juhle didn't want him to talk to this team. Since they'd been investigating Rush's murder, they didn't appear to have made much, if any, progress. And, as Glitsky had suspected from the beginning, no one seemed to be pushing them with any sense of urgency. This case was simply going to disappear if he or somebody else didn't keep the heat on under it. "I don't mean to crash your parade," he said, "but would you mind letting me know if you get a hit on any of those searches? And also, his girlfriends."

"We'd be glad to," Royce said. "But if you don't mind, what's your particular interest in this case?"

Gomez added, "Not that we don't appreciate all you've done so far, but you've got to admit it's a little out of the ordinary."

"It is, I know. It's just one of those times something gets under your skin. Rush was a client of one of the firms I work for and we're certain he didn't kill Paul Riley. If nothing else, the powers that be there would like to see if they could help clear his name. And if that brings his killer to justice while we're at it, so much the better."

"And how'd Jack and Jill take that?" Hardy asked.

Glitsky had swung by Hardy's house on his way home and now the two men were taking advantage of the rare warm night with lawn chairs on Hardy's back porch, just outside his kitchen door — Diz with his gin and Abe with his usual iced tea. The sky above was still bright blue, and in front of them, dozens of windows in the west-facing buildings sparkled in a glorious light show, reflecting the sun as it started to go down behind them.

Abe nodded. "They probably weren't exactly thrilled to hear that I was going to be sniffing around what really is their territory. But what are they going to do? I'd just brought them the best leads they'd seen so far. They spit in that bowl at their own peril."

Hardy sat back in his chair. "And you really think this was about jealousy?"

"It's as good a bet as any, and better than most. And if the warrants don't turn up somebody coming to Doug's address on

Tuesday night, that means somebody he knew came by to pick him up in their own car."

Hardy shrugged. "It might mean that."

Glitsky gave him a querulous look. "Don't be so negative. Here I drop by to share with you my brilliant detective work, all based on a bona fide clue on a magazine cover, of all things. I thought you'd be a little more enthusiastic, if not to say celebratory."

Hardy chuckled. "I'd break out the champagne, except I know you don't drink. Meanwhile, since it's not in your nature to wait for anything, what's your next move? I thought you'd eliminated any connection to Paul."

"Not definitely. Not any connection. Just the most obvious one."

"Which is?"

"James Riley — Paul's dad — as Doug's killer."

"And how did you get all the way to definite on that one?"

Glitsky settled back, crossing his legs. "Look at what James would have to pull off Tuesday night to get away with killing Doug. He wouldn't have risked a phone call, setting up an appointment. Doug wasn't a fool and that could only have meant one thing. That leaves James simply coming by Doug's apartment uninvited in the middle of the night. He rings the doorbell, same thing. Doug sees who it is and he doesn't open the door."

"Getting a little farfetched here."

"Okay, but just for fun, let's even go one step further: say James somehow gets inside the front door downstairs, then, even more unbelievably, gets Doug to open his apartment door, where James gets him at gunpoint and says, 'Come with me. We've got to talk.' "

Hardy came forward in his chair and shook his head. "That couldn't have happened."

Glitsky agreed. "Correct. Not in a million years. And that even leaves out how they could have driven together — James at the wheel of his car all the while he's holding his gun on Doug — until they get out to the park, fifteen minutes away. And then they take a walk like two old buddies? Which they are not." Glitsky shook his head. "Anyway, that's how I get to James not being Doug's shooter. Logistically, it just couldn't have gone down like that or any variation thereof."

"I love it when you sound like a lawyer," Hardy said, " 'or any variation thereof.' "

Glitsky tipped up his glass. He chewed

some ice, then said, "So I've eliminated James for good. And Jack and Jill ought to get to the bottom of Doug's love life in the next day or two, certainly by Monday."

"So you're done," Hardy said. "Congratulations again. Take the weekend off. Last chance for champagne."

"I would, but I'm still not drinking. And," more seriously now, "somehow, even if we get a hit on the girlfriends and/or the husband and one of them did kill Doug, it still doesn't feel like I'm even close to the bottom of this thing. And if the girls turn out to be a dead end after all . . ."

Hardy said, "I know the feeling. You get somebody off at trial and then you find out he actually did it."

"Right. And no matter what we get on Doug, we're still left with Paul shot dead, aren't we? Can it really be that Doug gets charged with Paul's murder and then he gets shot the day before his trial? We don't believe in coincidences, right?"

"Nope."

"But they happen."

"I've heard the rumors," Hardy said, "but I remain unconvinced."

Glitsky chewed his last piece of ice and put his glass down on the chair's armrest. "You had a list of questions from the file, didn't you? Relationships that Paul had in prison or at work that might have gone bad?"

"Not an actual list. I just jotted some notes. And before you get all excited about what you might find, let me remind you that it's likely none of these folks with a personal grudge against Paul Riley, if any of them even exist, are going to know Doug Rush. And even if you find somebody who had every reason in the world to kill Paul, nothing to do with the Exoneration Initiative stuff or prison or his life since he got out, you're still stuck with the same problem."

"Which is?"

"Which is trying to figure out how the murders of these two guys are connected. And if we write off coincidence, which we should, that's about the only game we're left playing."

"So essentially," Glitsky said, "you're saying that I'm where I started."

"Pretty much exactly." Hardy finished his own drink and nodded. "But here's a little bit of motivational karma floating out here in the ether."

"What's that?"

"If it is one guy and you get close, he'll probably try to kill you, too."

19

Jill Gomez called Glitsky at home first thing Saturday morning — seven thirty, to be exact — to inform him that they'd struck out on their search warrant requests in both San Francisco County and down the Peninsula in San Mateo County, where the community of Miramar was located. Two different judges in the two jurisdictions had refused to sign off on the warrants for lack of probable cause.

It probably didn't help, Glitsky realized, that Jack and Jill, in their haste to get things finally moving on their investigation, had themselves not yet so much as interviewed either of Doug Rush's lovers. They didn't, in fact, know if either of them owned a registered gun of the same caliber as the one that had killed Doug. The inspectors had not spoken to any witnesses who had seen either woman, or the pilot/husband Theo for that matter, with Doug in Golden

Gate Park or anywhere else on the night he was shot. In short, the search warrants were a pure fishing expedition. There was no evidence of any kind that would justify a judge's signature.

Gomez told Abe that she and her partner would set up interviews with all the principals in the next week and reapply for the warrants. But even that, Glitsky realized, might continue to be a hard sell. He was starting to understand that if this thing was going to get solved, it was going to be up to him.

"That didn't sound like your happiest phone call ever," Treya said as she came into the kitchen from their bedroom.

Abe, seated at their small round kitchen table, said, "Nope."

"It must have been important to call you this early."

A shrug.

"Want to tell me about it?"

"It's just some more of this Doug Rush nonsense." He gave her the short version of the Gomez conversation, concluding with ". . . but when they finally get to the girlfriends, it's probably not going to lead to anything anyway."

"But yesterday . . . ?"

"I know. Now I'm not sure at all."

"What's changed?"

"Talking with Diz last night. The improbability of the murders of Doug and Paul being unrelated."

"So what about your jealousy idea?"

"That could still, possibly, be part of it. Maybe. But how's it connect to Paul? I keep going back and forth. They have to be related. They can't be related. It's making me a nutcase."

He had his fists clasped on the table in front of him, and she reached out and put a hand over his. "It'll come to you," she said.

Glitsky spent the rest of his morning and early afternoon on the soccer pitch across from Crissy Field with his thirteen-year-old son, Zachary. Glitsky himself was not a fan of soccer, far preferring good old American football, but Zack had suffered a serious brain injury when he was three and Abe and Treya didn't want to risk another concussion or worse for their athletic son who, helmet or not, played hard and ran fast.

So soccer it was.

At two fifteen, having atypically called and made an appointment in advance, Glitsky was finally back in the private investigator business, flashing his license and introducing himself to Raymond Henry, who was behind the bar at the Lily Pad in Hayes Valley, where Paul Riley had worked after he'd gotten out of prison.

Mr. Henry's shift was just about over. He seemed to be about sixty years old, a little over six feet tall, maybe two hundred pounds, and clean-shaven with a full head of well-trimmed gray hair. It did not escape Glitsky's notice that in most of his all-important physical aspects, he could have easily been in one of the six-pack photos from which James Riley had twice picked out Doug Rush.

The restaurant itself — spacious and well-lit with large front windows and brick side walls — was vaguely industrial Japanese, with lots of raw and purportedly fresh fish among other items on display behind the counter at the bar. Most of the lunch crowd had cleared by the time Abe arrived, although perhaps a dozen uniformed staff were still in evidence, bustling everywhere, wiping down tables, resetting places, washing dishes, perhaps prepping a little early for the dinner shift.

After carefully inspecting Glitsky's ID, Henry flashed him a perfunctory smile and reached out his hand to shake over the bar. "Good to meet you," he said. "You mind if we go sit at one of the tables? My dogs are killing me here with all this standing around."

"No problem."

"Can I get you something? Water, tea, a beer?"

Abe waved it off. "Thanks, I'm good."

Henry shrugged, went down to the end of the bar, and came around to one of the newly wiped, though still not set, tables, where Glitsky joined him and sat.

"So what can I do for you?" Henry began.

"Well, first let me say that this is a heck of a nice place. I've never eaten here but I'm putting it on my list."

"Thanks. That'd be good. This town, it's hard to keep up with a new place opening every couple of days. A challenge, I tell you. But then again, that's the restaurant biz in general. You better be good and stay good and then get better. But hey, it's never dull."

"No. I can see that." Glitsky shot him his own imitation of a smile. "But as to what I'm here about, I have a few questions I'd like to ask you about Paul Riley."

Henry's friendly smile flickered and he shook his head. "Um," he said, almost as though he'd been punched. "Paul Riley."

"Not your favorite guy?"

"Not to speak ill of the dead, but him getting killed, it's not the worst thing that could have happened. But hell, might as well speak ill of the ones that deserve it."

"That's a pretty strong call."

Henry made a face of distaste. "He earned it."

"How's that?"

Henry looked around as though he suspected somebody might be eavesdropping. "You know who runs this place, don't you?"

"I thought you did."

"Yeah, well, I'm the manager, but we're run by Delancey. We're kind of a halfway house, or maybe three-quarters. Everybody you see in here," he said, throwing his hand up to include the whole room, "we've all done time. Hard time. Prison time."

"Even you?"

He nodded soberly. "Two strikes and twelve years at Avenal — burglary and attempted murder."

"Paul Riley was at Avenal, too."

"Yeah, I know. He started long after I got out, though. I've been out seventeen years." His own eyes a glacial blue, Henry met Glitsky's gaze. "I hope you're not trying to put me together with something he might have done. If you are, this talk is over."

"I'm not trying to put you together with anything. I'm only here about Paul Riley.

From your reaction, I gather he was some kind of a problem."

"Every kind of problem is more like it."

"You want to tell me some of the other kinds of problem he was? All the stories have him as this kind of folk hero, finally exonerated after a wrongful conviction and all those years behind bars. I'm gathering that's not the whole picture."

Pursing his lips, Henry looked like he was trying to decide about saying anything at all, and for a moment Glitsky thought he might have lost him.

Then he recovered. "I guess that's fair enough, that it's not the whole picture."

"So what's left out?"

Henry sat back and crossed his arms over his chest. Letting out a breath, he said, "Look, what you got to understand is that we've got a real short leash here, I mean *here* here, the restaurant. We don't get a second chance if we screw something up. That's just the way it is. People are always surprised they can even get a decent meal here, much less a pretty damn good one. But if any part of the service or cooking or attitude — anything — is unprofessional, then people say, 'Yeah, I saw that coming.' I mean, what else are you expecting from a bunch of ex-convicts? It's just a matter of time before any one of us goes back down for something. You can't change how people are, can you?" Henry sighed again. "Anyway, sorry, but like that. That's just the reality here, working with Delancey, trying our damnedest to keep it together. Every one of us. Every day, all day. The vigilance . . . if you want to call it that, it never ends."

"And Paul Riley threatened that?" Glitsky asked.

Henry nodded. "Man could have set us back a decade, or put us out of business forever. Smart and wily. He's only here a couple of weeks and he figures out a tip scam on credit cards that he tries to sell my waiters for a cut, like it's crack, but my peeps here, they're not buying, at least not at first . . . you good with this? Is this what you had in mind?"

"Go on."

"Okay, but first I got to tell you the main thing, which is the whole Exoneration Initiative situation with him."

Glitsky felt the pulse in his ear kick up a notch. "What about it?"

"Well, like I told you, everybody working here has done their time. When they get out, the smart ones come to someplace like Delancey and try to get straight and stay straight. It's not a ton of money, but it's regular, it's a salary — something many if not most of my peeps, they've never had before. But the main thing is . . . how do you call it, how we all get along together?"

"The culture?"

"There you go, the culture. They buy into the culture, which is you work hard, do your job whatever it might be, show up on time and clean — I mean physically clean — don't be high or drunk, and cooperate. But maybe most of all, we try to give everybody a chance to put their history behind them and be good citizens again. It's not always an easy road, and somebody like Paul Riley coming on board, with his status from prison sticking to him like white on rice, it's like poison in the well.

"Half the staff in here thought he was that folk hero you were talking about. You didn't have to follow our stupid rules, not when you could squeak by and cheat on the customer just a little, 'cause who's going to make a stink about an extra buck or two that somehow gets on the bill? That's what you expect, right? Cons ripping you off 'cause that's what they do, and it's only a matter of time before they're back in the slammer anyway.

"And that's not even talking about what

he did outside the shop here, which wasn't any kind of secret either. Better money and less hours with B&E. And what kind of sap wants to be a galley slave in here when there's a lot more easy pickins out in the real world?"

"Couldn't you just let him go? Fire him."

This brought a sardonic chuckle. "Are you kidding me? That boy was the absolute poster child for what we're all about, or want to be about. I mean, look at him, just out of I don't know how many years in prison and still, no hard feelings. He comes aboard here and he's living proof about how the system works. I hope I'm not painting too bad a picture, but I don't see how I could. The boy was nothing but trouble. You want my opinion, somebody did the world a favor putting a bullet in his head."

Glitsky shifted uncomfortably in his seat. "Let me ask you something, sir."

"Ray. Please. And sure. Whatever."

"All right, Ray. How'd they let a guy like that get out of jail?"

"What do you mean? The Exoneration Initiative got on his case and found a way to toss his conviction."

"Yeah, I get that. But if he was such a bad-ass — he must have been that way in prison 'cause, as you say, that's who he was. You'd think somebody would have noticed and passed the word back."

"Who cares? Certainly not the EI guys. They were only interested in the big crime media prize — exoneration on the rape and murder. They don't care what he's like as a human being or what else he did. I promise. They want to get him off on the high-profile stuff because that's their agenda and that's the story that plays and brings in the big donations. Whatever he actually did or didn't do isn't the point. All I can tell you is that he was that way when he got here, from day one. What's your question? How'd they let him go?"

"I guess that's it. Yeah."

Ray Henry looked up to one corner of the ceiling, then to another one. When he came back to Glitsky, he broke another small, somewhat apologetic smile. "They got him out because somebody else confessed to what Paul had been convicted on. That guy, the other guy — damn, I used to know his name . . ."

Glitsky remembered. "Deacon Moore," he said.

"Yeah, that's him. Deacon Moore. Not the sharpest tool in the work shed, I understand. But once he admitted that it was probably him who'd killed Paul Riley's victim —"

"Probably? Why are we in the realm of probably here? We ought to be talking definite, right? Deacon either did it or he didn't. And because he did, Riley got exonerated."

"Yeah, well, the EI people had Deacon going down for the same crime with Riley's victim and another victim anyway, so what's the big deal?"

Glitsky paused. "Forgive me, Ray, but you sound a little cynical yourself about whether the confession — Deacon's confession — was righteous. About whether Deacon really did it."

"Do I? Hmm. Well, Deacon confessed, so he must have, right? Even if he's barely competent to stand trial. Twice. And even if the Exoneration Initiative told him that in return for his confession, they'd represent Deacon Moore on all his cases and try and get him out on some kind of a mental health thing. So why wouldn't he confess?"

Glitsky leaned in and lowered his voice. "You're telling me that you think . . ."

"That Paul Riley was factually guilty as hell. Yep. But they got him released, the EI folks, which is a big 'W' for the home team. And that's all that matters. I wish I'd never seen the son of a bitch. Either that or that they'd spent the time and money and energy getting somebody out who was actually innocent, not just because of some bullshit scam. Seems like there's enough people rotting in jail who really didn't do what they got them in for. That's who these exoneration people ought to be working for. The truly innocent. And believe me, there's plenty of them. Unfortunately, not including fucking Paul Riley."

Glitsky sat back in his chair and let the silence build for a moment. "Can I ask you one more?"

"Of course. Let's have it."

"To your knowledge, does anybody working here own a gun?"

The question seemed to knock Henry back in his chair; when he came forward, he was almost laughing. "Are you kidding me?" he asked. "We're all of us, every one, convicted felons. We get anywhere near a gun and we're back in the joint before we know what hit us. Even in San Francisco."

20

"But, of course, what else is he going to say, Abe? 'Sure. Guns? We've got an arsenal of fifty guns back behind the kitchen. You want to come check them out?' " Treya's chortling resonated through the car's speaker system. "I just don't think that's happening."

"I don't know. I tended to want to believe him, though, especially the gun question."

"That's funny. It sounds to me like he wasn't Paul Riley's biggest fan by a long shot. If he did have a gun, from what you've been telling me, he might have been sorely tempted to use it on Paul and then just throw it away like I've heard some people do. But you're the cop . . ."

"Not anymore."

"Okay, but close enough. I'm going to concede that your instinct is probably right. He's a good guy who wouldn't go near a gun."

"Thank you."

"You're welcome, but I also have one last tiny little question."

"I should have guessed. Hit me."

"When they had Paul's death on the news and in the paper, did any of those reports give out the information that he was killed by a shot in the head?"

On this call with his wife, Glitsky was sitting at a red light on Masonic Avenue, and now suddenly her question laid claim to all of his attention to the extent that he didn't accelerate again when it turned green. Not until the car behind him slammed on its horn.

"Abe?"

"I'm here. No worries. Except it's lucky I'm not carrying a gun right now for this driver behind me to experience." He hesitated for another second or two. "But as to your question about Paul and the head shot, I'm sure some of the stories about his death must have had it. Because if they didn't, you want to know how Mr. Henry knew about that detail, don't you?"

"That thought crossed my mind, that's all. And with my husband out there on his own time looking for suspects and motives and all that stuff, I wouldn't be a team player if I let something I see get by you."

"Like the head shot. No, I get it. Team players are good and it's definitely something to check out. If I'm missing out on anything else, you have my permission to let me know. Except I have to tell you that these kinds of things — somebody you know getting murdered, for example — the details find a way to get out to, as we say, interested parties. Like Mr. Henry."

"Right. I can see that."

"But really, Trey, if you get any more ideas, I'd be happy to take them. I just liked Henry as a guy. I mean, everybody's a suspect until they're not and I don't want to write him off too soon, but there's nothing on him and not liking Paul Riley isn't much of a motive for murder."

"Well, before you cross him off the list, there's one other really last thing."

"You said that last time."

"This is really it, though. You've been trying to find some connection between Doug Rush and Paul Riley, right? Well, if Mr. Henry did in fact shoot Paul, then there's your connection."

"How do we get that?"

"Because even if Wes doesn't get Doug off, that trial's going to convince a lot of people that Doug didn't kill Paul. And if that's true, you know what that means."

"His killer — Paul's killer — is still at large."

"Correct," Treya said. "Which means he's still in jeopardy. But if he murders Doug before the trial . . ."

"Then the heat's off whoever it is. Nobody's looking for him anymore and the case just goes away."

"That's it. And don't forget. Nobody looks real hard for Doug's killer anymore either. It's a random shooting in the park at night. No known or even suspected motive."

"Low priority at best," Glitsky said.

"Right," Treya said. "Except for this one guy I've got a crush on. It's gotten into his head, and he's going to want to keep looking. In fact, he's looking right now."

Abe took a beat. "Not to worry," he said. "I get anything even remotely serious, I take it immediately to Jack and Jill and let them run with it. As, please note, I have done already on no more than a hunch that doesn't look like it's going anywhere."

"Note taken. I'm just saying —"

"I hear you. I am taking no unnecessary risks. Promise."

" 'Unnecessary' can easily be misinterpreted. Don't kid a kidder, Abe. You're still running a risk."

"Well, getting out of bed every morning is

a risk. Driving while talking on your phone is a risk, not to even mention texting."

"While we're at it, driving by itself is a risk."

"But often necessary, one must admit. The bottom line is that I think I'm the only one on the inside track here and I'd hate to lose my advantage."

"I understand that. Really. I just sometimes feel like I want to remind you to be careful."

"I'll consider myself reminded."

In spite of his protestations to his wife, Glitsky didn't really worry too much about the level of care he needed to cultivate as he went about his business. Having been a homicide cop for over twenty years, he'd investigated somewhere in the neighborhood of two hundred murders and in all that time had experienced only one close call with a suspect.

True, it was a bad close call — a bullet to his midsection that nearly resulted in his death — but he figured that this was his limit. It was sort of like people who survived plane crashes. It was pretty unlikely that they'd be in another one.

And in fact, he didn't know another cop who'd been shot in the line of duty more than once; since he'd checked that box already, he felt that he was much safer than many of his colleagues when he was out in the field.

He'd barely disconnected his phone call with Treya when one of those unexpected epiphanies that happened in almost every investigation made him pull over to the side of the road. With Jack and Jill's strikeouts on the Doug Rush romantic front and then the interesting but not particularly probative interview he'd had with Raymond Henry, he didn't have even a small hint of what he should pursue next.

There was no apparent trail.

This was either about the Exoneration Initiative or not, about Doug's love life or not. Neither was more likely at first glance than the other.

But then, suddenly and really out of nowhere, he remembered the substance if not the exact wording of a random comment by Martin Dozier, the semi-hostile EI attorney he'd spoken to earlier in the week.

Still sitting at the curb, he looked up Dozier on his phone and punched him up, only to get his voicemail — of course, it was Saturday afternoon. The man probably had a life. Glitsky left a message and pulled out again into the traffic on Masonic. But he hadn't driven two blocks before his phone chirped, and Dozier's name came up on his screen.

"Mr. Dozier. Thanks for getting back to me."

"Sure. What can I do for you?"

"This might be a little obscure, but when we talked last time, you said something that didn't strike me as particularly significant, but now it's kind of whupped me upside the head. You talked about your clients who got exonerated and released from prison and then, maybe within a few months of getting out, they got themselves killed somehow."

"Yeah. That's one of the tragedies we deal with from time to time. Suicide, overdose, continued criminal activity. It just seems to happen a lot."

"Do you know how many people this has happened to?" Glitsky asked.

"Not really. It's all pretty much anecdotal. A guy gets out, and a few months or a year later, you hear another one of these stories."

"And you said they got themselves killed. I think that's what you said, the words you used. So would these have been violent deaths? Do you have any statistics on what we're talking about here?"

"Well, certainly, not off the top of my

head," Dozier said. "It's not like an epidemic. As I said, it's more a grapevine type of thing, you hear about some guy shot in Illinois and then maybe a suicide in New York — I'd guess there'd be a pretty good number of suicides. Their compensation money doesn't show up, or they just can't adjust to living outside . . ."

"Do you have any idea of how many of these people there are in total?"

"I don't really know. I don't even know how I'd go about finding out, since all of us EI people are pretty much state by state. I know we've had Paul Riley, but he's the only one from California that I'm aware of. What are you getting at, if you don't mind my asking?"

"I don't really know. I just keep running up against these killings — Paul Riley and now my ex-client Doug Rush — in the context of the Exoneration Initiative. I don't have any hard evidence I can point at, but I thought there might be some pattern — some missing piece — that nobody was looking at."

"If there is, I'm afraid I don't know what it might be." Glitsky waited out the silence as Dozier paused. "You know," he said at last, "after you called me last time, I went back and reviewed the Paul Riley file."

Another silence. Glitsky didn't want to push. If Dozier had something to say to him, he'd find a way to get it out.

"You still there?" Dozier asked.

"Yes, sir."

"You know, we tend to get a little bit myopic when we get wrapped up in these cases. I mean, we're looking at procedural error or problems with the forensic evidence, someplace where we can go to a judge and point where clearly justice wasn't done, where the prosecution or the cops — no offense — overstepped or overcharged. Pushed ahead where they should have pulled back, or looked at some new evidence, like in the Riley case."

"Deacon Moore's confession," Glitsky said.

Dozier hesitated again. "I was probably going to call you in the next week or two. I had to decide whether I was going to trust you first. I've already made a couple of calls up to the city. You got a pretty good rep up there, you know that?"

"That's nice to hear."

"Yeah, well, I'm not all too sure that this needs to go beyond just you and me. I certainly don't want to call Paul Riley's exoneration bogus in any way. Innocent or not, his original defense attorney screwed up the trial in a big way by not taking a harder look at the DNA. Riley definitely at least deserved another trial.

"But let me just say that Deacon Moore's confession — the guy is lucky if his IQ gets all the way up to room temperature. If we — I mean the EI — were defending Moore against the charge that he killed Dana Rush, I think we could poke serious holes in the reliability of that confession. Any competent interviewer could have gotten him to admit to assassinating Kennedy. In fact, we'd sure as shit argue that even finding Mr. Moore competent to stand trial was a hell of a stretch."

"So what are you saying? That Riley did do it after all? Kill Dana, I mean."

"This is where I've got to trust you, Lieutenant. I don't have any idea. Deacon Moore isn't going to change his statement. He's already doing life and nobody is ever going to bother to try him for killing Dana. It would be a waste of time. But just between me and you, I'd have to say that I can't rule out that Paul Riley was factually guilty of killing Dana after all.

"Maybe Paul Riley got to Moore somehow," Dozier continued. "Called in a favor, or put some money on his book. Maybe one of our investigators told him the EI would try to help him out on all his cases if he confessed to Dana's killing. I don't know that any of that happened. I just know that Moore's so-called confession doesn't convince me of anything."

Grinding to a stop, Dozier then added, "I'll deny that I said any of this until the day I die. The EI does a shitload of good work. The system is rigged against the poor and the dark-skinned. They're disproportionally arrested and tried, and juries are stacked against them, so when we get our hands on a case like Paul Riley . . ."

"I hear you," Glitsky said. "Sometimes the cops and prosecutors don't follow the rules, and that's enough to get somebody out, even if he did it."

"Not just that, though," Dozier went on. "Most of the time, our exonerated clients actually and factually just plain didn't do it. We're all about proving that. But once in a while, I suppose we get it wrong, too. 'Cause that's what people do. They get things wrong."

"And you're saying that your people might have gotten it wrong with Paul Riley?"

Another wait while Dozier came up with how he'd phrase it. "I'm afraid I can't rule it out," he said. "And it just makes me sick."

■ ■ ■ ■

Charged up by Martin Dozier's revelations, Glitsky wasn't quite ready to call it a day and go home. He still wanted to explore the idea — although he didn't know what if anything it might mean — that other exonerated people might have "gotten themselves killed" within months of getting out of jail.

So fifteen minutes after the call to Dozier ended, he parked at the Ferry Building lot and walked in the still balmy late afternoon up to his office in the Audiffred Building. Glitsky couldn't help musing how much the '89 earthquake had transformed the neighborhood. The whole Embarcadero had been a gray and gloomy semi-slum tucked under the elevated freeway. When they tore the freeway down after the quake, it had become a beautiful, light and airy pedestrian bayside thoroughfare.

Fighting the crowd at Boulevard downstairs, he made it to the elevator and then up to his office and his cubicle with its gazillion-dollar view of the bay, the bridge, and Treasure Island.

At his desk, he logged in and started poking around on Google. Finding the relevant database took him far less time than he'd expected — the list of exonerated EI clients popped up immediately. Newly surprising, although he realized that he'd seen it before in the *New Yorker* article, was the fact that there had been just under four hundred people cleared by the Exoneration Initiative since its founding in 1989. Somewhere in the back of his mind he clung to the idea that the number was closer to ten times that — certainly, the EI had a profile high enough that it seemed to justify those higher numbers.

Still, nearly four hundred was a daunting number of people if he planned to follow up on any significant percentage of them. And there was no indication anywhere of what had happened to these people after they'd been let out of prison.

It was going to be a long slog, and to what end he didn't even know.

He slumped back in the chair in front of his computer, hands crossed behind his neck, half-staring again at the view.

Wondering what the heck he was doing there.

21

Monday morning, and the fog was back in.

Abe, Treya, and Wes were in Farrell's office, surrounded by the usual games and toys. Wes had just revealed to them today's T-shirt: *You can't make everybody happy. You're not an avocado.*

Glitsky gave it all the acknowledgment it deserved — a sardonic smile that ticked one corner of his mouth up a millimeter.

Treya couldn't even spare that much energy for it. "Good one," she said with an absolutely straight face. "No. Really. Funny. Very funny."

Wes gave her a mock frown. "That second 'funny' sounded a bit sarcastic, Trey. Almost to the point of cruelty."

"She can be way cruel," Glitsky said, then added helpfully, "but she breaks just like a little girl."

Treya cracked an unmistakable, albeit cold, smile. "You guys keep this up and I'll show you some breakage, I promise."

"Okay, we'll leave it," Wes said, finishing the buttoning of his white business shirt. "But I still love the shirt."

"That's what makes this country great," Treya said. "You can wear any dang shirt you want, even if your administrative aide doesn't agree with you."

"First Amendment, freedom of speech," Glitsky said with a nod. "Guaranteed right to free expression."

"Yikes," Farrell said. "You guys might want to take your act on the road."

"We've still got kids at home," Glitsky said. "They'd never let us go."

Treya nodded. "Abe's probably right," she said.

"Well, that'd be a nice change of pace." Glitsky sighed. "I haven't been right most of this past weekend, working the Doug Rush thing, where all roads lead to nowhere."

From his spot on the leather couch, Farrell picked up and shot one of the Nerf balls at the basket over by the bookshelves. Much to everyone's surprise, it went in. "There's a sign," he said. "Things are starting to turn around."

"Let's hope," Glitsky said. "I'm kind of out of ideas."

"What angle have you been working on?"

"Pardon the interruption, but on that note," Treya said, "I'm going to go check in downstairs with Gina. If you need me for anything, you know where I'll be."

After she'd left the office and closed the door behind her, Abe said, "I think she's getting a little tired of Doug Rush, and I can't really say I blame her."

"You do some work over the weekend?"

Glitsky shrugged. "Ten or fifteen hours. Or so."

"So call it twenty?"

"Close."

"That's a long weekend."

"There were a lot of exonerees to look at. Still are."

"And what, exactly, are you hoping to find?"

"That's the tough part. I'm not clear on that." Sitting back, Glitsky spun Wes his idea that some of the EI exonerees might have gotten themselves prematurely killed after they got out of prison.

"And what would that mean? In terms of Paul Riley?"

"I don't know. It's just a rock that's unturned."

"And how about Doug Rush?"

"I know." Glitsky shook his head with real

chagrin. "I'm not sure it would mean anything. And that doesn't much matter either, since in my twenty precious hours over the weekend, I've checked off about two hundred EI clients and haven't identified even one of these guys who might have been killed."

"And why again are you looking for them? What do you hope to prove when or if you do find them?"

"I don't know," Glitsky said. "I know — waste of time."

"Have you had any luck with Jack and Jill?"

"No."

"Nothing?"

Glitsky shook his head. "They couldn't get a judge to sign a warrant here in the city or down in San Mateo. They say they'll be trying again this week after they interview Doug's girlfriends, but I'm not holding my breath."

"How about Doug's other friends?"

"What other friends?"

"I don't know. Guy friends?"

Glitsky went still. "Guy friends," he repeated. "At least that's somewhere I haven't looked. Did he have any guy friends that you know of?"

"None off the top of —" Farrell stopped.

"Well, I don't know how friendly they were in real life day-to-day, but when Doug first got arrested, only about a month ago, his one phone call was to Nick Halsey. I didn't get the impression they'd seen a lot of each other lately, but during Riley's trial they were tight. I mean, that was long ago, so who knows? But if Halsey didn't hang with Doug, maybe he knows somebody who did. For whatever that's worth."

As he waited, freezing, in the line to enter the Hall of Justice, Glitsky was starting to feel a bit like he was actually working as a police inspector again. This was his third visit to the Hall in the past week. This time, instead of heading up to the fourth floor and Homicide, he hung a right after he cleared the metal detector, then turned left and walked down the long hallway to the Fraud offices. He'd called from Farrell's office, so Nick Halsey was waiting for him, had even procured one of the interview rooms so they could speak privately.

The two men had been in Homicide together years ago, but they'd never worked with each other or really interacted much before Nick had been booted out of the unit and transferred to Fraud in the wake of a scandal: one of his cases had been overturned on appeal when a court decided that Nick had coerced a confession and tampered with evidence. Several witnesses who'd identified his defendant at trial had later testified that Halsey told them what to say and even threatened reprisals if they wouldn't go along.

Abe remembered that there had been a week of dramatic and highly publicized testimony. Nick and several other officers denied the accusations of intimidation and pointed out that the statements were on videotape. But the eyewitnesses all insisted the intimidation had taken place off camera. In the end, the judge — perhaps with an eye on his pending reelection campaign — had ruled against the police and overturned the conviction.

The department had stood behind Halsey, but everybody knew he was through with Homicide. In every case he did after that, the defense would throw this judge's finding in his face. And so Nick got moved to Fraud.

Glitsky himself had never had any problem with Halsey. In the limited time he'd known him, he'd always seemed a straight-ahead homicide cop trying to do his job. It was Glitsky's personal opinion that Halsey had been screwed by the system, a victim of an overpublicized case and a weak judge. Even as they were shaking hands, saying hello, making some cop small talk, Glitsky was glad to see he had landed on his feet.

He was good-looking, still trim if weathered. The strong, handsome Nordic face housed a set of piercing blue eyes, but in spite of his friendly greeting to Glitsky today — he even, over Glitsky's pro forma objection, tried to flatter Abe by calling him "Chief," his highest former position — the eyes somehow did not convey warmth or real welcome.

But Glitsky wasn't there to judge the man. He'd clearly carved out a place for himself with SFPD, and like him intuitively or not, Abe would cut him all the slack and respect he needed as a fellow cop with a long history of service and everything that entailed.

After they'd gotten comfortable on either side of the small interview table, Glitsky got right down to it, thanking him for making the time to talk on such short notice.

Halsey had perfect white teeth, and he took the moment to show them off. "Hey, if it's about Doug Rush and the son of a bitch who killed him, you can have all the time you need, anytime you need it."

"I appreciate that. I gather you knew him pretty well."

"Well, lately, maybe not so much. But back in the day, during the trial and for a while later — a good while later, actually — we . . . yeah, I think I knew him pretty well. He was a hell of a good guy and his life was a mess. So he could use a friend, beyond dealing with all the bullshit around the trial. You know about his wife and then his daughter?"

"I do. Terrible stuff."

"Yeah."

"But I don't know much about what went on during the trial, which I gather was when you guys hooked up."

"He needed somebody he could let it out around. He couldn't handle sitting there every day while they piled the lies on what a good citizen Paul Riley was. Yeah, a good citizen with a couple of break-ins and assaults and a juvie record a mile long. None of which was admissible, of course. And you know, why should Doug have to deal with that? A couple of times, okay, he lost it in the courtroom, which wasn't going to get him anywhere with a jury, so I kind of got next to him and tried to keep him restrained. Mostly successfully, I have to say. He was just hurting, and no place to let out the frustration and the pain. Victims, you know. They get such a raw deal."

"Sounds like you helped him get through it."

"I hope so. It never seems like enough, with anybody who goes through what he did. Well, you know. You're a cop. You've seen it, maybe by now more often than I have."

"Did Doug think they weren't going to convict? Was that it?"

"That's always it. Right from the first, until the jury finally came back with the guilty verdict. It was my case, you know, and as solid as it gets. And still, up till the last second, we're thinking he — Paul — is going to walk." He ran a hand through his full head of white hair. "Jesus. And then, all these years later, they go back and let the fucker out anyhow."

"You're talking Paul Riley now."

"Yeah, him. Or any of those Exoneration Initiative people. Exonorees, they call 'em, like it's a badge of pride. So can you blame him?"

"Who's that?"

"Doug. For taking care of that business with Paul Riley once and for all."

"You're saying you think he did kill Paul?"

"Absolutely. Why wouldn't he? If I were him, I might have done it myself." This retelling of the Paul Riley trial was clearly getting inside Halsey's head. He pushed again at his hairline, wiped his forehead, put a palm flat on the table in front of him. "I know," he said, "I shouldn't let this stuff get to me so much." Letting out a long breath, he went on, "You know, I hadn't been in Homicide for a long time. Even so, when I heard about Riley getting out, it really got to me. It was the perfect case, evidence through the roof, and then it all went up in smoke and he got what they call exonerated."

Halsey took a moment, then sighed again in resignation. "You know, my mother was killed on a B&E" — breaking and entering — "when I was fourteen. They never caught the guy." He looked into Glitsky's eyes across the table. "I don't know why I'm telling you this. But whatever Doug Rush did around Paul Riley, that kid was guilty as hell and he got what he deserved."

Glitsky kept his peace for a long moment. At last he said, "The medical examiner tells me that Doug didn't kill himself. So that's the homicide I'm investigating. Whoever killed Doug."

"All right, if you say so. And hey, sorry about the walk down memory lane. But this stuff never goes away."

"I hear you. You might be better off out of

Homicide. It's only gotten worse."

"Okay, so take two. How can I help you?"

"I'm wondering if Doug Rush had friends, people he hung with, maybe somebody who had a reason to kill him, nothing necessarily to do with Paul Riley."

"I can't say that I spent much time with him around other people. We'd just usually go out someplace and get toasted, but probably not in the past six or eight years. Other than that, he had his biker friends, I suppose, but I didn't ever meet any of them personally."

"He had a couple of girlfriends."

"A couple? Well, good for him. Doesn't surprise me, but I don't know them. Did you check his phone, or his computer? Search his apartment?"

Glitsky nodded. "This is where not being a real cop anymore has its drawbacks. Homicide will get there when they do, with warrants if they can get them signed, but in the meanwhile, I'm cooling my jets."

"Always a good time."

"Isn't it, though?"

Glitsky remembered from his search of Doug's apartment that he had a leather jacket in the closet with the initials YBMC across the back, which had to stand for the

Yerba Buena Motorcycle Club. So half an hour after he left Nick Halsey's office, he pulled up and into a miraculous parking spot directly across Folsom from the bikers' storefront home.

He checked his watch. It was a few minutes before eleven and the sun was beginning to battle with the fog — since this was the Mission District, the sun would win in the short term. Four motorcycles were pulled up at the curb in front of the entrance across the street. In spite of the weather, a gray-haired couple in heavy leather sat at one of the six sidewalk metal-mesh tables, drinking out of coffee mugs.

Glitsky got out of his car and crossed over, nodded at the couple, and walked inside. The place was fairly well-lit from the large windows that faced the street. Three guys who could have been identical triplets sat around one of the six interior tables, close by the door.

A young guy with a luxuriant beard — Raymond Earll Shine, by the name patch on his shirt — was wiping the bar, and Glitsky held up his PI license (next to his phony badge), and said hello. He introduced himself and said he was hoping to talk to some of Doug Rush's friends, if they were around and/or available, or if Doug had had any.

"Sure," Raymond said. "Everybody knew Doug. It's a damn shame what happened to him. It's, like, hard to believe that somebody actually shot him. I mean, he got along with everybody. He was a pretty mellow dude."

"Some people think it had something to do with the guy who'd allegedly killed his daughter getting out of prison."

"That would have been Doug, then, doing the shooting, wouldn't it? Not somebody shooting him."

"Yeah. That's where my investigation is slowing down. It's possible that there's no connection at all between the one and the other."

Raymond snorted a little laugh. "Ha! If you believe that one . . ."

Glitsky shook his head. "Not saying I believe it. Or don't. I'm just wondering if there was something in Doug's life that was going south as well. Maybe if he was in some kind of trouble that one of your members here might know something about."

"Well, he was going on trial for murdering that guy, wasn't he?"

"Yes, he was."

"Well, I'd call that trouble."

From behind him, Glitsky heard the scraping of a chair. Half-turning, he found himself facing one of the triplets and the other two were up and falling in behind. All of them were about Glitsky's height and maybe a third again his weight. In a different context, they might have been intimidation incarnate, but for the moment, they were hanging back out of Glitsky's personal space, apparently wanting to be cooperative.

"How you doing?" the first of them asked, then extended his hand, which Glitsky took. "I'm Jon Dunleavy. I was a friend of Doug's. Hell, we're all friends of Doug's. Or were. If the city lets the body go, we're hoping to bury him on Friday next to his wife and daughter. Otherwise, Monday. But either way, we're the closest thing to next of kin that he's got. So what are you asking about?"

"I'm just trying to get a sense, maybe the same as all of you, of why somebody would have wanted to kill him. Everybody seems to have liked him."

"Except maybe somebody in the family of that kid he killed. Revenge for that."

"For him killing Paul Riley, you mean. Maybe. But I don't believe Doug killed Paul."

All four men surrounding him shared a

knowing smile. Jon said, “I guess you’re going to believe what you want.”

“You think he did? Kill Paul?”

“The short answer is yep, no doubt. He talked about it all the time. The kid deserved it. Nobody ever said he didn’t actually kill Doug’s daughter.”

“Well, let me ask you this: When he was out on bail, this last month before he got shot, did he talk about it? Killing Paul?”

“No.” He looked around. “Guys?”

Everybody shook their heads.

“There you go,” Jon said. “But what’s he gonna do? He’s going to trial. He’s not stupid. He’s not going to be telling snitches who can testify that he’s been bragging about it. Anybody asks, he just says he didn’t do it. Even if he did plan it out here for all the world to hear.”

“He did that?”

“Let’s just say he talked about it before Riley got killed. And then after it happened, it was just like his story was that somebody else must have beat him to it.”

“And who would that have been?”

“I don’t know. Santa Claus? One of the elves?”

Glitsky took in the group. “So none of you ever heard him confess afterward? Maybe in the last month?”

Head shakes all around. "Never, not close," Jon said. "But that's what you'd expect."

Outside on the street, another motorcycle pulled up to the curb and another old white guy dismounted. Somewhat to his surprise, Glitsky realized that with the exception of Raymond behind the bar, each of the men he'd been talking to looked enough like Doug Rush to confuse James Riley about his identification.

What if one of these big, tough guys had gone after Paul Riley to avenge the death of Dana Rush for their motorcycle brother?

The new guy came through the door, noted the knot of men gathered by the bar, and stopped in his tracks. "Everything cool?" he asked.

"All good," Raymond said. "Just talking about Doug Rush."

"That poor fucker," the guy said. "You still pouring coffee?"

The new arrival introduced himself to Glitsky as Jerome Walker, and he had evidently been a better friend to Doug Rush than any of the other three. Raymond served coffee to all the men (and tea for Glitsky), and now all of them were gathered in chairs around another table.

Glitsky started out on Jerome. "You said

that Doug talked all the time about how he was planning to kill Paul Riley."

"Yeah," Jerome said, while the others nodded.

"What took him so long?"

"What do you mean?" Jerome asked.

"Well, Paul got out of prison in December and he didn't get shot until much later. What took Doug so long to get around to it? Once he found out that Paul was being released, what was he waiting for?"

"I know that one," Jerome said. "He wanted to be sure. He wasn't going to kill the guy if he really was innocent, like I mean really didn't do it, period, end of story. He didn't want to have any doubt at all, reasonable or otherwise."

Jon inserted himself back into the discussion. "He had, like, a whole library of articles about the case. He wanted to make sure he got it right."

"I've seen them," Glitsky said. "Those articles."

"Well, Doug told me that they finally convinced him," Jon went on. "He told me he just couldn't get to absolute certainty, and so he finally decided to let it all go — it just wasn't going to be worth it." He lowered his voice a notch. "Of course, there's always the possibility that this was his story and he was stickin' to it. That way if the cops came and asked us about it, we could truthfully say that we believed he didn't do it, or at least that's how he'd left it with us."

"But you still think he did it? Killed Paul?"

Jerome let out a sigh. "We can't ever know for sure, I don't think. All I can tell you is that if it was me, all of the above notwithstanding, I would have blown him away."

22

So far today, Glitsky had talked to two friends of Doug's — Nick Halsey and Motorcycle Jerome — who both believed that Paul had raped and killed Dana Rush, and that if it had been them, they would have taken out Paul Riley themselves. They'd used almost the same exact words.

Saturday, he'd talked to Martin Dozier, who, much to his own consternation and against his professional self-interest, had become very nearly if not absolutely convinced that Paul and not Deacon Moore had killed Dana.

It was getting on to lunchtime, and maybe it was all the tea he'd consumed, but Glitsky had no appetite. He didn't much feel like going into his office either. So without really planning to, he found himself on the freeway heading south, with no destination in mind — although he was subliminally not unaware that should he continue, he would in an hour or so reach the city of Santa Clara, which was the Northern California home of the Exoneration Initiative.

By the time he passed the airport about twenty minutes into his drive, he'd realized that he was wasting a lot of time on the question of Paul Riley's ultimate guilt. Now he felt that there was some kind of unanimity on that question: Paul had in all likelihood killed Dana.

Period, end of story, as the bikers might have said.

Likewise, Glitsky realized that in spite of Doug Rush's arrest and the opinions of his friends in the YBMC, he hadn't killed Paul. He had, to Glitsky's mind, a perfect alibi, spending his day — the day of Paul's murder — with the beautiful Bridget Forbes down in Miramar.

By the time he'd made Belmont, about halfway down the Peninsula, he had become nearly desperate to draw any conclusions from all of his investigating. Most critically, he still was unsure about whether the deaths of Paul and Doug were related. It seemed impossible that they wouldn't be, yet he had no evidence tying the two together. The only glimmer of light in that scenario was that assuming the same person had killed Paul and Doug led to the only theory of the two deaths that worked for Abe — for some unknown reason, Paul Riley had been killed by X, who at first was happy to let Doug be arrested for that crime, but later realized that the trial would probably somehow incriminate him as a murderer, so X had to kill Doug as well, to shut him up, and to get it done before the trial.

Labored though this interpretation of events might be, it was the only one that made any sense; though it left open and unresolved the motive for killing Paul, it also supplied a critical insight into Doug's death: he must have known X well enough to feel comfortable walking with whoever it was through the Shakespeare Garden in the middle of the night.

In fact, regardless of whether or not X was the same person who had killed Paul, he simply must have been a friend of Doug's. But let's pretend, Glitsky thought, that he had killed Paul as well. At least then he had a coherent narrative.

At last, Glitsky took the Santa Clara exit, found the address on his GPS, pulled into the adjacent lot to park, and walked into the offices of the Exoneration Initiative.

Not surprisingly, Martin Dozier wasn't exactly enthusiastic in his welcome of the uninvited ex–homicide inspector. And he certainly wasn't going to have him come back to his office where his colleagues might pick up a sense of what Glitsky was there about. So after a muted greeting, Dozier pretended for the receptionist's benefit that Abe was his expected lunch companion and suggested that they go out to a Mexican place around the corner and grab a bite. Glitsky said that sounded good and waited while Dozier went back into the offices, returning a minute later with his briefcase.

In person, Dozier was a short, pasty, heavyset man with a deeply lugubrious expression that did not vary much from minute to minute. A thick white brush of a mustache claimed pride of place over his mouth. He wore his completely gray hair in what Glitsky thought was a frankly anachronistic Prince Valiant bowl haircut that covered the tops of his ears. He couldn't have been much over forty years old.

They hadn't made it to the nearest corner when Dozier asked, "Something big going on?"

"What do you mean?"

"I mean you and me, we've been getting along fine on the telephone for the past few days, and now you're here in person. Makes me think somebody's turned up the gas."

They walked a few steps before Glitsky

said, "I wish I could say that you're right, because then I could tell you what it was and you could point out where I was wrong. Or right. It almost wouldn't matter which. But the real answer is, I wasn't getting anywhere interviewing people in the city so I thought I'd get out of Dodge and let the brain go on autopilot for a while. I'm sure it's trying to tell me something, but whatever it is, it's not making it easy."

"Sure, because what would be the fun in that?"

The two men stepped off the curb, crossed with the light. When they hit the other sidewalk, Dozier said, "Well, your autopilot got you down here after all. Maybe it picked up something the last time we talked."

"I'm listening."

Dozier chuckled. "This may be pure coincidence, but I had pretty much decided that I was going to call you this afternoon."

"I like the sound of that."

"You might like it better after lunch."

They fell into the end of a line of perhaps a dozen people, standing out on the sidewalk in front of Julio's. "This is a great place," Dozier said. "Everything's good, but the burritos are the best in town, totally worth the wait. Go with the *carnitas.* But watch out for the super-hot hot sauce. It can take your skin right off."

"Not my skin," Glitsky said.

"All right, but that's what they all say. Consider yourself forewarned."

"I appreciate it." They moved up a couple of steps. "But you were saying something about calling me this afternoon?"

"I was."

"Where did that come from? What changed your mind?"

Dozier ran his right hand down over his mustache. "I'm not going to lie to you, Lieutenant. That talk we had over the weekend shook me up. The idea that we spent all that time and energy to get Paul Riley out of prison, when in all likelihood he was factually guilty of murder — it's my worst nightmare. We don't want to get people off who did it. That's not what the EI is about at all. You can scoff at the idea if you want, but the mission is really about justice."

"I'm not scoffing, but welcome to the prosecution side. Believe it or not, in theory we're about justice, too. Not just numbers."

"That's not exactly been my experience with you guys."

"I could say the same thing about your guys, too, but we're getting along so well, maybe we want to leave that for now and have a debate later."

"I can do that."

"Good call. Let's."

They got to the window and both men ordered the *carnitas* burritos with the super-hot hot sauce. They got a warning from the young woman taking their orders — *muy picante.* She didn't change their minds. Glitsky took a further walk on the wild side by ordering not iced tea, but a quart bottle of lemonade. A sidewalk table underneath a green and yellow umbrella opened up as they stood looking for a spot.

"It's our lucky day," Dozier said. "I'll grab the table, you get some sauces and chips." He pointed to the condiment shelf on the far side of the window. "It's all good."

"Got it."

In a minute, they were both seated and digging in. "So what do you have," Glitsky asked, "that you were going to call me today and not make me wait until next week?"

Dozier chewed, swallowed, swigged at his Coke, then blew out against the blast of spice. "Well, after we got off the phone Saturday, I don't know why it got inside my head, same way apparently that it got into yours, but I started thinking about your original question: How many of our exonerees got themselves killed within a year or so

— maybe less — of getting out?"

"Yeah," Glitsky said. "I went on Google and got through about half your exonerated list over the weekend. I don't know why I spent the time or what I hoped to find. But there I was, checking out two hundred or so of these guys. But no luck — not even a nibble. I was planning to get through the rest of them over the next few nights if I could. But there was no telling how to find whoever might have been killed. I mean, maybe if I do nothing else for two or three days, I might be able to identify at least a couple of them, but since I don't even know why it would matter . . ." He shrugged and took another bite.

Dozier chewed thoughtfully. "I don't know why it would matter, either. But it got my curiosity up, so I started making some calls to colleagues around the country." He put his burrito down and reached under the table, bringing up his briefcase, which he put on the table, and assayed a bright smile. "I found twenty-three of them," he said with more than a trace of pride.

Glitsky put his burrito down, nodding in appreciation. "Twenty-three is a big number."

Dozier nodded. "And that's in the last ten years, which was my own arbitrary cutoff date, since the guys before then, I wouldn't have much in the way of following up. Memories of witnesses fade. Attrition kicks in on people just generally dying off, so they'd mess up our database. But still, twenty-three out of maybe four hundred — that's a pretty good sample."

"It's unbelievable," Glitsky said. "How'd you do it?"

"Well, we've got more complete files than Google has, believe it or not. Its files don't keep up on our exonerees once they're out, whereas we do. Plus, yesterday after I got the first few, I called some colleagues who I thought I remembered they'd been the source of the bad news about our clients dying off, the anecdotal stuff I was telling you about. I'm guessing you didn't have any access to anything like that."

"You're guessing right. Other than the bare facts that your clients got out, there wasn't anything about what happened to them next."

"Well, anyway." Dozier reached over and unsnapped his briefcase, extracting a two-inch pile of paper in manila folders that he put on their table. "I thought you'd want to look at this, see if any of it sang for you."

"If you insist." Glitsky pulled the stack of paper over in front of him, flipping through it perfunctorily. "You put some serious work in on this."

Dozier shrugged that off. "Well, as I said, curiosity got the better of me. Once I got started, it was pretty hard to stop."

"You get anything like a pattern on any part of this?"

Dozier killed a moment going back to his burrito. Food, drink, swallow. Then he said, "I don't much like what I came up with, so I thought I'd wait to see if you picked anything up — if anything jumped out at you — after you'd gone through this stuff."

Glitsky sat back, sipped at his drink. "If you don't mind, Martin, I'm a long way behind the eight ball here — Doug Rush was shot a week ago tomorrow, so I'd rather save the time. If you see a pattern, let's start there. If I don't like what you found, I promise I'll just kick the can on down the road."

"All right. And remember that this might be nothing."

"I'm tuned in to nothing."

Dozier nodded and said, "Of the twenty-three exonerees who died within a year of their release, eleven of them died of what we called natural causes — cancer, heart attacks, strokes, general old age, other diseases catching up to them. Two were apparently murdered in gang-related violence. Two more died in car accidents. Four of them killed themselves."

"How'd they do that, the suicides?"

"One guy hanged himself. Two — or three, if you count the last guy, who washed his Vicodin down with most of a half gallon of Wild Turkey — were prescription drug ODs."

Glitsky grimaced. "That'll put you out of your pain."

"No shit."

"And that leaves four."

"Yeah, it does. I thought you'd catch that."

"And these last four, they've all got something else in common?"

"You could say that." Dozier picked up his drink, swallowed and sighed, and put it back down. "Oh, and Paul Riley is one of them. They all got shot in the head. No surrounding criminal activity, no mutual combat, no robbery, just shot in the head, assassination."

Glitsky's burrito stopped halfway to his mouth. "You've got to be kidding me."

"I wish I were."

Picking up something in his tone, Glitsky said, "What else?"

"Well, once I had these four last guys, I kind of felt I was onto something, so I spent most of yesterday reading up on their files, soup to nuts." He tapped the stack on the table between them. "They're the top four folders here."

"And they have something else in common?"

"Yep." He drew in a deep breath, gathering himself. "Two reasons nobody put these four guys together were because they all happened in different states — Illinois, New York, Georgia, and then Paul Riley here in California — and the second reason was that they were spread out over the last decade. The first one was nine years ago — just about missing my deadline. The second one was two years later, seven years ago. Then three years after that was another one. Then finally Riley."

Glitsky put his hands over his mouth in a prayerful attitude. "Lord," he whispered.

Dozier went on, "Yeah, but I'm afraid we're not done. And this is the part that I really hate. After I'd isolated these four in their own category, I read up on their cases to see if anything else jumped out at me that might tie them all together somehow."

"Something tells me you found it."

Dozier nodded. "It took a while because this stuff isn't really that obvious. But I knew I had these four exonerees who'd gotten hooked up with us at the EI, so we must have thought we had a reasonable case on each of them. So I bored down, starting with Jaquis Randall, the oldest case, the guy shot in Chicago in 2011. You with me?"

"Every step."

"Okay. So back in 2005, Jaquis was up for killing a couple of white kids, thirteen and fifteen years old, who walked into the wrong neighborhood to deal drugs on Jaquis's turf. During jury selection, one of the original jury pool women shows up with like a baseball card she's wearing stuck to her cap that says 'Free Jaquis Randall.' Then it turns out she's also given these cards to a bunch of her homies in the gallery. So, naturally, the prosecutor takes her peremptory challenge and dismisses this woman from the jury, as any reasonable DA would do."

"I'll bet I know what happened," Glitsky said. "Some appeals court down the line found that poor Jaquis couldn't get a fair trial because the prosecutor was prejudiced against Jaquis and probably Black people in general."

"Yeah, exactly right. But the prosecutor was Black herself."

Glitsky held up a hand. "Couldn't be clearer," he said. "I've seen this a hundred times."

"Yeah, well, I must say this isn't exactly the kind of appeal that the EI has built our reputation on. I don't have any idea why my colleagues in Chicago took this case, but they did, and then they sold it on appeal and got the ruling exonerating Jaquis. When, really, there wasn't any doubt that he was actually guilty of the murders. But we got the win, if you want to call it that, after Jaquis had done six years while looking at life without." He let out some air and met Glitsky's gaze. "And it's gracious of you not to remind me that this was pretty much the way it went for Paul Riley."

Glitsky gave it a beat; when he spoke, he kept his tone neutral. "I'm assuming that your two other guys who got shot were factually guilty, too."

Dozier's jaw was clenched in frustration. "I tell myself that four out of about four hundred is still pretty good. If we're getting it right ninety-nine percent of the time, you tell yourself you're doing all right. You're making a difference." Suddenly, he seemed to run out of steam. "We don't want to think that this happens at all."

"You said it earlier," Glitsky said gently. "People make mistakes. It's a species problem." He took a last bite of his burrito. The salsa hadn't gotten any less spicy. He reached for the lemonade and tipped it up. When he'd swallowed, he reached out and tapped the pile of folders. "You mind if I take these with me?"

"That's why I brought them out. They're all copies."

"That's a lot of work," Glitsky said. "I appreciate it."

"Don't mention it." Dozier leaned in and broke an ingratiating smile. "I'd appreciate it if you let me know if this stuff leads anywhere. Or if it makes things better for anybody."

"Absolutely. You'll be first on my list."

"This has been a bit of a wake-up call, you know."

"Yeah, well, you can just look at it as another F.O.G."

"F.O.G.?"

"Fucking opportunity for growth."

"Thanks, Lieutenant," he said. "I'll keep that in mind."

When he pulled back onto the 101 heading north, Glitsky couldn't help but see that the fog — not the F.O.G. fog, but the real thing — was launching a massive assault on the city, karmic payback for the recent days of warm sunshine. A dark-gray smear of cloud blocked the view of everything but the airport; by the time he'd made it to there, he was in the middle of it.

It took him an hour and forty-two minutes to make the sixteen miles from the airport to his parking spot across from the Ferry Building. Picking up his thin stack of the four manila folders that he'd brought away from his meeting with Dozier, he got to his cubicle at four o'clock on the dot.

The Hunt Club office was atypically bustling with its full complement of regular, full-time employees. Usually, the five investigators and their boss, Wyatt Hunt, were out in the field, but this afternoon every desk and cubicle was filled. Who wanted to be out and about in this weather anyway?

Abe had barely put his stack of folders down at his desk when Pam Robison showed up at his elbow. She was the charming and über-friendly middle-aged admin who worked in the Hunt Club offices piling up credits for the hours she'd need to qualify for her license as a private investigator.

"Hey, stranger," she said. "If you've got a minute, Wyatt wondered if you could drop by and say hello when you got in."

"Am I in trouble?"

"I don't think so."

"Darn."

"Darn?"

Glitsky nodded. "If I'm not in trouble, my life must be too boring. Maybe I'll make him wait a while."

"Well. Your call, doll. I'm just delivering the message."

With mock exasperation, Glitsky said, "Oh, all right. I'll go check in."

Hunt's office, all the way to the back of their workspace, was the only one with a door. It was closed when Glitsky got to it, so he knocked and Wyatt told him to come on in.

"You wanted to see me?"

"I did. Give me a second here. Have a seat." He hit a few keystrokes, then pushed the keyboard away from him. "So how's it going?"

Wyatt was in his ridiculously handsome midforties, though he looked ten years younger. He worked out most mornings with a six-mile roundtrip run down to the Golden Gate Bridge and back. He also windsurfed every chance he got, played better than decent guitar, and had half a basketball court set up in the converted warehouse he called home. A couple of years ago, he'd married the wonderful Tamara Dade, and now they had a one-year-old, Virgil.

Glitsky thought it would only be fair if everybody hated Wyatt on general principle, but this, alas, proved very hard to do since on top of his good looks and awesome playthings, he was a charming human being — fair, loyal, honest.

"It's going pretty good," Abe said. "I may have gotten some kind of break at last in this Doug Rush case. I'll do some follow-up tomorrow and see if anything pops. Meanwhile, Pam said you wanted to see me."

Wyatt sat back in his chair. "I had a cup of coffee with Devin this morning down at Lou's, and it's more or less about the same thing. He asked me how you were making out on this stuff you're working on, and wanted me to remind you that this is still an active homicide case and if you came across some new evidence — or any evidence at all — your first stop should be to check in with Jack and Jill."

"I already did that, Wyatt. Last Friday, I gave them everything I had, including what I thought were some good bets as suspects, but they couldn't get any judges to sign off on the warrants to search anybody's houses. Maybe they will this week, but who knows? Or maybe it'll be this year, but I'm not inclined to wait on that."

"So that break you mentioned that you're

going to follow up on? What's that about?"

Glitsky shook his head. "It nowhere rises close to evidence. If those judges thought Jack and Jill's search warrants didn't make the evidence cut, they're never going anywhere near this stuff." Relaxing back into his chair, he crossed his legs. "That said, though, as far as leads go, it's pretty seriously cool. You want to hear about it?"

"With that intro, like I'm going to say no?"

"I didn't think you would. So anyway . . ."

It took the better part of five minutes. By the time Glitsky was finished, he'd come forward on his chair, elbows on his knees, the light of excitement in his eyes. "So how 'bout them apples?"

"I like them," Hunt said. "A lot. And your theory based on all this is what?"

"Well, that's where things fall apart for now. But it's just too much coincidence; this stuff can't *not* be connected. Can it?"

"That would be a long shot. But the question is how?"

"That's what I'm hoping to find out. But meanwhile, I think you'll agree that it's too soon to share any of this with our colleagues in Homicide, including Devin. It's just another fishing trip that would waste their precious time."

"Right." Wyatt grinned. "We wouldn't

want to do that. That would be wrong."

"That's what I thought, too. I don't want to come across as unprofessional."

"Perish the thought. But okay, seriously, I've got a quick one for you: What made you start thinking in the first place about this original pool of twenty-three guys who'd died?"

"I wish I knew, Wyatt. I wish I knew."

Part Four

23

"Jesus Christ, Abe. Pick up your goddamn phone!"

Glitsky, barely back at his own desk after his discussion with Wyatt Hunt, had no trouble recognizing Wes Farrell on his voicemail, and he punched in to cut him off.

"I'm here," he said. "What?"

"Have you been listening to the news?"

"Sure. In my spare time. But really no. What's going on?"

"You remember Bridget Forbes?"

"Sure. What about her?"

"What about her is that she's dead."

Glitsky felt his head go light and brought a hand up to squeeze at his temple. "I don't want to hear that. What happened?"

"The whole story's not out yet, or maybe almost none of it. So it's possible nobody knows. I just heard it on the news, where they had it as a murder/suicide."

"Don't tell me . . ."

"I don't think I have to. But I can't help but think that what happened is that Theo must have gotten home from France."

"I'm going down there right now. Please tell Treya I'm going to be getting home late. And you might call Jack and Jill and give them a heads-up. They're going to want to be part of this, jurisdiction or not."

With the fog and the late-afternoon traffic, Glitsky didn't make it down to Miramar until six thirty. It was still light, but barely. On the way down, he'd been passed twice by police cars, their sirens blaring and lights glaring. Fighting the impulse to pull in behind them for the draft effect if nothing else, he clutched at his tightening stomach and kept to within ten miles per hour of the speed limit.

At long, long last, he turned onto Bridget's street off Highway 1 and saw to his relief that the house was apparently still an active crime scene — an ambulance blocked half the street. There were six San Mateo County police cars, a coroner's wagon, a couple of Highway Patrol units, and several more of what must have been city or county vehicles. The vans from two television stations had arrived as well. Most of the available parking space was taken anywhere near the building and Abe wound up pulling into an open spot about seventy-five yards from Bridget's driveway.

Letting himself in under the yellow crime scene tape, Abe walked up to a young man in uniform with the name LEFFERTS stitched above his breast pocket and introduced himself, fabricating only just a bit. "I believe that one of the victims here is one of my clients, and I was thinking I might have some helpful information for your inspectors."

"I'm sorry, sir," Lefferts said. "I'm afraid you'll have to wait until we get the okay that nonpolice personnel can be allowed inside. The Crime Scene unit doesn't want to disturb whatever evidence is there."

"Sure," Glitsky said. "Of course. I understand."

He liked it far better when he was falsely recognized as a working inspector in San Francisco. But there was nothing he could do at the moment, except maybe learn something by inadvertence.

Officer Lefferts wasn't going to let him in, so he wandered back to a circle of perhaps a dozen people who'd gathered around the TV vans. Reluctant to introduce himself to the reporters lest he himself become some part of the story, he moved off a few yards, got out his cell phone, and punched up a Hail Mary of a number.

She picked up on the first ring. "Gomez."

"Inspector," he said. "It's Abe Glitsky. I wanted to make sure that Mr. Farrell got to you about this Miramar thing."

"He did, thanks."

"Where are you now?"

"Down at the scene."

"So am I. Are you inside?"

"Yes."

"How is it?"

"Terrible. I feel . . . never mind. It's just terrible. How can I help you?"

"Do you think you might talk to the officer guarding the front door to let me in?"

After a short pause, she said, "Let's give it a try."

Even though the crime hadn't happened in her jurisdiction, Gomez had an inspector's badge, and evidently her word about Glitsky's acceptability in the house was good enough for Lefferts. Once he was inside, no one seemed to care what role, if any, he was going to have here. Just so long as he stayed out of the way, which was something he knew how to do.

After a few minutes, though, the energy in the room shifted and one of the older men came around from where he'd been standing by the door to the bedroom. Jack and Jill fell in a few steps behind him as he walked up to Glitsky and said, "I'm Glen Tipton. This is my crime scene. And you are?"

"Abe Glitsky." He held up his ID. "Private investigator. Thanks for letting me in."

"Not a problem as long as you're on the log. But I must say it's not exactly crystal clear to me why you and your people think you need to be here."

Glitsky threw a glance at Jack and Jill behind Tipton and said, "They're not my people. I'm former Homicide in the city. They're the active inspectors."

"Okay, then. So do you want to tell me why you're here?"

"I'm in private practice now. I interviewed one of the apparent victims — Bridget Forbes? — last week and it turned out she had some information that made her and/or her husband persons of interest in a homicide in the city."

"Well, it looks like you flushed them."

Glitsky grimaced. "I'd like to think that's not what happened."

"Why don't you tell me what you think did happen?"

Abe tossed another glance over Tipton's shoulder, toward the bedroom where the killings had apparently gone down. "As I said, I was here to interview the Forbes woman last week. She was the alibi for my client who was up for murder. You might have heard about the Paul Riley case? The Exoneration Initiative guy who got shot last month?"

Tipton's eyes widened in surprise. "You're telling me Forbes in there was part of that?"

Abe nodded. "She was my client's girlfriend. Her story was that they — that's Bridget and my client, Doug Rush — they were together down here when Paul Riley was getting shot. This was while her husband, Theo, who was a pilot, was in France at the same time. So for obvious reasons she preferred that her relationship with Mr. Rush wouldn't get out. Especially to her husband."

"It looks like it did, though," Tipton said. "And you think that's why he shot her?"

"That's one reason he might have had," Abe said.

"He knew she was having this affair?"

Behind Tipton, Jack Royce cleared his throat. "Excuse me," he said. "I believe he must have known that for at least a week."

"Why is that?" Tipton asked.

"Because we've got to consider the possibility — no, the probability now, I think

— that Theo shot Doug Rush last Tuesday night, too. In which case, jealousy would definitely have been the reason."

Tipton said, "You're saying Theo killed Rush . . . ?"

Gomez put in her two cents. "Then flew to France, where he had a day or two alone to think some more about how much his life was ruined. I mean, his wife's betrayal with his best friend, the fact that he was now a murderer and would undoubtedly be caught and face trial and at least years in jail if not the rest of his life —"

Tipton cut her off. "Why would he think he'd be found out?"

Jack and Jill exchanged glances; then the latter spoke. "Because he knew we were close."

"How's that?"

"Because we came down yesterday to talk to Bridget, and Theo was here. So he knew we were onto something."

Glitsky shared Tipton's surprise. "Wait a minute, Jill. You're saying you came down here and talked to Bridget yesterday? I thought you couldn't get your warrant."

She nodded, matter-of-fact. "Well, we don't need a warrant to interview people, Abe. So that wasn't an issue. And after you left the office on Friday, Devin came by and made it clear that we should feel free to speed up the investigation if we had anything to roll on. We weren't supposed to get hung up too much on protocol."

"We got the impression," Jack added, "that you'd lit a fire under him, which was why we went after the search warrants right away, for all the good that did."

Tipton quickly took in the three San Francisco interlopers, his impatience starting to simmer visibly. "So you showed up here yesterday and talked to one of our victims in there?"

Jill corrected him: "Both of them, actually."

Tipton shot back at her, "And you're saying that suddenly, because of that, Theo knew he was made for the Rush shooting last week, so there was nothing left for him to do except kill his wife and then himself."

"We feel pretty shitty about it," Jack said, "but it hits all the notes. We just happened to walk into the middle of this melodrama, and I think it must have pushed him over the edge."

Glitsky was standing up straight, his hands in the pockets of his leather aviator jacket. "That could work," he said. Turning to Tipton, he went on, "But I've got an outstanding question or two."

"Let's hear them," Tipton said.

"All right. When I was down here last Friday, I asked Bridget if she and Theo had weapons in the house. She came out with a twenty-two Beretta, and said that Theo had another gun. So my question is, I'm assuming that you found a gun in there by the bodies. Is that the case?"

"Yeah," Tipton said. "Still in his hand, as a matter of fact. But it wasn't a twenty-two Beretta. That one was in a cubby next to the bed. I've got the apparent murder/suicide weapon bagged into evidence on that table over by the door."

"Could you identify it for sure?" Glitsky asked.

"Of course. So could you if you want to check it out yourself, but no doubt it's a Glock forty. Clean and efficient. Two rounds shot."

"Theo's gun. Registered to him."

Tipton nodded. "Undeniable."

At ten fifteen on this cold, windy, foggy Monday night, the Little Shamrock boasted eight customers, four of them in the back room throwing darts, three at a table under a Tiffany lamp by the restrooms, and the last one, Wes Farrell, sitting alone at the front corner of the bar, nursing a Lagavulin. Drinking a Black and Tan across from him on the other side of the bar, Dismas Hardy sat on a stool and found himself explaining that sitting down was something he did not tolerate with his regular bartenders, but due to his age, legs, bullet wounds and wisdom, and the fact that he owned over 50 percent of the place, he made an exception for himself.

Farrell clucked in disapproval. "You can't expect people to follow you if you don't set a good example." He showed Hardy today's T-shirt: *Outside the box? I am the box.*

Hardy suppressed a grin. "How about if I don't want people to follow me? How about if there's a different set of rules for the owner than there is for the employee who wants to maintain his job status by keeping up to standards set by the owner, among which is that we don't sit on a stool when we're on duty behind the bar?"

"That's the way society falls apart," Farrell said. "Different rules for the elite and the masses. Next thing you know, revolution."

"Over sitting on a stool?"

"It's got to start someplace. Just sayin'."

Hardy tipped back his pint glass, eased himself off the stool, and walked down to pour himself a refill at the taps. Since a well-poured Black and Tan takes at least five minutes to settle out, he walked back to where the stool sat, shook his head, and said "Fuck you" cordially to Wes. He then picked the stool up and carried it down the length of the bar, finally bringing it out to its previous spot on the customer side, where it belonged.

When he got back to Farrell, he said, "This is not about the amazing guilt trip you've just laid on me about my absolute right to sit on my barstool back here. This is all about me expressing solidarity with the common folk with whom I empathize deeply."

"I'm much more comfortable among you commoners," Farrell said. "And I know Abe will be, too."

"Abe is never comfortable," Hardy said. "And how'd you talk him into meeting you here where, if memory serves, we make drinks?"

"Mostly because it's on his way home. Plus, he's had a tough night. He might even want a real drink."

"I'll bet you he doesn't."

"No. You're probably right. I'd have to give you odds. How about five to one?"

"Ten to one on twenty."

"Ten! The guy hasn't had a drink in a year. Seven."

"Okay, seven. He orders a drink and you owe me a hundred and forty bucks."

"I hate to take your measly twenty bucks," Farrell said, "but it's a deal."

They shook on it.

"What's he been doing that's so tough? While you're thinking about your answer to that, I'll go get my refill."

When Hardy got back, standing now since there was no stool, pint glass in hand, he took a good drink. "So what's up with Abe?"

Farrell, his reservoir of humor finally getting dangerously low, sighed and started in. "One of the witnesses that he interviewed last week — hell, that we interviewed together — this truly gorgeous babe down in Half Moon Bay, she got herself shot today by her husband."

"Killed?"

"Deader than hell. And then — you gotta love it — her husband killed himself."

Hardy blew out in commiseration. "That is a bad day."

"No shit. What makes it worse is Abe thinks he might actually have had something to do with it. Which means I did, too, which I'm going to just flat-out reject."

"Why would he think that? I mean, a husband-wife murder/suicide. That's hardly going to be Abe's fault?"

"Well, it's the Doug Rush case, maybe, is why. If we hadn't decided to keep going on that . . . shit, I don't know. He tried to tell me over the phone driving up here, but he kept breaking up. So I'll let him tell us if he ever gets here. It's slow going out there in this soup. It took me twenty minutes to go ten blocks from home."

"You should have walked."

"Oh, okay. Thanks. I will next time."

Hardy leaned around and looked out the large front window. "And speak of the devil."

Glitsky, hunched over against the cold, pushed the door closed behind him. Turning around, he nodded to Farrell, then looked at Hardy and said, "I'm assuming you know how to make an Irish coffee."

"Hah!" Farrell held up his fisted hand, and Hardy said, "Shit."

Glitsky sat next to Wes at the bar, his hands trying to get warm around his coffee drink.

"It's not us," Farrell said. "It wasn't us."

"Except that it feels to me like it was, Wes. We're the ones who told her we could keep her secret about Doug, and the next thing you know, I'm up in Homicide telling Jack and Jill all about it. They need to go get a warrant so they can search Bridget's house, and Julia's, too, while they're at it. That's not what I call keeping a secret.

"And then when they strike out on the warrants, they take it upon themselves — because I've been pushing Devin Juhle, who is in turn pushing them — to go by Bridget's place yesterday. Little do they know that Theo's going to be there, but as soon as he sees Jack and Jill, he knows the jig is up, that they're onto him for killing Doug; it's only a matter of time before they take him down. And he decides he's not going to live, or let Bridget live, to let them do that to him. He's going to do what he's now done."

"Yeah, okay, Abe," Farrell said, "but let's not forget that he'd already killed Doug a week ago —"

"Do we know that? Has that been established?"

"Damn close enough, don't you think? Motive, means, opportunity . . . and our old friend the Glock forty. And he did that — killed Doug, I mean — long before you and I had ever even heard of Bridget Forbes."

"And that means?"

Hardy seemed to have it all figured out. "It means," he said, "that Theo already knew the secret about her and Doug way back then, so giving up her secret in actual fact didn't make any difference. If he hadn't known about Doug, okay, then you can beat yourself up, because maybe Jack and Jill showing up at their place hurried things along. But if Theo already did know about Doug and Bridget's affair — and he probably did — then what he did wasn't about us giving away any secrets. It was the poor guy reaching the end of his rope and deciding to take his cheating wife along with him."

24

At a little after noon the next day, Tuesday, Glitsky pulled his car up to the curb in front of Doug Rush's apartment building on Green. The sun hadn't even made a feeble attempt to burn the fog off, and if anything, it was colder than it had been yesterday. On the drive over, Glitsky'd had his windshield wipers on low; once he opened the door and stepped out into it, the mist was thick enough to feel like rain, but it just hung there, unmoving.

He rang the doorbell for number one, Julia Bedford. Buzzing him inside right away as usual, she was standing in her half-open doorway, arms crossed, wearing a blousy camo shirt tucked into her well-worn, well-torn jeans, plus the usual Birkenstocks. Her long gray ponytail hung halfway down her back. She could have been one of the motorcycle people, riding on the back of Doug's hog.

"Okay, Mr. Glitsky," she said by way of greeting. "Here I am, awakened from my beauty sleep as promised. What's today's mission?"

"Well, first, it's Abe, all right? I wanted to thank you for agreeing to see me again."

"Sure, no problem. It's not like my dance card was full. You want to come in, where it's neither cold nor dark nor wet? If you're not going on up to Doug's right away?"

"I'm not. Inside sounds good."

With a little flourish, she said, "Entrez," then stepped back to let him pass in front of her. The inside of her apartment was, in fact, well-lit and warm. Closing the door behind them, she turned and said, "Coffee, tea, or me?"

Startled — was she coming on to him? — Glitsky flashed her a quick look.

She smiled. "Just kidding about that last part."

"Tea would be good," he said.

"Be right back. But all kidding aside, you can take off the jacket. You'll smother in here."

"Will do."

He shrugged out of his jacket and watched her walk to the kitchen, just behind them, where she filled a kettle at the sink, then put it on the stove and turned on the gas.

Closing some of the space between them, Abe said, "I thought I owed it to you to tell you right away that the police have pretty much closed the book on Doug's death."

She turned toward him, her face suddenly clouded over. "Pretty much? What does that mean?"

"It means they're pretty sure they've got who killed him. But if you blink you might miss it on the news."

"What's that about?"

"It's about this case always being an embarrassment for the cops, right from when they beat Doug up arresting him. It'd be better all around if it just went away."

"And you're saying it has? Gone away now. They know who killed him?"

"That's why I wanted to talk to you. I thought after all your cooperation with us, you deserved to hear it in person."

"That's nice. Thank you. Does this mean that I'm not a suspect anymore?"

"What do you mean?"

She gave him a sideways glance. "Don't shit a shitter," she said. "Are you trying to tell me you didn't know that some inspectors came by and talked to me on Sunday?"

"I didn't know that, although maybe I should have."

"You guys ought to talk more to one another."

"Did they accuse you of anything?"

"Not outright. They just wanted to ask about my relationship with Doug. So I told them what I told you, which is that we were basically friends with benefits. They asked me if I knew that he was having another affair. I told them — again — that what we had wasn't that heavy. We liked each other. I assumed he liked some other women as well. No big deal. I mean, come on, we're all grown-ups on this bus."

Glitsky scratched at his chin. "What else did they ask you?"

"Not too much. I think I cut them off at the pass."

"How'd you do that?"

"They started to ask me about the night Doug got killed, and I'm all 'Whoa, you've got to be kidding me?' But clearly they weren't, so I told them no, I hadn't gone out with Doug in the middle of the night. I don't even own a car and I've never driven a motorcycle. There's no way I could have driven him anywhere, and as for shooting him, among the things I also don't own is a gun. The whole idea that I could have hurt Doug in any way, much less killed him, is ridiculous. Did you know that they were going to come and hassle me?"

"I thought they'd be coming by with a search warrant, but they went ahead without one."

"To look for what? If I had a gun?"

"That would be my guess."

She chuckled. "Like I'd be stupid enough to keep a gun if I'd used it to kill somebody. So what else would they be looking for?"

"Your phone records, probably, to see if you'd called a cab or an Uber or Lyft."

She shook her head in disbelief, finally letting another chuckle escape. "That's really beyond crazy. And on a personal note, I wish you would have just asked me, even if I had nothing to tell you. Are they going to come by again, with a warrant next time?"

"No. I don't think so. As I say, the case looks like it's closed up."

The whistle blew on the kettle, and Julia took the opportunity to collect herself as she poured the boiling water into the two waiting mugs.

"Because you need to follow up on every lead?" she asked ambiguously.

Glitsky nodded. "It's nothing personal."

"To you, maybe, Abe. To me, it feels personal. Like you don't believe me."

"Julia. Listen to me. You had a close relationship with a murder victim. The inspectors found out that Doug was seeing another woman. Jealousy happens. They had to make sure this wasn't one of those times."

"But this is me, the person, Abe. I couldn't have hurt Doug. I wasn't jealous of anybody. You should have known that. How could you not have seen that?"

"For what it's worth, I felt like I did know it. And for the rest, I'm sorry. It's moot now anyway. They've got their theory and it's not you. I agree with them. It's not you. It never has been you. But now, if you don't want to kick me out of here, I'd like to pick your brain about Doug's last few months."

"Would you believe what I tell you? What you might find out?"

Glitsky held up his right hand as though giving an oath in court. "I will."

"Well then, of course. Sure." With a heavy sigh, she dropped in the tea bags, then handed him his mug and picked up her own. "But let's go sit first. I think way better sitting down."

He followed her out and sat across from her at a small table in the front room, but really hadn't even gotten comfortable before she said, "From the way you talk about it, it sounds like there are still some questions about who killed Doug?"

"Not a lot. Not if you ask the police."

"And who was that? His killer, I mean."

"Theo Forbes."

She sucked in a breath in surprise, then nodded. "The pilot."

"That's the guy."

"You're saying that Theo killed Doug?"

"I'm not saying it," Abe said. "But that's the party line."

"But why? He was one of Doug's good friends. He loved Theo."

"Well, this may be hard for you to hear, Julia, but apparently he also loved Theo's wife, Bridget."

She sat back, took a breath, and closed her eyes for a moment. "I'm afraid I don't understand. You're saying what?"

Glitsky took a long beat while he sipped at his tea. Finally, he said: "Yesterday, Theo shot Bridget and then took his own life."

"Oh my God." She couldn't find her voice for a moment. "I heard about the murder/suicide couple down the Peninsula, but I didn't pay any attention to the names and never put it together around Theo. Or Doug, for that matter."

"I told you, they're playing it close."

"And how does Doug fit in?"

"Apparently, Theo found out about the affair between Doug and Bridget."

Julia clearly wasn't finding a place to

process this. "And so he killed Doug? What, he drove up here and picked him up and they drove out to the park so he could kill him there? Why would he do that?"

"I don't know. But that's what they're saying. That's their theory. And I must say it's not really so ridiculous on the face of it. It's defensible, at least."

"But this was last week, when Doug died. And then Theo waited — what? — almost another week before he shot Bridget? Why would he do that?"

"He flew to France in the interim. Maybe he thought about it over there and decided what he had to do when he got back."

"Really?"

"I don't know, Julia. There's another part of the theory, if you'd like to hear it. Theo got desperate because he believed that the cops had already pegged him for Doug's murder. And he learned about that when the homicide inspectors came by his place down in Miramar on Sunday. He was going to go to prison for the rest of his life. So he had no other choice."

Julia lifted her mug, sipped, put it back down. "God," she said. "God. This is just so horrible. I can't believe that Theo would . . ."

"There isn't really any doubt about that

part," Glitsky said. "The gun was still in Theo's hand when they got to the crime scene."

"And what about Doug?"

"What about him?"

"Well, if they have Theo's gun, can't they just do . . . what do you call it? . . . ballistics to see if it was the same weapon?"

"There's no way to tell that. First, they don't have the bullet that killed Doug, and even if they did, they probably couldn't match it with Theo's gun, which is a Glock. And Glocks don't work for ballistics, which is one of the reasons they're so popular. On the other hand, we can't rule out that Theo's is the same gun that shot Doug. But we'll never know for sure. And that's about as close as we're going to get on that."

Julia closed her eyes, took another slow and deep breath. And another. Glitsky let her live with her new reality around all of this. He wasn't finished with her yet — he hadn't really come by to give her the courtesy heads-up about Doug's death and the murder/suicide. He was here because there might be something she knew that she wasn't aware of, and maybe he could coax it out of her.

Reaching over, he touched her hand.

"How are you doing?" he asked in a gentle tone.

Another breath. "I'm okay. I'm very upset."

"I don't blame you. It wouldn't be natural if you weren't."

At last she opened her eyes and brought them up to meet Glitsky's gaze. "So what I'm getting is that this is probably the last time I'm going to be hearing about Doug's death?"

"It very well may be."

"But you're still having problems believing that it's what really happened?"

"Some. If I were back working as an inspector, I'm sure I'd be satisfied. There's an answer for every question. The point is whether enough questions got asked."

"Like what questions?"

"Well, the first one is really small and possibly completely irrelevant. Theo shot Bridget once and then shot himself, and when they found him he still had the gun in his hand with two bullets out of the magazine."

"Isn't that what you'd expect?"

"It could be. I can't deny it. It's right there and, as I say, it's an answer. But since the homicide inspectors are presuming that he shot Doug with the same gun, wouldn't there be three bullets missing from the magazine?" Glitsky asked. "That one woke me up in the middle of last night. Of course, he could have shot Doug and then just reloaded. Or what about if he just carried the gun with a full magazine and one in the chamber? I probably never would have considered it at all if a lot bigger question wasn't hovering out there."

"Which is?"

"If Theo shot Doug, there's no way I can figure that it had anything to do with Paul Riley's murder, and I just can't seem to shake the idea that these two killings — Doug and Paul Riley — must be connected. Or put another way, I find it much easier to believe that Theo did in fact kill Bridget — no doubt about that — but had nothing to do with shooting Doug."

Julia's brow furrowed. "But wasn't that the motive? That Theo found out about Doug seeing Bridget?"

"Yep. But that's another problem."

"What's that?"

"Well, you brought that very thing up earlier. The whole idea that Theo came up here to the city, shot Doug, and then took a few days, most of a week, in fact, planning this murder/suicide before he shot Bridget."

"Okay, but you had the answer to that: he

went to Paris to think it over."

"Maybe — and again, an answer to a question, just not the right one. Definitely, he could have flown to France and mulled it over for a week. But doesn't it make more sense that he shoots Doug, comes home from that when his blood is still running high, kills Bridget and then himself? It plays better as a heat-of-the-moment situation to me. It also absolutely depends on the fact that Theo knew about Bridget and Doug and their affair on that Tuesday that he drove up here to kill him. Wouldn't you say?"

"And didn't he?"

"To me, that's a real hard sell. And getting harder the more I think about it."

"Why is that?"

"Because when I talked to Bridget last Friday," Abe explained, "she told me that there was no way in the world that Theo knew anything about the affair, not on that Tuesday night. If he had found out somehow, he would have confronted her with it. That's just who he was. Instead, on that Tuesday night, the night Doug got killed, they went out to dinner at this restaurant down the street from their place and Theo stayed on there to listen to the music while she went home. There was no discussion over dinner of anything like a marital problem. Theo just didn't know anything at that time. No way, nohow."

"But then how did he find out?"

"He was home on Sunday when the inspectors came around to their house to corroborate Doug's alibi for the time Paul Riley was shot. Theo put two and two together then, on Sunday, and by Monday morning had worked himself into a rage enough to start shooting. To me, that timing works way better. And leaves Theo shooting Doug out of the picture altogether."

"Okay, but that leaves me with a question: Couldn't Bridget have said that she and Doug spent the alibi day just hanging out together, not in bed or anything?"

"Sure, but that's the kind of fact that tends to come out if somebody makes the accusation and gets things going in the first place. Maybe Theo accused her and Bridget just spilled it all. All I'm saying is that Theo finding out about the affair on Sunday is a more likely scenario than him waiting around for almost a week after killing his good friend before he decides to end everything with himself and Bridget. And that interpretation also leaves open the probability that the killings of Doug and Paul Riley are related."

"That again?"

"I'm afraid so. My gut's just not willing to let it go."

"I should probably tell you now," said Julia, "that it wasn't me who killed Paul, either. Joke alert."

"Good one," Abe said. He broke his own weak smile. "You should probably know that I've got a few pals who have an Indian nickname for me, like Dances with Wolves. It's People Not Laughing. Because wherever I happen to be, people are not laughing."

"Funny, Abe."

"Yeah, a laugh riot. And for the record, I don't think you killed Paul, either. But I think there's a reasonable chance you might know who did."

"I promise you, Abe, I don't."

"I don't think you can make that promise, Julia. You can know something and not be aware of it, or its significance. Did you hang with him among his motorcycle gang very often?"

"Sometimes. Not every day. I'm a wimp, and it would depend mostly on the weather."

"But you knew some of those players, am I right?"

"Sure. Most of them, I guess, over time. It's a good group, mostly."

"It's the 'mostly' I'm concerned with."

"What do you mean?" She pointed at his mug. "Refill?"

"I'm good, thanks."

"Well, if you'll excuse me for a minute," she said, pushing her chair back, "I've got to go see a man about a horse."

Glitsky waited, the frisson of a developing case playing havoc with his state of mind. Suddenly, he pushed his own chair back, stood, and walked into the living room, where he brushed aside the diaphanous white curtains hanging in front of the large bay windows. Through the lingering fog outside he could barely make out the cars parked along the street. He realized that he'd broken a light sweat in the warm room and dragged his fingers over his forehead, wiping them dry on his pants.

From close behind him, he heard her say, "You think it was somebody in the club . . . ?"

He turned around. She was standing way inside his comfort zone, maybe eighteen inches from the front of his shirt. He could hardly not notice that the top two buttons on her camo blouse had come undone, the fabric hanging slightly open over her breasts.

He took a step backward. "This fog's never going to lift again," he said, reaching for the drapes just to be moving away from her.

She was definitely sending a strong signal if he wanted to acknowledge it, which he didn't. But he was out of practice. No one had even remotely come on to him for at least a decade. Plus, he'd been married and faithful to Treya for twenty years and didn't feel at all inclined to break that streak.

Still, he could not deny his completely unexpected arousal.

He felt himself flush and swiped at his forehead again.

She reached out and gently touched his sleeve. "Excuse me." Passing in front of him, she brushed lightly against him as she went by. "I need to crack one of these windows," she said, "or we're going to faint in here."

He barely had room to retreat as she leaned over slightly, unlocked then lifted the window a couple of inches. He found it difficult to take his eyes from the view she was presenting to him.

Was she just waiting there, pausing for him to react, or to come closer?

Finally.

Finally, she said, "Better," and turned. She smiled with an unmistakable invitation and a real warmth in her eyes. "So where were we?" She touched his arm again.

Giving him every chance in the world.

He dredged the answer up from what seemed a long way down in his psyche. "Doug's friends in the bike club. Mostly good guys."

She continued to look up at him in extreme close-up. "The man forgets nothing." She let out what might have been a disappointed sigh. "Are you thinking anybody specifically? Who might not be one of those good guys?"

She waited one more beat and then — the moment having suddenly passed — she shrugged and stepped away, back to her seat at the round dining room table.

Glitsky, still somewhat light-headed, got back to his own place and forced himself to speak in a normal tone. "Here's my own latest theory, if you can stand another one. See how it plays for you, who knows the culture down there very well."

"Not all that well."

"More than the average citizen, I'd bet."

"Okay. Maybe that. What do you want to know?"

"I want to know if there's an enforcement arm."

Julia sat back in her chair, thoughtful.

"Enforcement? I'm not sure what you mean."

"I mean like the Hells Angels, for example. You screw up and break one of their own codes or rules, you get disciplined."

"Disciplined how?"

"It varies. Kicked around, thrown out of the gang, beat up, raped if you're a woman, sometimes — rarely but it happens — even killed."

Julia shook her head. "I think with Doug's group, it's mostly social. Lots of couples, like that. Doug and I, we just liked to cruise up to Tomales Bay and eat oysters, and I think most of the other members are like that. What made you think about this enforcement thing?"

"I went by the club headquarters out on Folsom the other day to ask some general questions about Doug. Some guys were hanging out there who didn't seem like your friendly social types. They had a definite edge to them, ready to mix it up with me if I was thinking about causing any trouble. I wasn't there to threaten anybody, so everything turned out all right, but there was a minute where I got the strong impression it could have gone another way."

Julia cocked her head, thinking about it. "Well. That's not something I ever had anything to do with, but yeah, now that you mention it, some of the guys come across as pretty tough . . . not to me or the other women, of course, but just in general, like if we're getting hassled by the anti-bikers. Or cops. But that doesn't happen too often, and I never saw anything like that with Doug being involved. That I knew about, anyway."

"Okay, but how about this? Everybody I talked to knew about Doug and the whole Paul Riley situation. And all of them had the same story, which was that Paul had in fact killed Dana and the exoneration thing was just bogus. He deserved to be killed, and Doug had every right to kill him. Or somebody did."

"You're thinking one of his biker brothers?"

A nod. "On the assumption that it wasn't Doug himself. But an enforcer in the gang? Jon Dunleavy, for example. Taking Doug's revenge for him when he didn't have the guts or the will to do it himself."

"It's not very brotherly of Jon to let Doug get arrested for something he didn't do, is it?"

"That's true." Abe scratched at the table.

"And also, how do you account for Doug getting shot? The same guy — okay, call him

Jon — shot Paul Riley, then kills his biker brother Doug, who he avenged by killing Riley a month before? Why would he do that?"

"Because, brother or not, Doug was probably going to give him up at the trial."

Julia shook her head back and forth, back and forth. "If Doug knew or even thought he knew who killed Paul, why didn't he just give up that person while he was out on bail?"

"I don't know. *Omertà*?" Glitsky broke a tight half-smile. "I like to tell myself that eliminating possible suspects is progress."

"But this doesn't feel like it?"

"Not in the least bit," he said. "Not even close."

25

When Glitsky got back to the Hunt Club's offices, it was midafternoon and the place had reverted to its usual daytime state of near desertion. Only Pam Robison sat at her workspace and she was busy, only pausing to give him a perfunctory wave as he reached his cubicle, then getting back to her work.

The emptiness suited Abe; he felt somewhat like it was the mirror of his soul.

He had been gone all day and had accomplished little to nothing. He had spent most of the ride back to the office beating himself up for his reaction to Julia Bedford's flirtatiousness. Though he had done nothing even remotely compromising with her, it roiled his guts that he had even noticed the open buttons on her shirt, the disconcerting proximity, the curve of her ass.

He even was questioning whether he'd had a legitimate reason to drop by to interrogate her again in the first place. He had wanted to talk to her about the Yerba Buena Motorcycle Club and any role it might have played in the Paul Riley murder, but Julia had dismantled that whole line of questioning in about two minutes, leaving Abe to wonder if he'd really had anything pertinent to ask her at all. Or if he was just spinning his wheels.

Now he unlocked the lower right-hand file drawer in his desk and pulled out the four files that Martin Dozier had given him before he'd gotten the emergency call about Theo and Bridget Forbes yesterday afternoon. He had barely glanced at them, and that omission made him feel if possible even more stupid and inept than he had upon leaving Julia's apartment.

Maybe, he thought, he should retire after all. He was clearly no longer a competent inspector, and he felt with a deep sense of unease that his meddling — telling Jack and Jill about the discoveries he'd made in his investigation — might even have played a significant role in Theo's discovery of Doug and Bridget's affair, and hence the murder/suicide.

Dozier's file on Paul Riley was on top of the small stack. Abe picked it up and, leaning back in his chair, opened it up, flipped through the pages. It felt odd and disorienting to be reading about Wes Farrell and Nick Halsey, both of whom were at the heart of the prosecution team that had sent Paul down all those years ago. And then for Doug to have called on Wes as his defense attorney . . .

No wonder Wes had been so reluctant to believe that Doug was innocent. During Paul's trial, Wes had seen firsthand the temper and anguish of Doug Rush, how it had played out in the courtroom. If he didn't eventually kill Paul Riley after Riley's release, he certainly had every reason to. And yet, they had all now come to believe he hadn't done it.

Turning more and more pages of courtroom testimony, he skipped over most of them, only slowing down as he got to Nick Halsey on the witness stand. On these pages, Nick came across mostly like a serious professional cop, although the defense attorney objected several times to his apparent inability to use the word *alleged* when talking about Paul.

The jury will disregard . . .

The witness is reminded that the defendant is innocent until . . .

But Abe already knew all of this and it wasn't getting him anywhere.

Closing that file, with a weary sigh he picked up the next one, Jaquis Randall in Chicago. It was more of the same — arrest record, police reports, forensics, autopsies of the young men who were the victims, witness transcriptions, the trial itself, the appeals, several local articles about the Exoneration Initiative and its fight for justice for this unfairly incarcerated Black man. And then finally several newspaper articles after Jaquis had been shot.

Glitsky read all of these articles in their entirety. When he'd finished, he went back to the first page and started flipping through the file again. When he got to the end the second time through, he closed the file and sat back in his chair, his hands templed over his mouth. It appeared very obvious to him that Jaquis had been wrongly exonerated — as opposed to the Paul Riley case, some of the articles in this file raised that very point.

Suddenly, he sat up straight and came forward in his chair. "Idiot," he said.

"Maybe not a complete idiot," Dismas Hardy said over the phone. "More like a part-time idiot."

"I shouldn't have been wasting my time going through all those files," Glitsky said. "I don't care about these trials that got appealed."

"Sure you do."

"Actually, not so much. What I care about is the homicide investigations on these guys who got shot in the head."

"And have you found anything?"

"Not yet. I've got a time-zone issue. Chicago's later than us. Did you know that?"

"I've heard something about it."

"It's true. Two whole hours. New York and Atlanta are three each."

"Good to know."

"So the bottom line is that nobody's home."

"Somebody ought to be in the office at Chicago Homicide, wouldn't you think?" Hardy asked. "Doesn't Chicago have about ten murders a day? I don't see that as a nine-to-five job."

"Well, I left a message. Somebody ought to pick it up."

"I'm sure. And when, again, was this Chicago killing, this Jaquis guy?"

"Two thousand eleven."

Hardy lowered his voice. "Two thousand eleven? You're talking eight years ago."

"Give or take."

"Either way, it's a long time. Is your case even still active?"

"I'm hoping so. If they've got a perp for Jaquis sitting in prison someplace, I'm back to square one."

"And if they don't have a perp?"

"Then I'm still in the investigation business."

But for the moment, there wasn't anything to investigate. The last two exonerees had been killed six and three years before, and in New York and Atlanta, respectively. Abe had already left messages and didn't expect any replies until the next morning at least.

Sitting at his desk, he wondered if he should make a call to Jack and Jill to see if he could enlist their aid in connecting to the police departments in Chicago, Atlanta, and New York. After all, they were active-duty homicide cops, whereas Abe was a meddling private investigator who would probably turn out to be nothing but trouble.

When he'd been running San Francisco's homicide detail, he and his inspectors had not exactly welcomed with open arms the assistance of private investigators. Most of the time they contributed nothing of substance, even on those rare occasions when they were working for the prosecution side.

After another minute or two of contemplation, he picked up the phone again and put in a call to Devin Juhle, only to reach yet another voicemail — at least this message was in his own time zone. At last, a wave of frustration brought him to his feet. Walking back to the coffee machine, he made himself a cup of tea and blew on it to cool it down. He must have been exuding dissatisfaction, because Pam stopped what she was doing at her desk across the office and said, "Are you okay, Abe? Is everything all right?"

"Peachy," he said.

"Somehow you don't look like it."

"I was being a little sarcastic."

"I picked that up. Are you stuck?"

"That's a good word for it."

"That's almost always a part of it, though, isn't it? You get stuck, eventually you realize you've got to kick something a little harder, break out of it."

"I feel like I've already done that part."

"Well, I don't mean to pry."

"No. You're right. I really ought to go out and kick some tires while I'm waiting for people to call me back. And then wait some more."

"Nothing's worse than waiting."

Abe nodded. "The thing is," he said, "I thought I had something when I woke up this morning."

"What was that?"

"You got an hour?"

She looked down at her wristwatch. "I've got ten minutes if you talk fast."

"All right." Somewhat to his surprise, he found himself telling her not about the ex-onerees who'd wound up shot around the country — there was no way he could do anything about them until he got some callbacks, probably tomorrow morning at the earliest — but about his suspicions of Doug's motorcycle pals and the YBMC.

They were closer and a lot more easily checked on; yet he'd essentially been talked out of his working theory on Doug's situation with the club because Julia had raised one objection, namely that if Paul's killer was a member of the club doing Doug's avenging for him, he would never have come back later and murdered Doug. On the other hand, Glitsky wondered, again, why wouldn't he do just that if he thought Doug would rat him out? It might not be his first choice, or even any real choice at all, but why should they eliminate one of the brothers as a possibility completely?

What had been Julia's answer to that?

That damn Julia and his unexpected reaction to her had been messing with his thought processes all afternoon. He'd wanted to leave her apartment as quickly as he could, get away from the temptation, so he'd talked himself into agreeing with her argument against the YBMC being involved because it was the easiest way to get himself out of there.

Finishing up with Pam, he said, ". . . so anyway, I guess I talked myself out of thinking it could have been one of the bikers."

Pam said, "It doesn't sound farfetched to me. Especially if Doug sold all his club brothers on the idea that Paul really had killed his daughter."

"He told that to every single one that I talked to."

"I could easily see why one of them would just step up and do it, maybe for the honor of the club if nothing else. I mean, these are motorcycle people, not kindergarten teachers."

"And what about Doug?" Abe asked.

"What about him?"

"Why would they have killed him a month later?"

"Maybe he found out about it and didn't approve. Maybe they couldn't be sure he'd keep his mouth shut. In fact, any number of reasons, maybe having nothing at all to do with Paul. Like, for example, you said yourself that the guy was a serious ass-bandit. Maybe he was hooking up with one of their women. I mean, imagine the rage if you'd put yourself so far out on the line by taking care of Paul for Doug's vengeance and honor, and then next thing you know, this same guy — Doug — steals your old lady, so you pretend to be his friend to talk last-minute trial strategy, but instead you shoot him. What about that doesn't work?"

"Nothing." Glitsky thought for a second. "In fact, it could resolve the whole question."

"There you go."

Abe's tea had gone cold and he realized that he no longer wanted it anyway, so he emptied the cup into the sink. "Has anybody ever told you you're a genius, Pam?"

"Are you kidding?" she said. "All the time."

26

The wind pushed the fog around, dissipating it slightly, but it also knocked the temperature down into the forties. The parking gods on Folsom delivered a spot less than two blocks from the YBMC headquarters, but Abe was still well-chilled by the time he arrived where he'd parked last time directly across the street. He couldn't help but notice that as dusk neared, the place had a completely different vibe than before, when in the fitful sunshine it had seemed vaguely welcoming.

Now it was frankly, albeit subtly, forbidding. Part of it was the weather, of course, but a phalanx of six bikes blocked easy access at the curb. No surprise, the tables out front sat empty. Bodies in leather were packed up inside against the windows, which were dripping with condensation.

The door was closed but not locked, and Abe walked right in, excusing his way through the packed crowd and the tables. The Grateful Dead was singing "Casey Jones" — "Drivin' that train, high on cocaine" — at a reasonable volume and the smell of beer was pervasive, with bottles on every table and, seemingly, in every hand.

This was not, as Pam the genius had suggested, a bunch of kindergarten teachers.

A few of the members kept up the press as they pushed back at him, some with what seemed like true aggression, as he shouldered his way through, negotiating his way to the bar. He might have imagined it, but the room seemed to get marginally more quiet as the members became aware of his presence. It probably did not help, he observed to himself, that he was the only person of color in the place.

He ignored that as best he could. Raymond from yesterday was behind the bar again, busy passing out more Budweiser longnecks, which seemed to be the only selection. There wasn't any visible cash register, and Abe realized again that this was a private club, not a bar, even if they did serve beer.

Finally, flashing the all-purpose and truly meaningless badge he kept in his wallet, he got Raymond's attention and leaned in over the bar so he could be heard. "Is Jerome

Walker in here? I've got a couple of questions for him."

Much to Abe's surprise, Raymond nodded, took a few steps off to one side, and knocked on an otherwise invisible panel in the wall behind him, which turned out to be a door that opened inward. Raymond poked his head in, said something, listened to the response, and then came back to where Abe stood. "Around the side here," he said.

Abe made his way down the remaining length of the bar and then went behind it. Raymond hadn't closed the panel completely, so Glitsky knocked once and pushed it enough to fit past, then pulled it closed behind him, all but shutting out the music.

Abe had checked the Internet briefly before coming down here, but hadn't been able to learn much about the club's administrative structure, if any. But from his visit yesterday morning — to say nothing of his talk with Julia earlier today — he'd decided to go on the assumption that Jerome Walker had some rank, and now it looked as though he was right.

The windowless room had a low ceiling, but decent lighting from low-hanging overhead fluorescent bulbs. Jerome Walker sat at the beer-bottle-laden table in the middle of the room with a large and hard-looking but nevertheless attractive younger woman next to him and the triplets from the other morning, including Jon Dunleavy, sitting around. Looking at Abe, Walker nodded as though verifying something to himself, then indicated one of the empty chairs and told Abe he could take a seat.

When Abe had done so, Walker started out cordially enough. "You're putting in some long hours, Officer. Can I offer you a brewski?"

"I'm fine, thanks. And maybe this is a good time to tell you that I'm not a cop. I'm a private investigator. Sometimes showing the badge opens some doors. Some people can't read my ID, but everybody knows what a badge means. I hope you don't mind."

Walker chortled and everyone else at the table joined in. "I could sometimes use one of them myself," he said.

"Yeah, well, just so you know, it's illegal to impersonate a police officer, so you've got to weigh the risks."

"I'll keep that in mind. You're . . . Glitsky, is that right?"

"That's it. Abe Glitsky."

"Good to know, in case I have to turn you in." He tipped his bottle up. "So what can we do for you? I'm gathering this is about Doug Rush again."

"Yes."

"Didn't we cover that yesterday?"

"Maybe not all of it."

"Don't take offense at this, but if you're not a cop, what's your interest?"

"He was a client of the firm I work for. There are some insurance questions," he lied. "They don't know why he was killed."

"I thought we had all agreed that somebody in the boy's family — I mean the kid he killed — took him out for revenge."

"That's a good theory. His name, by the way, the kid, was Paul Riley, and nobody thinks Doug killed him anymore."

"Well, sure he did." He looked around the table for corroboration, and everyone nodded in agreement. "What else makes sense? They had an eyewitness, didn't they? He was going to trial just last week if he hadn't gotten himself shot first."

"All true," Abe said, "except he wasn't in the city when Paul was shot, which kind of takes him out of the equation."

His beer halfway to his mouth, Walker stopped and carefully placed the bottle back on the table. "What do you mean? He wasn't in the city?"

"It's pretty straightforward, Jerome. He

was down in Miramar with his girlfriend all day."

"So why didn't she say so right after it happened, when they arrested him?"

"For obvious reasons, she would have preferred it if her husband didn't have to find out. She was afraid it would break up her marriage and she didn't want that. I don't know. Maybe if push came to shove, she would have changed her mind and agreed to testify; probably it would have caused a big stink and a continuance for late discovery, but no judge would have completely excluded an alibi in a murder case even if it delayed the proceedings. Given James Riley's shaky ID to begin with, her testimony would have gotten Doug off. There's no doubt. He couldn't have done it."

Walker threw a weighted glance at the young woman beside him. She was frowning, her forehead creased with concern. "I don't see," she began, but Walker shifted in his chair. Then, moving ever so slightly, he held a hand low over the surface of the table, wordlessly ordering her to shut up.

Glitsky had come down here with the intention of kicking the tires harder, getting out of being stuck in the rut he'd dug for himself. Now, he felt, he had gotten them primed and it was time to make his move. "So knowing what I knew," he said, "after I thought about the time I spent here yesterday, I found it interesting that all of you were so unanimous about what you thought had happened —"

"That's because everybody knew what had happened. Nobody'd heard of any damned alibis. In fact, even now, I don't know what the fuck you're talking about. I still hadn't heard of it until you just showed up here, and I don't see any reason I ought to believe it. I don't know what you're even getting at."

"I'm getting at Doug not killing Paul Riley. Which leaves my investigation wide open. And that in turn leaves me wondering about who might have done it, anyway, since for sure it wasn't Doug. If it might, for example, have been somebody he rode with."

"You're out of your mind. Why would anybody do that?"

"Because he truly believed that Paul had killed Doug's daughter, and so Paul needed to die. And if Doug himself wouldn't shoot Paul, or couldn't make himself do it, for whatever reason, one of his brothers could make it happen as a matter of honor. Misguided honor, but even so. And the rest of your club here, the ones who knew about it, kept it to themselves to protect the secrecy of the brotherhood."

"You can't prove any part of this."

"It's funny how often guilty people say that. And then how often they're wrong once the real investigation starts."

"You don't have a real investigation. You started off here telling us you're not even a cop, so why is anybody going to listen to anything you've got to say?"

"They'll figure it out, once they get a clue about where to look. And now we know where that is. And that's not even talking about who killed Doug."

Walker took his time with his beer, tipping it up until it was gone. "You're saying somebody here did that, too? You think that's funny or something?"

"We'll see how funny that is when the inspectors come around."

"I'll show you how funny it is." Holding his beer bottle by the neck, in one quick and practiced movement he smashed it against the table, shattering the thick end. Suddenly on his feet, knocking his chair to the ground in the process, he brandished the makeshift weapon like he knew how to use it.

Glitsky was instantly on his feet, backing

away toward the door.

Walker took a short charge but brought himself to a stop a few feet before he could have actually hit Abe, and rasped out: "We're done here — and right now — if you want to leave on your own feet."

Glitsky had what he thought he needed and had come for — the lower threshold of what might drive somebody like Walker or one of the other members of the gang to violence. He wasn't about to take on four men and one woman who undoubtedly had more experience at hand-to-hand contact than he did. Reaching behind, he got a grip on the doorknob and pulled it open.

"You're nowhere near done," he said, and got the hell out.

In the ensuing silence, Walker looked with some surprise at the glass neck of the bottle he was still holding. His breath came almost in gasps as he lowered himself into one of the free seats. The woman got up and came over, pulling a chair close to him, massaging his shoulders.

"That man needs to be discouraged," Walker said while the others waited for him to recover. He took his time, meeting the eyes of everybody else in the room. "Too much going down here, I think we all know, even if we didn't kill no Paul Riley or Doug Rush. We don't want him feeling welcome whenever he or his troops feel like stopping by."

The biggest of the triplets picked up an empty bottle and said, "They's only two ways he can go outside and there's three of us."

"Sounds right." Walker nodded.

The other two triplets picked up their own empty bottles and Jon Dunleavy pulled at the door, opening it up.

His own blood loud in his ears, his heart pounding, Glitsky excused his way slowly through the crowd — now frankly hostile, or maybe that was just his imagination. Whatever, once he got through the front door and outside, he paused for a breath, two, three of them — calming down, trying to relax. At last he stepped off the curb by the phalanx of bikes.

Crossing the dark street through the freezing wisps of fog, he got to the other sidewalk when his legs suddenly almost went out on him. Turning, he leaned back against the façade of the closest building.

The biggest mistake he'd made, he realized, was not bringing his gun. If he had, it would have leveled the playing field. And he'd usually made it a rule during his time as an inspector to be carrying heat when interviewing murder suspects, in case things got out of hand as they sometimes did.

Still, it had worked out well this time — close to dangerous but with no real harm done. At least Jack and Jill would now have something to talk about if they came down here, and they would pretty much have to do that when they'd heard about the discussion Abe had just had with Jerome Walker, and — more importantly — his reaction to Abe's accusations.

Obviously Walker and the gang were hiding something, and maybe a lot of illegal somethings, and clearly, at least higher up in the ranks, the YBMC was not the benign social club that it pretended to be.

Half a minute or twice that later, the shaking and weakness in his legs finally let up and he turned to his left and started walking again. All of the streetlights seemed to be out of order and the street was mostly dark except for the random storefront — a Laundromat, a pizza place on the other side, an ATM at the first corner, the tiny neighborhood grocery.

Glitsky stood in the brief shadowy corner light and searched the parking places on both sides, hoping for a glimpse of his own spot that had seemed so close when he'd driven up. But he figured he still had another long half block at least.

He stepped off the curb again, just as a young couple walked by in the middle of something that was making them laugh, the guy's arm around his girlfriend's shoulders. Glitsky heard their footfalls fading behind him.

And then the sounds coming back closer for a moment — they must have missed their turn at the last corner.

But no.

It was someone else behind him, one person from the sound of it, heading in the same direction as Abe, but faster — late for something.

And here was Abe's car where he'd parked it. No windows smashed. Everybody else in the world, it seemed, was suddenly driving his exact same Subaru, so he stopped to make sure it was his license number.

Leaning over to check — yep, his plates, his car . . .

He straightened up.

Footsteps . . .

Part Five

27

"He didn't want me to call you," Treya said to Hardy as she let him into their home.

"I'm not surprised."

"He said you'd only just give him grief."

"He's probably right. How is he, though, in real life?"

"Not good. He's in and out of consciousness. Right now he's out on the couch. He's probably got a concussion at the very least, but I thought I'd get a second opinion — that would be you — and then together we could convince him to go to the ER."

From the living room, they heard Glitsky's voice: "Not happening."

Hardy made a face and spoke to Treya. "That sounds heartening. Like his old self."

She grabbed Hardy's arm and led him around the shoji screen that delineated their living room from the front doorway. As advertised, Abe was lying down on the couch, his eyes closed and his body draped with a comforter from their bedroom. He had one ice pack across his forehead and another one around the back of his head.

Hardy pulled an ottoman up beside him and let himself down on it. "We know you're awake," he said. "And you look like shit."

Glitsky opened his eyes, barely shook his head, then closed them again. "Good to see you, too. But I'm good."

"I told you," Treya said.

Hardy shrugged. "So what happened?" he asked.

"Somebody whacked me. Maybe twice."

"Definitely twice. At least," Treya said. "You can feel the bumps pretty good."

"Do you know who it was?"

"Generally, yeah. The Yerba Buena guys. I'd just been seeing them, muddying the waters about Doug Rush . . . and when I left they were pretty unhappy."

"And so you were on your guard, is that it? That's how this happened?"

Glitsky shook his head, very slightly, again. The pain showed in his face. "I know," he said. "Stupid. It just never occurred to me they'd do this."

"Have you called anybody?"

"Yeah, Treya called you."

"No. I mean called somebody like the police?"

"And say what?"

"What you just told me."

"How can I do that? I never saw anybody. What am I supposed to say? They just came up and hit me from behind and I was out."

"And when did this happen?"

"Seven thirty, quarter to eight, somewhere in there."

Hardy checked his watch. "Two hours ago?"

"I think I was out awhile, Diz."

"Nobody tried to help you?"

"It wasn't like the street was crowded. It was dark and mostly empty. And otherwise, I'm a dark-skinned older person lying on the sidewalk, probably homeless. Why is anybody going to think to help me?"

"Jesus," Hardy said. "This city. So how'd you get home?"

"You'll love this," Treya put in.

"You want to steal my thunder and tell him?" Abe asked Treya.

"No," she said. "It's your beautiful story."

He shrugged. "I drove."

"Smart move," Hardy said, "with a traumatic head injury, going in and out of consciousness and all."

"Hey. The car's in the garage downstairs. The door is closed behind it. I'm here, talking to my wife and my pal and everything, and I don't think I've lost consciousness again since I woke up on the street."

"Yes, you have," Treya said.

"I faked it for the sympathy vote," he said.

"Sounds like that worked really well," Hardy replied. "But sympathy or not, don't you think it might be a good idea to have a medical person take a look at you?"

"Not really, no. They'll just tell me to get some bed rest and take it easy for a week or whenever and don't hit my head again. That whole concussion protocol, whether or not I have one. Like anything I do is going to make a difference."

"Okay, but what if it's worse than that?" Hardy asked.

"Thank you for bringing that up," Treya said.

"It probably isn't," Abe said.

From behind them, they heard Zachary's voice. "Yeah, but what if it is?"

"Hey, bud," Glitsky said, looking across the room at him. "That's very unlikely."

"Okay, yeah, but you guys made me wear a helmet until I was six. You can't mess with your brain. You only get one shot. You said that a million times."

Their daughter Rachel picked this moment to step out from behind Zachary. "I can't understand why you're being so stubborn about this, Dad. You got hit in the head a bunch of times, and now what if it's bleeding internally and you get a stroke or an aneurysm and die? Wouldn't that be worth going to the ER and finding out before it can happen? So they can stop it before it's too late." The tears that had been gathering in her eyes now spilled over onto her cheeks and she started to sob. "Don't you even want to be around to see us grow up? We love you and we need you to get better. Don't you see that? We love you so much, Dad. So much."

"Out of the mouths of babes," Hardy said.

After some more relatively intense debate, Treya and the kids agreed to let Hardy drive Abe down to the emergency room at St. Mary's. That way, there would be no wait for an ambulance to arrive, and Abe did not seem to be on the verge of blacking out again. Abe convinced everybody that they wouldn't admit him to the hospital after they'd taken a look at his brain. He'd be back home in a couple of hours.

They got the patient down to the car, which Hardy had parked blocking Glitsky's garage. They lowered the passenger seat to a steep recline and put him in, and Hardy got rolling. They'd just turned onto Lake —

one block from the Glitsky home — when the patient moaned.

"Hey!" Hardy said. "None of that. If you die while I'm driving you down, your family's going to kill me."

"I'm not going to die."

"Yes, you are, someday. Let's just not make it tonight. And speaking of which, do you think they were trying to kill you?"

"Probably not. If they wanted to, they could have easily enough. Don't you think?"

"I don't know. I wasn't there."

"I don't think that was it. They just wanted to warn me off and to keep the inspectors from coming by and asking questions."

"If you say so."

"I do."

Hardy pulled up at a red light. "Put your head back down," he said. "You're thinking too hard."

They released Glitsky from the ER at 1:15 a.m. with the expected diagnosis that he had a concussion and should take it easy for the next few days. The doctor also recommended that, given the source of his injuries, he should probably call the police. Abe thanked him for his time and advice and told him that he'd get right on both recommendations.

Though he'd slightly leaned on Hardy for the walk into the hospital, by the time they came out, Abe was walking under his own power, seemingly with no balance problems. When they got back to the car, he readjusted the passenger seat so that he would be sitting up, and as soon as he'd gotten in, Hardy said, "Maybe it's just me, but I detected a note of insincerity in your relations with the good doctor."

"How can that be?"

"I don't think you're going to go slow, and I don't think you're going to call the police."

"It's just you," Abe said. "You tend to see the worst in everybody. I'm sure that sometime in the not too distant future I'll call the police. Maybe just not about this."

"That'll be helpful."

"I try to be."

"Still, though —"

Glitsky held up a flat palm. "Please. Can we leave this alone? I've been hurt way worse than this playing football. The doctor didn't think this was too serious. I came in mostly walking on my own, no memory issues, eyes not too dilated. I'm good to go."

"I like the 'eyes not *too* dilated' part. Also walking *mostly* on your own."

Glitsky shook his head, slowly. "I'm fine, Mom," he said. "Just fine."

Back at Hardy's home at a little after 2 a.m., Frannie woke up, turned on the light over her bedside table as Hardy was crawling into bed, and asked how it had gone. Was Abe all right?

Hardy snorted, puffed up his pillow behind him, and sat back into it. "If cantankerous is any indication of robust health, then I'd say he really is fine."

"But you did take him to the ER, at least?"

"Absolutely, but only after both of his children threatened to immolate themselves if he didn't go. What if he died and left them fatherless?"

"Playing the orphaned-child card. That's always a good one. So what was the real prognosis?"

"They let him go home, and I don't think they'd have done that if there were outstanding issues. As to whether he's going to try to take it easy for a week or so, I'd say probably not."

Frannie tsked. "So does he know who did this to him? Or why?"

"He's got a theory about Doug Rush's motorcycle gang, but he can't be completely certain. He got knocked out from behind and never knew what hit him."

"And so, of course, being Abe, he's going back again to rattle their cage?"

"He says maybe not."

"Do you believe him?"

"Not entirely, but he seems to be going on the assumption that these guys warned him off on purpose. They could have killed him if they wanted to, but they didn't."

"And this means what, exactly?"

"According to Abe, it means they also didn't kill Paul Riley or Doug Rush. And it's obscure enough that I'm not sure I completely get it, but he might be onto something, even if it's simply eliminating more suspects."

Frannie huffed out a breath. "Eliminating suspects, I love that. Until there's only one of them left, and whoever that is eliminates Abe."

Hardy shook his head. "Let's hope not." He leaned back into his pillow.

She leaned over and kissed him. "Are we going to sleep now? You want me to get the light?"

Hardy sighed heavily. "Maybe not right yet."

"Okay," she said wearily. "Is there something else?"

"Actually, there is." He took a breath, let

it out heavily.

"Are we going to play Twenty Questions?" she asked.

Hardy gave her a weak smile. "Probably not necessary. It's about another witness — a woman named Bridget Forbes — who Abe and Wes went to visit last week down in Miramar."

"What about her? Although I'm not too sure I want to know, do I?"

Hardy broke the news about Bridget and Theo as gently as he could, but there was no disguising the fact that two more people connected to Doug Rush were dead. "I'm telling you this," he concluded, "first because you need to know, and second because I think you're right."

"About what?"

"About an unacceptable amount of violence around this case for everybody involved in it. This thing — whatever it is — has suddenly begun spinning out of control. And all of this stuff that Abe's been engaged in is really not something he should keep pursuing. These are all police matters and that's who should be handling this investigation."

"I've been saying that all along."

"I know. It's why I'm talking to you."

"So what are you going to do?"

"Well, I've got to talk to Wes and Gina first, but I'm going to suggest that we cut off Abe's funding and give all of his findings over to Jack and Jill."

"Who?"

"Oh, sorry. Those are the homicide inspectors who need to be involved in this, and in fact took over for Waverly and Yamashiro. Royce and Gomez. Jack and Jill."

"They must love that."

"Well, I wouldn't care if it was Romeo and Juliet, just so long as they can take over this investigation. I don't care what Abe says about it — that Doug's motorcycle buds could have killed him if they wanted to — I still think it's a miracle he didn't get himself killed tonight, and I don't want to give anybody else another opportunity. Or the motivation."

"You don't think that's already in play?"

"I sure as hell hope not, but I can't fool myself any longer. You were right from the beginning. Something's going down here that is serious and dangerous. Abe's done a lot eliminating some suspects, but keeping him on this when Homicide has all the advantages just doesn't make sense anymore. Although he'll probably make a stink when we call him off."

"Better stink than dead."

Hardy nodded. "My thoughts exactly."

28

Glitsky woke up to an otherwise empty house at 9:30 a.m.

Treya had left a note on the kitchen counter, encouraging him to go back to sleep, no matter what time it was. She mentioned that she loved him. The note also told him that she had taken their car, which he interpreted correctly to mean that she believed he had no business being behind the wheel of a moving vehicle. Next to the note she'd left a bottle of Extra Strength Tylenol, of which he took two tablets, thought for a couple of beats, then took another.

He put some water on to boil, then dropped a bag of Earl Grey into his favorite mug and walked first to the bathroom, then turned for the short walk back down the hall to his bedroom. He vaguely remembered Dismas Hardy getting him to the front door in the deep dead of night, and

Treya opening up to let them in, but he had no memory whatever of anything beyond that, including getting into the sack.

His frown deepened as he stared at the bed, trying unsuccessfully to recall any part of going to bed or falling asleep. Only then did he realize that he was still wearing yesterday's clothes, which he'd slept in. He reached around the back of his head and gingerly touched the sites of the trauma, suddenly no longer sure that he'd been hit only twice.

And what, if anything, would that mean?

Lowering himself through a small wave of dizziness, he sat on the edge of the bed, his bare feet flat on the floor.

The kettle whistled as the water boiled back out in the kitchen, and he stood up — slowly, slowly — retracing his steps from a few minutes before. He filled his mug and placed his full weight on his palms on either side of it on the counter.

With closed eyes, he leaned into his arms and waited.

Not sure what, if anything, he was expecting. Some of last night's memories to return? Some sense of normalcy in his home?

Opening his eyes, he leaned down and inhaled the fragrant steam from his tea, picked up the mug, and went for a quick tour of the living room. Nothing seemed out of place, except that his comforter was still draped over the couch. Pulling the ottoman around and sitting on it, he drank some tea, trying to will away the headache.

That exercise wasn't working too well.

When he'd finished the mug, he brought it back to the kitchen sink and set it down carefully. All of his movements felt awkward and clumsy; when he turned to go back to the bathroom to take his shower, he felt more comfortable holding on to the counter, small step after small step.

Ten minutes later, showered and shaved, he sat on his bed in his bathrobe and noticed something that he told himself he should have seen as soon as he'd gotten up — his cell phone was plugged into a charger cord on the side table. Of course, he realized, he had no memory of putting it there. As he leaned over to reach for it, another dizzy spell nearly knocked him off the bed, but he pushed himself back, got his hand on the phone, and straightened up.

He had turned it off, and now, punching the side button, he waited yet again. When the screen finally lit up, he saw that he had a ridiculous seven voicemails — Dismas Hardy, Wes Farrell, Pam Robison from

Wyatt Hunt's office, Julia Bedford, Jack Royce, Glen Tipton from Miramar, and Martin Dozier.

When it rains, it pours, he thought.

Yet even with all of that activity, none of the calls were the ones he was expectantly awaiting from law enforcement people in Chicago, New York, and Atlanta.

Dismas Hardy: "This is just a friendly reminder that the doctor in the ER and your lovely wife both told you that you need to stay horizontal and try to get some sleep. Or even a lot of sleep, at least for the next day or two. Frannie told me that there was no chance you would actually do that, but I told her you were a responsible adult and would follow the doctor's instructions religiously. When she stopped laughing, she bet me ten bucks and I took it, so don't let me down. Meanwhile, when you're all the way awake and not before, call me. We need to talk."

Wes Farrell: "Hey, Abe. Sorry to hear about your head. Or is it your brain? Treya says you're basically all right, but need to lie low for a while and get some rest. To facilitate that behavior, I talked to Diz and Gina when they both came in and we all agree that we'll be cutting off the funding for the Rush matter, effective now. So don't call me back. And get back to bed. You've got nothing you need to do except get better."

Pam Robison: "Just calling to check in how it went with the bikers last night. If you need anything from me, just let me know. I'll be around the office all day."

Julia Bedford: "Abe, this is Julia. Bedford? I don't mean to bother you but I've been thinking about what you said yesterday, that you actually suspected I could have killed Doug. I have to tell you honestly that it's really gotten inside my head. That you could think that about me. I couldn't sleep for most of the night, and I've just been wondering if there's anything I can do so you can completely rule me out as a suspect. I'm sorry to keep bothering you. But it's just . . . I can't believe. If you can talk sometime, maybe I can make you believe I couldn't have done that. I'm just not that kind of person. Okay, then. Bye."

Royce: "Lieutenant, Jack Royce here. I just wanted to give you a courtesy call to let you know that Jill and I went down to the Miramar Beach Inn — the restaurant — last night, where they had the same Tuesday music lineup as they had last week, the night Doug Rush got shot. So we asked the two guys playing there if they remembered hanging out with Theo and/or Bridget? The short answer is yes. Bridget went home early. Theo got pasted on tequila, then stayed till near two o'clock and helped them break down their gear. He was completely shitfaced, couldn't even walk. All of which means no way did he drive to San Francisco to pick up Doug Rush and shoot him and then drive home. Give me a call if you'd like to talk some more. But this was pretty compelling and conclusive. Later."

Glen Tipton: "You probably already know this, but your inspector colleagues have eliminated Theo Forbes as a suspect in the shooting of your client, and I just wanted to let you know that we concur with that decision. So don't feel like you've got to come on down here and double-check to make sure we got everything right. Not that we don't appreciate all the professional help, but this one's really cut-and-dried. In any event, the coroner has ruled it a murder/suicide, and I hope that's the end of your concern with the matter. Of course, if you do have any questions and would like to discuss this further, you've got my number. Take care."

Martin Dozier: "Lieutenant, this is Martin Dozier and I'm just following up to see if anything has turned up in your investigations. I'm around if you need me."

When Glitsky opened his eyes, he was lying on his back on his bed, still holding his cell phone in his hand. Miraculously, it hadn't rung in the two hours since he'd come in and listened to his messages. He didn't remember deciding to lie down, but here he was, wrapped in his bathrobe. Lifting his head an inch off his pillow, he checked for dizziness and found that he was pretty much okay, so he came all the way up and swung his feet over so he could sit up.

In no time, he was dressed. Back in the kitchen, he took a couple more Tylenol and sat at his kitchen table, sipping water from a Mason jar. He played the voicemail messages back again and this time allowed himself to react.

Diz and Wes could both bite him, he thought, if they thought they were going to pull the plug and call him off the investigation. Not when he was this close. That just wasn't happening.

Pam Robison was a joy; he was starting to see that she was someone he could depend on.

Julia Bedford would be happy to hear that she wasn't any kind of suspect.

If Abe had anything that he believed about this case, it was that the same person had killed both Paul and Doug. And because James Riley's identification — flawed though it might be — did not allow for another interpretation, that person was a man.

Jack and Jill were probably right eliminating Theo Forbes as Doug's killer, and therefore he hadn't been Paul's killer, either. In any case, Glen Tipton's snotty and condescending tone did not bode well for any further cooperation between San Francisco and San Mateo Counties, and this was as it should be, since both the Paul Riley and Doug Rush homicides were in San Francisco's jurisdiction, whereas Bridget and Theo were on Tipton's ground. Theo might have killed himself and his wife, but he hadn't killed Doug Rush and Paul Riley.

And finally, Martin Dozier remained a hidden if inexplicable ally.

Abe got up and made the circuit of his house looking for his soft leather briefcase into which he'd put the exonerees' files yesterday before heading off to the YBMC. Stymied on his first pass, this time he went down the hallway leading to his kids' rooms, then back through the foyer by the front door, around to the living room . . . before remembering that those files were in the trunk of the Subaru that Treya had driven to work that morning.

Lowering himself again onto the ottoman, Abe leaned over and put his elbows on his knees, then rested his head in his hands. As he sat, a wave of fatigue and vertigo broke over him. Taking a heavy breath, he closed his eyes, almost nodded off, then started back to full consciousness.

He got to his feet, walked back through the kitchen and down the hall to his bedroom. Going to the safe on the middle shelf of his clothes closet, he spun the dial a few times, then pulled the door open and lifted out the holster holding his HK 40, his favorite handgun.

Laying the package on the bed behind him, he turned back around and took down and slipped into his Kevlar, heavy and awkward, but Glitsky knew from experience that when you needed it, you were glad you had it on.

Finally comfortable, he tucked himself into his shoulder holster, pulled on his leather aviator jacket, and touched the Uber app on the face of his phone.

He called Treya from the Uber car and told her he'd be in the Freeman Building's garage in fifteen minutes and would she mind meeting him down below where she'd parked their Subaru in one of the visitors' spots.

"It doesn't sound like you're getting that all-important bed rest the doctor recommended right now," she said.

"I already did. I slept the morning away and then slept a little more."

"No, but really."

"Really, Trey, I'm just going down to the office, where I will sit quietly and review my notes. The problem is that you've got my notes."

"The other problem," she said, "is that Diz and Wes and even Gina don't want to pay for your time anymore."

"They're just bluffing."

"Not really so much. They think that this should be turned back over to Homicide. You've done your usual ace of a job and eliminated about half the city as suspects, and now you need to step away and let them do what they do."

"Like when they arrested Doug?"

"Maybe better next time."

"I'll consider it, but first I'm going to review my notes and see where I stand."

"Abe. Please. Think about last night. Give it a day or two, and meanwhile, go back to bed. Make a decision in a couple of days when you're feeling better."

"I think we're breaking up," he said. "Treya? Treya?"

"Don't do this, Abe."

"Well, if you can still hear me, I'll meet you down at the garage. Otherwise I'll be forced to go break into the trunk and cause all kinds of havoc."

29

Now in his cubicle in the Hunt Club's offices, Abe had just spent the last two hours going over the copies of the files that Dozier had given him. In that time, his head had gone back to pounding and he'd gotten two more phone calls — Raymond Henry from the Lily Pad restaurant and another one from Julia Bedford — neither of which he'd answered. He felt like he was fighting himself to stay in the zone. There was a lot of information to keep track of, and he didn't want to derail his train of thought.

But despite his best efforts, he couldn't deny that he wasn't making any real progress. He thought by now he knew everything imaginable and relevant about the four exonerees (counting Paul Riley) who'd been killed within a year of their release from prison, but there really wasn't much that they had in common. He reasoned that it must be somewhere here in these files, but he couldn't find any real correlation between them, except for the fact that each had died from a single gunshot wound to the head.

Finally he gave up and walked on back to Pam's desk — they were again the only two people in the office — to clear his brain and to run his methodology by her. When he'd finished, she waited awhile, picking her words, before she said, "No offense, Abe, but since you asked me, I've got to say that it sounds like you're going at this a little backwards."

Abe, who'd boosted himself onto the desk directly across from her, broke a deep frown. It was all he could do not to react as a spike of anger and pain shot across the back of his head. Summoning all the calm he could muster, he quietly asked her, "How's that?"

"Well, all these guys, the exonerees, you've been reading over these files, concentrating on what their original crime was and how the Exoneration Initiative got involved and set them free."

"That's because that's what happened."

"Right. Sure. But then they got shot, which is more or less where all of these file entries end. Wouldn't you say?"

"I would, but that's because they were dead."

"But you want to know who killed them, don't you? I mean, that's your focus. You don't really need to care about all the trial and appeal stuff, or even the Exoneration Initiative. What you need to do is talk to the people who investigated these deaths. I'm talking the homicide inspectors. It seems to me that with all these files, you've gotten hung up on the trial side. But you don't want the DAs who charged these guys or brought them to trial. They're not the people you need to talk to if you want to find out what happened on these homicides. You've been going at it bass-ackwards."

Back at the desk, a couple more Tylenol on board, Abe called the Chicago Police Department, identified himself as who he really was, and told the dispatch officer that he had some information on the nine-year-old homicide of an Exoneration Initiative exoneree named Jaquis Randall.

He got forwarded to another answering machine — it was after five o'clock in Chicago — and left a message for an Inspector Rupert Marchand. Although it was an hour later in Atlanta, he got patched through there to a Detective Billie Acosta and she picked up the phone on the first ring.

"Acosta. Homicide."

Glitsky identified himself, made sure it was clear that he was a private investigator, and jumped right in. "I'm calling about the murder of one of your Exoneration Initiative exonerees back in 2011."

"Got to be Franklin Piersall. Tell me somebody confessed to killing him dead and you'll win a prize," she said.

"You know about that case?"

"It's your lucky day. He was my case. You said you're calling from San Francisco? What's his connection to you out there?"

"I don't know, to tell you the truth. Maybe nothing. But that's why I'm calling you."

He gave her a short rundown of the situation, but hadn't quite gotten all the way through when she said, "Hold it, hold it. You're telling me that there are three other of these exonerees in the country who've gotten shot?"

"Yes."

"Well, you know, these exonerated guys — and particularly Mr. Piersall — they're not necessarily altar boys."

"Or kindergarten teachers," Glitsky said.

"I'm sorry?"

"Nothing. Just another handle for them. But regardless, you're saying that Mr. Piersall wasn't really much of a sweetheart?"

"To put it succinctly, I'd go with that."

"So after he got out, he made enemies?"

"Let's just say that he didn't make too many friends. He was just an abrasive guy. According to pretty much everybody who knew him. Which, of course, isn't necessarily a reason why you have to go and get yourself killed."

Glitsky hesitated. Then: "Did you have a suspect who went to the head of the class?"

"That's the frustrating thing, as you probably know. The investigation never really went anywhere. He had a live-in girlfriend with some of the usual issues, and a couple of guys he hung with who were pure trouble, but all of those people had rock-solid alibis for when Franklin got shot. And, of course, no witnesses either."

"So how did the actual shooting go down?"

"Pretty much no-nonsense. His girlfriend was at her job — she was a hairdresser — and he was alone at her place watching television in the middle of the afternoon. He was on the third floor and we're theorizing that Franklin opened the door and before he could say boo took the hit in the middle of his forehead. One shot. Very professional. No lands or grooves, so probably a Glock. No shell casing at the scene, so no ballistics at all."

"That sounds exactly like my guy here in San Francisco. And I'm guessing nobody saw the shooter come or go?"

"You're guessing right. And while you're guessing, you're right again, the apartment didn't have any cameras, and neither does the general neighborhood. Not then, not now. Our killer just took his one shot and disappeared and nobody saw him. Magic."

"Good prep."

"That too. Although I couldn't run into any scenario that supported the idea of some kind of hit. Basically, all in all, it was a shutout, and the case is still open, and that's not my favorite. So anything else you got, I'm all ears."

"All right. This might not seem relevant, and maybe it isn't, but I've talked to one of the EI lawyers at some length, and he's come around to the opinion that one thing these four exonerees have in common, besides the head shot, is that they may have been factually guilty of the crimes they were originally charged with."

"You got an EI lawyer to say that? The ones I know, they never in their collective lives ever made a mistake like that. All their convicts are innocent, which is why they got off."

"I hear you, and it's the same here. But my guy, I didn't have to twist his arm. He saw it himself and didn't like it even a little bit, but he finally realized that sometimes the politics get in the way of the truth."

Acosta chuckled over the phone. "You shock me!"

"I know. It's hard to believe. But to bring us back to Franklin Piersall, did you get any whiff during your investigation that his original conviction might have been right after all?"

"You're asking what if he were factually guilty and got off on a technicality and not because he was innocent."

"Yep."

"What would that mean?"

"Well, maybe nothing. But it might mean the same motive . . . I mean, that was the case with Paul Riley — my guy — some vigilante thing could have been in play. So a guilty guy gets let out on a technicality . . . somebody, maybe one of the vic's relatives, might take it into his head to balance the scales."

Glitsky picked up the incredulity in her voice as she said, "You're not saying you think it's possible that your killer and my killer might be the same person?"

"I am starting to think that it might not be impossible, yes."

"That sounds like a hell of a reach. I mean, Atlanta and San Francisco?"

"Okay, maybe more realistically, two guys who have the same motive, maybe in contact with each other through something on the Web? I'm just wondering if there was anything in your investigation that had some miscellaneous hanger-on taking up space where he didn't obviously belong."

"Nobody springs to mind, to be honest with you. But I promise, I'm going back and looking again. And you say there are two other exonerees with the same profile? Where are they?"

"Chicago and New York."

"You wouldn't want to share some names, would you?"

"Sure. Chicago is Jaquis Randall." Glitsky spelled it out. "Killed in 2011. And New York is Alex Losciavo." He spelled it out again. "Killed in 2016."

"And your guy, Paul Riley. This year."

"Last month, to be precise, but you got it."

"Do you mind if I check in with the inspectors handling these cases?"

"Not at all. I'm going to reach out to both

of them, but knock yourself out. Though I would appreciate it if you could keep me in the loop if something pops on your end."

"Goes without saying." She hesitated. Then: "Do you think it would be helpful if I talked to your EI lawyer?"

It was Glitsky's turn to chuckle. "That would be a big can of 'nopes.' If his name ever got out around this — I don't even want to think how he'd take it. Not well, I'd guess, and I can't say I'd blame him. He's a good guy, but I guarantee he's reached his limit about going to bat for the prosecution side. If this got out, he'd be ostracized for heresy."

"Okay. I'll leave him."

"Deal," Glitsky said.

Closer to home, Raymond Henry from the Lily Pad had what he thought was interesting news. One of his waiters, Donovan Keating, hadn't come into work yesterday — Tuesday — and it turned out that he had gotten caught in a routine search by his parole officer. Glitsky knew they did random searches of parolees from time to time just to keep them honest. It turned out that Donovan's parole officer — his PO — had found a handgun in his possession, which, as Mr. Henry had acknowledged when Abe had talked to him before, was an automatic go-back-to-jail card.

"But the thing is," he was saying, "and why I'm calling, is that Donovan was one of the guys who got a little caught up in blowing the whistle on the credit card scam that Paul Riley was trying to get going here."

"I remember," Abe said. "What's your point?"

"Well, somehow — nobody knows how — Riley got a picture on his phone of Donovan with a gun. Riley swore that he was going to snitch him off if he didn't come on board with the scam. But Donovan didn't want to risk his job here. It got heated."

"Between Keating and Riley?"

"Yeah."

"So, what? Riley was going to tell Donovan's parole officer that he owned a firearm? Did he ever get to that?"

"I don't know. That might have been the beginning of the sting I'm talking about that just went down yesterday. Things go a little slow on follow-up with these POs sometimes. Riley might have actually ratted out Donovan back in April or so, but they didn't get around to moving on that until now."

"Raymond," Abe said, "let me get this straight. You're telling me you think that this guy Donovan had both a motive and a weapon to kill Paul Riley?"

"I am. I think it's at least worth checking out. You asked me to tell you if I got any new information. This seemed to fit the bill."

"It does, you're right. Thank you." Glitsky thought for a moment. "Let me ask you one more quick one. Do you have employee records of when people were working on any given day?"

"Sure. We're all high-tech savvy. I got a computer and everything."

"Good. Are you near it?"

"Close enough."

"You want to look up April second, see where Donovan was or wasn't?"

"Give me a minute."

Glitsky waited. The throbbing in his head had eased during these past phone calls, but now it surged back with a vengeance. He closed his eyes, rubbed his forehead, went around the back of his head until he got to the bumps, which were still sensitive to his touch. He exhaled heavily.

"Glitsky, you there?"

"Right here."

"You'll like this. Donovan didn't work at all on April second. He worked a double — lunch and dinner — on the third."

"All right, one more."

"You already said that for the last quick one. You don't normally get two last quick ones."

"Let's make an exception this one time. I'm trying to save myself some footwork."

"I hear that." A sigh. "All right, one last quick one, take two."

"What does Donovan look like?"

"What do you mean?"

"I mean, we got a supposedly positive ID for Doug Rush as Riley's killer. If Donovan doesn't look a lot like Rush, then he most probably didn't shoot Riley. So what's he look like?"

After a short pause, Henry said, "Something like me, I'd say, though not as good-looking. I mean, he's white, grayish hair over his ears, sixty-ish, maybe two hundred pounds, give or take. More than that, you can look him up yourself on the Delancey website — we feature our hero waiters all the time. And Donovan had — has — a lot of fans."

"All right, Raymond. Thanks. You've been a help."

"I try."

"Julia, this is Abe Glitsky."

In a breathless voice, she started right in: "Thank God you called me. I've been a wreck just sitting here thinking that you really believed that I could have shot Doug, but Abe, that just isn't who I am. I could never do anything like that. I don't even know how to shoot a gun. I'm just an old peace and love hippie chick. You must have seen that already. I thought we were getting close to being friends, at least. I would never lie to you, ever. And I don't want to bother you while you're so busy, but it's really important to me to know that you believe me. And if you don't, how can I convince you?"

Thinking that the lady doth protest too much, Abe still found it difficult to imagine that she had played any role in the murder of Doug Rush. Lowering his voice to reduce the threat inherent in it, he said, "Julia. Listen. You don't have to convince me of anything. Part of this whole process of what investigators do is consider all the possibilities, even the most unlikely ones. It's not personal. You've been a cooperative and helpful source of information about Doug right from the beginning and I'm very grateful to you. So stop beating yourself up over whether or not you're a suspect. At least in my eyes. To my mind, you're a good citizen and a very nice person on top of that. It's certainly not your fault that you've found yourself in the middle of a murder investigation. You've handled it very well, all things considered. Better than most people. You can rest easy about that. Really."

Abe felt that he could almost hear the relief seeping out of her. "That is such a load off my mind. I suppose I shouldn't have let it get to me so badly, but —"

"Julia. Julia. Easy. I'm telling you that I don't have any suspicions about you at all. I'm not lying to you. You don't have to let yourself go into any more of a tailspin. Just take a few deep breaths and let it go."

"I'll try to do that. But I want you to know that I'll be thinking about this, about who killed Doug, and I hope you won't mind if I call you if I get any ideas."

"You can call me anytime you want with anything you have."

"I really did like Doug a lot, Abe. I want you to find out who killed him."

"I do, too, Julia. I'll let you know if I make any progress."

30

Bang! Bang! Bang!

Something close by, getting slammed in the pitch dark.

"Abe! Abe! Are you all right?"

"Yeah." Where was he? He couldn't see a thing. "Just a minute. Where am I?"

"In the nap closet."

The nap closet didn't exactly ring a bell.

"The door's locked. Can you get up?"

"Yeah. I think. I must . . . Hold on." He put his hand to his head.

Pushing himself up to a sitting position, he finally saw the crack of light bleeding under the door. He slid down to the end of the cot, reached out, got to the knob and turned it, pulling the door inward toward himself.

A female figure stood silhouetted in the doorway, but his eyes had popping little pinwheel explosions of light at the periphery of his vision, and he couldn't make out more than her shadow.

Then Pam — of course it was Pam — was on a knee in front of him, holding him up.

"What's going on?" he asked her.

"That's what I was going to ask you," she said. "I thought you'd gone to the bathroom, but then when you didn't come back to your desk after a half hour . . ."

"I don't remember coming in here or lying down or anything else."

"Yeah, well, here you are. How are you feeling?"

"Run over by a truck, if you must know." He closed his eyes and tried a breath or two before he opened them again and looked around. "When did this closet get here?"

"We've always had it. Tamara added the cot when she was pregnant and we decided to keep it."

"It must have looked good to me, too."

"Must have."

"A half hour?"

"At least."

He went to stand, but she tightened her grip on his arms. "Maybe you want to give it a minute or two before you get up. Do you feel like you need to lay yourself all the way down?"

"I don't think so. I'm afraid I'd just go back to sleep."

"And would that be so bad?"

"It might be."

"Why?"

"I feel like I'm this close, you know. This Doug Rush case. I'm almost there if I can just keep at it."

"If you can just keep living."

"Yeah. That too. But that'll probably happen." He closed his eyes through a couple more breaths. "Would you mind doing me a favor?"

"Sure. Whatever."

"I've got some Tylenol in my desk drawer, upper right. And some water."

"I'm on it."

As soon as she got up, he leaned forward, put his elbows on his knees, and rested his head on his hands. The light show in his eyes had dimmed and the intensity of the throbbing had scaled itself down a notch. It struck him as likely he would survive.

But maybe last night's doctor, his wife, his kids, and his best friend were not all wrong about the whole bed rest thing — he seemed to be spontaneously defaulting to that every couple of hours anyway.

Pam came back with his pain meds and he swallowed a couple, then risked standing up. He was fine, he told himself. Not dizzy at all. Looking around behind him, he nodded. "Nice room," he said.

With a half hour to go in the theoretical cop workday, Glitsky showed up in the homicide detail and was pleased to see that Jack and Jill were at their adjoining desks, tapping away at their computers. He had called them both earlier, separately, but neither had returned his calls. Their lieutenant, Devin Juhle, had not been in his office when Abe stopped by as a courtesy to ask permission to bother the inspectors again. As it was, Juhle couldn't accuse Abe of trying to circumnavigate the chain of command.

He had walked from his office to the Hall of Justice, thinking that the exercise and cold air might help his headache, and so far it had been working. Although, he had to admit, it might also have been the Tylenol.

But now here he was.

Both inspectors greeted him cordially enough, showing no sign that they'd purposely been stiffing him on his phone calls.

"I just thought I'd stop by to keep you guys in the loop with my own investigation. I got a call a while ago from the manager of the Lily Pad restaurant, Raymond Henry. Ring a bell?"

"Not really," Jill said with a distinct lack of enthusiasm.

"That's the Delancey Street place," Jack added, "right? Do I remember that Paul Riley worked there?"

"That's the spot," Abe said. "I talked to Henry early on to see if Paul had a beef with any of the other workers, all of whom are ex-convicts, by the way."

"And what did he know?" Jill asked impatiently.

"Not much, back then. But then yesterday, one of his waiters — Donovan Keating — got busted on a parole violation. Possession of a firearm."

Jack nodded. "So he's going back to prison." Not a question.

Abe nodded back. "He might already be there, depending on how they're doing the processing. But he's definitely in custody. You guys ought to be able to find him better than I could."

"And I'm guessing now" — Jill was shaking her head in frustration — "you're going to tell us that he had a problem with Paul Riley. At this restaurant?"

"You got it," Abe replied, then launched into the story.

By the time Abe finished, Jack had rearranged himself to be sitting on the corner of his desk. "So," he said, "this guy Keating had a reason to kill Riley?"

"And a pretty good one, too. The old proverbial falling-out among thieves. If Paul was going to rat him out to his parole officer, and it looks like that's what he might have done . . ."

Jill wasn't buying what Abe was selling. "But by then it would have been too late, right?" she asked. "If Riley had already ratted him out with his PO? Killing him wouldn't have accomplished anything, would it? So why would he shoot him?"

Her partner answered: "He's pissed off, that's why. He knows he's screwed and Riley did it to him. That sings for me."

Glitsky nodded. "All I'm saying is that I think it would be worth talking to Mr. Keating, wherever he is. He had a motive; he had a weapon. He wasn't working on the day Riley got shot. He looks a little like Doug Rush —"

Jack snorted. "Who doesn't? Rush could be Everyman."

"I know," Abe said. "It's a crowded field out there. In any event, long story short, I thought it was worthwhile giving you both the heads-up around Keating, see what he has to say."

"Sure," Jill said. "We'll jump right on it."

"But maybe not, huh?" Glitsky called her on her attitude.

"I hate this," she said. "There just is no evidence anywhere, even with this guy Keating." She held up a hand, stopping Glitsky before he started. "I know, I know. Don't get me wrong, Abe. We'll go and talk to this guy, of course. But the fact that he wasn't working on the day Riley got shot isn't what I'd call a compelling argument for anything. Likewise, owning a gun, even if he's an ex-con, is a far cry from shooting somebody who may or may not have ratted him out to his parole officer."

"Jill is still upset about Bridget Forbes," Jack said.

Her eyes flashed in anger. "Damn straight I am. And Theo, too. We should have seen . . . we should have . . . oh, never mind. But here again we've got a possible suspect who hasn't left one shred of evidence, a shell casing, nothing. There's no case here, unless you think we can get him to confess, which is not going to happen."

"Hey," Jack said. "If he's one of the Delancey guys, he's done serious prison time in a rich educational environment. He's learned how to leave a crime scene without a trace."

"You could say the same thing about a

cop," Jill said. "When I decide to kill you, for example, nobody is going to be able to prove it because I wouldn't have left anything to connect me to you."

"There's a consoling thought," Jack said. "If you —"

Glitsky's cell phone rang and he pulled it out. "I've got to take this," he said. "Good luck if you talk to Keating."

"We'll get right on it," Jack said.

Jill sat back in her ergonomic chair, her arms crossed over her chest. She was shaking her head, shaking her head.

"Mr. Glitsky. This is Inspector Rupert Marchand out in Chicago." He had one of the deepest speaking voices Abe had ever heard. "I got your message and I've just had a talk with a Detective Acosta in Atlanta. She's got herself a cold case about the murder of one of the Exoneration Initiative exonerees. She tells me that it's possible that it's also connected to a case out your way in San Francisco. And maybe another in New York."

"That's correct. I've pretty much established that there are four people who seem to have gotten out of prison on the EI's appeal and then were shot in the head within the following year, maybe sooner."

"You're talking about Jaquis Randall."

"Yes, sir. As I told Detective Acosta, he was one of them."

"And the hitch," Marchand said, "is that they were apparently released and exonerated in spite of the fact that they were factually guilty of the crime that had sent them down."

"That's it, in a nutshell. My question to you is whether in your opinion Jaquis fits into that model?"

"Perfectly. It was the stupidest appeal I've ever seen in my career, but somehow they made it work and got him out. But regardless of that, Jaquis, he was a bad apple. It didn't surprise me at all, him getting hit."

"By 'hit,' do you mean that you think it was a professional job of some kind?"

"Absolutely. This is Chicago, after all. People be getting hit here all the time. You see something so clean, that's your first choice who did it. Then again, in this case, he killed two boys dealing on his turf. Their folks, either one, looked good for it, my first choice, but there was no putting anything on them. And you know, frankly, the word had gotten out about Jaquis and nobody here in the police department lit any fire around finding who'd done him."

"We're a little the same way out here."

"I looked. I gave the investigation most of a month, but between you and me, I can't say I blame anybody. The parents of those boys had every right to their rage. Notice I'm not saying the word 'vengeance.' If I could have built a case, I would have brought in somebody."

"But there was no case?"

"Nothing."

"Beyond the parents?"

"Not even. Jaquis didn't have friends, and he went right back to his hood when he got out. So it could have been . . . I mean, I interviewed no less than a dozen of his acquaintances, but nobody even made the first cut. I could send you the transcripts if you want to see them."

"Thanks, but not necessary," Glitsky said. "I'm just still trying to piece this thing together. There's a lot of moving parts."

"I hear you. But just between us?"

"Yeah?"

"Jaquis deserved killing, and I don't much care who did it."

In the course of the phone call with Marchand, Glitsky had moved out of the open bullpen where he could be heard and into the glass-enclosed adjacent space where the homicide detail kept file binders and bankers' boxes and other random, mostly paper junk on library tables. By the time they ended their conversation, he had pulled around a wooden chair and now sat half-hidden behind some of the boxes.

His head no longer hurt, but a heaviness behind his eyes seemed to be daring him to close them for just a minute. Pulling in closer to the table, he dropped his head and let it come to rest on his arms.

And then suddenly, he was sitting up straight, his heart pounding in his ears. If what he'd just thought was the explanation he'd been looking for . . .

If . . .

He knew exactly where he could go to find out.

Shirlee Harris was in her twenty-seventh year of service as HR and records coordinator in the Hall of Justice. Originally, her third-floor office was the repository of several hundred square feet of file cabinets, but ten years ago, when Evidence and the Police Laboratory had moved into their new facilities near Hunters Point, Shirlee's department had moved downstairs to the basement. Shortly thereafter, the metal file cabinets had started to disappear as the contents of them went digital. And now

Shirlee presided over a modern computer room with her own desk and ten cubicles with their own monitors for her staff.

Glitsky knocked on the open door to the hallway and advanced to where she sat at her desk, the only employee in the room. She could have checked out and gone home at least forty-five minutes ago, but her job was her life, and Abe knew from long experience that she almost never left until six. He gave her a smile and a casual salute.

Returning both, she stood up and stretched a hand out over her desk. "Lieutenant Glitsky," she said. "As I live and breathe."

"Hey, Shirlee. How are you and life here in the beating heart of the building?"

"Keeping up to date and moving on down the line," she said, giving him a quick once-over. "But the real question is how have you been? I haven't seen you in forever."

"Doing well. Treya and I are still together and still happy. The kids are getting older. Same ol', same ol', but all good."

"And how's the department holding up?"

And this, Glitsky knew, was the crux. Clearly, as he had hoped, and even as she was nominally in charge of all the personnel records both in and outside the building, she was among the many who hadn't seemed to process the idea that Abe had actually retired and didn't work here anymore.

"I've just come down from there," he said, basking in the smidgen of truth. "I must say, it seems to keep on running like a Swiss watch."

"Leadership," she said.

"Not so much," he said. "Mostly good people."

"And modest to boot."

"I'm going to blush," he said.

"All right, I'll stop. But what brings you down here after all this time? What can I do for you?"

31

By the time Abe made it back upstairs, it was dark outside and Homicide had completely cleared out. Nursing a low simmer of frustration, he pulled a chair around, sat down, and hit the Call button on his phone. This brought him to Jack Royce's voicemail and he left an urgent message: if he and Jill were by any chance on their way to interview Donovan Keating wherever he was being detained, they should put that conversation on hold until they'd had a chance to talk to him. In fact, no matter what the inspectors were doing, they should cool their jets until they'd talked to Glitsky.

He had no sooner left that message than he called Jill and reached her voicemail, too. This didn't surprise him — she'd made it clear that she'd run out of patience with him and his unfounded theorizing. Abe couldn't blame her.

Still, he left the same message on her

phone as he had on Jack's. It was urgent. Please call immediately. He would explain as soon as she got back to him.

His call to Devin Juhle with the same message made the trifecta — nobody picking up anywhere. Everyone going to their voicemail.

Glitsky wondered if they'd all been talking to one another, deciding among themselves to stonewall the meddling Mr. Glitsky.

He sat dead still, hunched over, his cell phone in his hand.

"Come on," he said aloud through clenched jaws. "Come on."

Nothing.

At last he tried another number. To his surprise and relief — the universe might not, after all, be conspiring against him — Wyatt Hunt picked up on the first ring. "Abe. What's going on?"

"You remember the other night when you asked me to keep Devin and his team in the loop on this Doug Rush case?"

"Sure."

"Well, I'm finding that a little tough because nobody's here at the Hall in Homicide and nobody's answering my calls."

"So what do you want me to do?"

"Well, I'd like you to call Devin and see if he picks up for you."

"Okay. Then what?"

"Tell him I need to talk to him."

"You want me to call Devin right now?"

"If you wouldn't mind."

"Because he isn't picking up for you?"

"Right."

Hunt's sigh over the phone came in loud and clear. "All right. Hang in there. I'll get back to you in a minute."

"I'm not going anywhere."

Devin Juhle wiped his dinner plate with his last slice of sourdough. The kids had already been excused and now were in the downstairs playroom under the guise of doing homework, although it sounded suspiciously like their homework involved television.

But you had to pick your fights, and from Connie Juhle's perspective, homework wasn't going to be tonight's existential battle. Ever since her husband had taken the phone call during dinner, Devin had been preoccupied and quiet, and she knew that it would fall to her to talk him down from the latest precipice.

"There's one last half-serving of spaghetti left," she said.

"Thanks. But I'm good."

"Is the spaghetti okay?"

"Perfect as always."

"Although I notice you're not having seconds as you always do."

Devin met her gaze and let out a deep sigh.

"Who was on the phone?" she asked.

"Wyatt."

"Bad news?"

He shrugged. "More a moral dilemma — my favorite. Evidently Abe Glitsky thinks he's solved the damn Doug Rush case for about the hundredth time. And really, all I want it to do is go away. I mean, how much more can go wrong?"

"You don't want to ask that. The answer, always, as you know, is more than you think."

"I do know. But this one's been snakebit since Waverly and Yamashiro beat the guy up while they were arresting him. Then our perp gets himself killed the day before his trial was scheduled to begin. And then it looks a whole lot like Jack and Jill might have jumped the gun on some interrogations and maybe played some peripheral role at least in that murder/suicide down the Peninsula. It's like textbook on how we can screw things up, and I just don't think we need to be reminded about it every day or so. And Abe just won't go away."

"So what's your moral dilemma?"

He mopped up more sauce with a swipe of bread. "I told Wyatt that I'd talk to Abe tomorrow. That whatever it was ought to keep until then."

"Okay. And that's true, right?"

"It could be, perhaps."

"Uh-oh."

"Yeah. But what if it's not? If Abe really thinks he's ready to move, and he is no babe in the woods, you put it off for twelve hours, it might all go away somehow. And in any event, I'm not doing my job if I don't at least find out what we're dealing with. If Abe's really got it this time, I really can't justify not following up and maybe letting another disaster happen on my watch."

"So are you going to talk to him? Abe, I mean."

"I don't see how I can't."

Headache? What headache?

Glitsky wondered where it had gone as he took the elevator down and went out to Bryant Street to call his Uber car. He must have gotten enough of the bed rest everybody was harping about in small increments that had finally done the job.

Maddeningly, when he went to punch up his Uber app, he discovered that the power on his phone was gone; he would have to take a cab. It didn't really matter anyway, since he'd told Treya after his catnap in the Hunt Club's closet that he would probably be late getting home.

He was close to the end. He was all right, pain-wise. She shouldn't wait up.

Of course, this was before he'd met up with Jack and Jill at the Hall, before what he'd unearthed in Records, before he'd learned that Devin Juhle was apparently through with him and his investigation, at least for today.

Well, all right, he thought, to heck with them. If he could expect no cooperation from Juhle or Jack or Jill, he could at least solidify his position around proving that the killer of Paul Riley had also murdered Doug Rush. The package would then be complete.

It had been a long time since he'd taken an actual taxicab, but there was a small line of them parked on Bryant, right in front of him, and he flagged the first one, hopped in, and gave his driver Julia Bedford's address on Green Street.

"I would have called for an appointment but my phone ran out of gas. If this isn't a convenient time . . ."

"No. It's fine," Julia said. "It's good to see you again. I was just wondering how your investigation is going, if you've had any luck getting it all straight."

"As straight as these things go," Abe said. "Now it's a matter of making the case air-tight."

"It's not there yet?"

"Not quite, but close."

"I hope you're not back to suspecting me again."

"No. To tell you the truth, you were never high on my list."

"But, I know, you had to make sure."

"That's the job," Abe said.

"I get it. So would you like to come in?"

"That'd be nice."

Julia held the door back and let him pass in front of her. After closing it behind them, she said, "I'll put on some tea."

"Sounds good." He took a seat at her now-familiar round dining table.

She spoke from the kitchen. "So to what do I owe your dropping by?"

"Actually, I wanted to see if you would be able to help me close this case for good."

"Really? Are you kidding?"

"Not at all. And let me say at the outset that there is absolutely no pressure. You can say no right now, and I'll drink my tea and be out of here and won't bother you any-more."

"Well, not saying it's a bother, but it's not the kind of thing a girl gets asked every day. I mean, to help play some real role in a homicide investigation. And it sounds like that's what you're talking about, am I right?"

"Yep."

"You want to give me a minute?"

"As much time as you need. And while you're considering, I'd be lying if I told you there was no element of risk involved."

Julia laughed, hearty and unforced, as if this were some kind of new game. "Now you really are kidding me," she said.

"I'm not." Abe held up three fingers of his right hand. "Scout's honor. I'm serious as a heart attack."

The teakettle sang in the kitchen and she said, "Let me get that."

As she went to make their tea, force of habit had Abe reaching for his cell phone before he remembered that it needed to be charged. Turning in his chair, he asked if she had a charger handy.

"Somewhere around here," she said. "Or you could plug yours in. Whatever."

He got his own cord out of his leather briefcase and plugged it into the outlet under the table. When he straightened up, she was coming forward with their steaming mugs in hand. “Service with a smile,” she said.

“Thank you.”

“You’re welcome.” Sitting down, she said, “You were just saying that there was an element of risk. Can I ask you, by risk you mean real danger?”

“Not to put too big a spin on it, Julia, but I’m talking about taking down somebody who conceivably may have killed at least five people. So yes, real danger.”

This straightforward response from Abe visibly got her attention, where suddenly and clearly things shifted away from anything like a game. The expression on her face all but shut down into a tight frown. “Five?” she asked. “Okay, Doug and Paul Riley, I’m assuming, but three more?”

“At least. If I’ve got the right guy, we’re dealing with a stone killer who’d kill both of us as soon as look at us.”

Julia paused again, took in a deep breath, let it out in a sigh. “And you think that I can help you bring him in?”

“At the moment, you’re my absolute best chance.”

“How’d I get to be that?” She reached out and put a light hand on Abe’s arm. “Not to complain, but here I was, just sitting in my apartment minding my own business. And now suddenly I'm in the middle of this thing? How could that possibly happen?"

"You're not there yet, Julia. There's that potential, though, if you decide to come on board with me. But until you do, as I said before, there's no pressure, and no penalty if you decide to pass. I wouldn't blame you, even."

"So am I in danger already?"

"No. That's why you're in the perfect position. Our killer would never see you coming."

"But then when he does, he shoots me?"

"Unlikely, but possible. You wouldn't be alone. We'd have you covered all the way."

"Who is we? I thought this was just me and you."

"No. If we decide to go ahead, we'll need some backup. That means police."

On the table between them, Abe's cell phone beeped, telling him he had missed a call from Devin Juhle, who had left him a voicemail while his phone was down. "Speak of the devil," he said to Julia. "I need to get this."

"Abe." The phone was on speaker. "This is Devin. I told Wyatt that I wouldn't be talking to you until tomorrow morning, but on reflection I wanted you to know that if you've really got something urgent going on tonight, I'll leave my phone on so that you can reach me anytime. Just remember that the key word is 'urgent.' Not less than."

Julia said, "Who was that?"

"Devin Juhle. Head of Homicide."

"He sounds like he wants to be with you on this."

"It's probably not his first choice. But at least he sounds ready to help."

"Are you going to call him back?"

"I'm not sure. It still depends."

"On what?"

"You."

32

At nine thirty, an hour and a half after Glitsky had returned Devin Juhle's voice-mail, Julia Bedford sat back in a reading chair in her living room and looked around her apartment with a sense of absurdity and disbelief. Was this really happening to her?

Before Glitsky would make that call to the head of Homicide, he'd told her he had to be certain that she fully understood her role in this trap where she would be the bait.

Dangerous didn't begin to cover it.

After she'd listened carefully to the case he had prepared, she'd realized that Abe was correct. There was every reason to believe that he had identified the "stone killer" for whom he'd been searching the past week. But his case, he'd explained to her, was fatally flawed because he had no physical evidence.

He'd made it clear to her: the bare fact that his suspect had a motive to kill all five victims and the opportunity to be in the places where they were killed, even combined with the fact that all of the victims had been killed by a single shot to the head by a Glock forty, didn't remotely meet the standard of proof needed to make an arrest, much less get a conviction.

In none of those other cities had investigating officers found any evidence that would place Abe's suspect at the murder scenes. Just as the San Francisco inspectors had found nothing.

This killer knew how to leave a completely sanitary crime scene, no matter the city in which he was operating. A couple of days to plan the attack, get the lay of the land, then a quick strike. The biggest problem would probably have been acquiring an unregistered gun, but even this probably wouldn't, and no doubt didn't, prove much of an obstacle on the street.

Whatever he had done, it had worked and left no trace every time.

Glitsky had told her that they would somehow have to lure him into a trap, and this was where Julia came in.

It was called a pretext phone call.

After Abe had described it, her immediate reaction was that she couldn't possibly do what he was asking. She was not sure that she had the strength, the wit, or the courage to pull it off. But she did tell him that if it meant apprehending and ultimately punishing the man who'd killed Doug Rush, to say nothing of the others, she was game for whatever role Abe wanted her to play.

Only then had Abe placed the return call to Juhle.

This time, the lieutenant had picked right up.

Now Glitsky and Juhle sat at Julia's round dining table. Glitsky had already explained to her that they were both armed, their weapons loaded. Outside somewhere in the dark streets were other officers; unclear to Julia exactly how many, or what their role was. She had a recording device attached to her telephone.

Glitsky nodded to her, and she placed the call, leaving it on speaker so everyone could hear.

He answered.

She replied, "Hi. This is Julia, Doug Rush's girlfriend. I'm not sure if you remember."

"Sure. How are you doing?"

"I'm all right. I miss Doug."

"Yeah. Terrible thing. He was a good guy."

"He was."

She felt the tremor in her voice and hoped it wasn't too much of a giveaway to her state of mind. Both of her hands shook, and her stomach churned.

"So . . . what can I do for you?"

"I just . . . I wondered if you and I could talk for a little while."

"I would have thought that's what we're doing already. You don't mind my asking, how did you get my phone number?"

"Doug had it on his phone. He gave it to me when he got out on bail. He thought I might need it if the cops beat him up again, or whatever might happen. If he got into trouble, he wanted me to call you. He thought you were one of his true friends."

"He's right. I was."

"That's what I thought, too."

Julia found herself at a complete loss for words. She looked over at Abe with a panicked expression, shaking her head.

His voice breached the gap. "So, again, how can I help you?"

"I wanted to ask if you are planning to go to the service? Is there going to be a memorial of some kind?" she asked. "Do you know anything about that?"

"I hadn't heard. Wasn't the bike club doing something? It should be on their website. Listen, Julia, you caught me in the middle of —"

"Please. I need a little closure here. I need to talk to you."

"I don't know what you're asking or, really, how I can help you. I'm sorry if this is so painful. My heart goes out to you, but I don't see what you need from me. I don't know what you mean by closure."

"Of course you do." She hesitated, took a breath, and came out with it. "Listen. You don't have to play games with me. Doug told me that it was you who killed Paul Riley, and like you I think he probably deserved it."

"No probably at all. But if Doug said it was me who killed him, he didn't know what he was talking about."

"No. He did know."

"Couldn't have. Didn't happen."

"You didn't tell him you were going to kill Paul if he ever got out?"

"Okay, but that was before he actually did. Get out, I mean. I hated that son of a bitch and the Exoneration Initiative that got him off. I think it did Doug some good for somebody to let him rant about the system and how fucked up it is, and then rave alongside him. But that doesn't mean I killed anybody. You ask me, I still say it was Doug."

"Maybe you didn't hear, but Doug was in Half Moon Bay the whole day when Riley got shot."

"I heard that that was his story . . ."

"It wasn't a story. It's the truth."

"Even if it is —"

Julia's voice went up half an octave. "There is *no doubt.* No doubt. And that leads me to why I needed to make this call." She paused for a moment, then sobbed a real sob. "Why did you feel you had to kill Doug, too? How was he a threat to you?"

A silence descended, lasting so long that everyone listening thought that he might have hung up. Glitsky held up a finger, and no one in the room made a sound.

At last, the voice spoke, so quietly it was barely in the audible range. "You need to get ahold of yourself, Julia. That's a hell of an accusation."

"I know it was you. Doug left me a voice-mail the night he was killed saying you were on your way over to talk about the Riley killing. He said he suspected it was you, and as much as he hated Riley, he wasn't sure he could justify shooting Paul down in cold blood. You were here at our building that night. I saw you come up the stairs outside. I heard you and Doug talking when you were going out a few minutes later. After midnight. What more proof do I need?"

Now there was no mistaking the threat in his voice. "You don't want to go down this road, Julia. What are you trying to get out of this?"

"I told you. Closure."

"That's an overused word. And this conversation is over."

Before he could ring off, she blurted, "Don't hang up or I'm going to the police."

"Julia —"

"The problem was, you were his friend. I just couldn't believe you really did it. I couldn't fit it in anywhere. I mean, you seem like a normal person, a good person. Even when I finally realized why you came by here that night, like you did, it meant that it had to be you. There's nobody else it could have been. Don't you see that? But how could you do it? How could you let it get to that? To killing your friend?"

He snorted. "Friend, my ass. He was all apologetic, but told me he was going to roll all over me at his trial. Evidence or no evidence putting me near Paul Riley. I'd understand, wouldn't I? I mean, in his position, who wouldn't have done the same thing? It was just strategy, he said. The jury would let him go because they'd think I'd done it, and there wasn't any evidence they could connect to me. So it would be win-win. Even if I was the one he ought to thank for finally getting rid of the fucking guy who raped and killed his own daughter. Not saying I was. Doug should have left it alone, but he just couldn't and he deserved whatever he got. Both of them did — Riley and Doug."

"And so you killed them both?"

"You'll never prove it, and I never said it," he replied. Then, his voice softening: "Look, Julia, I think you were right in the first place. We need to talk about this face-to-face. I can be there in fifteen minutes if that works for you. Just please wait until we've had a chance to talk before you take this any further."

"All right," she said. "I'll wait."

And the connection went dead.

Juhle picked up his phone and punched in Jack Royce's number. Jack and Jill were parked half a block down the street from their suspect's stand-alone home on Quintara Street. When the inspector picked up, Juhle asked, "What do you think? We got enough?"

"He sure as hell sounds guilty," Jill said. "But that might not do it."

"I wish we had a judge listening in," Jack

added. "We could play the tape tomorrow."

"I wouldn't call any part of it a confession," Glitsky put in, "much as I'd like to put cuffs on him right now. But let's hear it for Julia. That was a great job."

Julia, tears running down her face, nodded in acknowledgment. "He really did it, didn't he?"

Glitsky nodded. "And he even told us why. But still, if nobody reads that as a confession, there's nothing more we can do unless he makes another move. Devin, it's your call."

Juhle hesitated. "I say we let him get here. Julia told him she was going to go to the police. He's got to process that and see how much time he has, how long it will take her to actually do it. If it were me, it wouldn't take very long. And besides, he said he was coming over here. I think that if he actually shows up in the middle of the night after that conversation, we've got enough to arrest. After that, it's up to the DA.

"And Julia, by the way," Juhle added, "thanks for everything. That was a great job, but now maybe we want to get you set up somewhere else tonight."

She looked first at Abe, who shrugged.

Making up her mind, she said, "Not a chance. I've come this far. If something happens and you need me again, I have to be here."

"I appreciate that, but I really wasn't asking," Juhle said. "Things might get tricky if —"

"Hey! Lieutenant!" Jill's voice came up through the phone. "Are you still with us?"

"We're listening," Juhle said. "What's up?"

"His garage door just came up," she said. "He's moving."

Goddamn.

He never thought that ridiculous hippie chick knew he was even alive, much less friends with Doug. No way did he think that she was keeping tabs on either of them, their comings and goings. She was just sometimes *there,* sometimes visible, sometimes not.

He couldn't believe, after all his other plans and calculations had worked so perfectly over most of a decade in three other states, with no hint of suspicion falling on him, that he was going to be threatened with exposure now by this nonentity.

She undoubtedly wouldn't even care about the issues, about justice, about what he had done. When it should be all right, even heroic, to take the lives of these bastard heartless killers who had not only committed these heinous crimes but had been convicted, found guilty in the courts. If the system then let them go after their five appeals — thank you, Exoneration Initiative — where was the justice in that?

They ought to be giving him a medal!

Who in the hell was ever going to miss the four exonerees he'd eliminated? It wasn't farfetched to believe that he'd probably saved more lives in the future than he'd taken in the past. These were evil people; it was only a matter of time before they killed and raped and caused all kinds of mayhem again and again, casually ruining the lives of everybody they touched or dealt with.

The only one he felt bad about was Doug. He really hadn't considered carefully enough, how of course Doug would be the natural first suspect. Back during Riley's trial, Doug had been out of control in and out of the courtroom. After they let Paul Riley out with all the attendant hoopla, Doug had all but advertised his intention to kill Riley and balance the scales of justice. But he hadn't had the guts to pull it off himself.

So it had fallen to him to avenge Dana Rush.

He'd given Doug almost four months to take out his daughter's killer, and finally he had come to realize that he'd never get to it. Justice delayed was justice denied, so finally he'd decided that enough was enough. Paul Riley getting up every morning and having a job and doing some regular breaking and entering; all of that ate at his insides like an ulcer.

Of course he knew, if he was being honest, that he should have gone to a little more trouble to change his look somehow. He was operating in his hometown, after all, where people knew him, and not across the country in other cities where he was a complete stranger. And worse, he'd never even considered the broad-stroke similarity between his and Doug's appearances that might cause someone to misidentify Rush as the killer.

James Riley, Paul's dad, had of course seen him in the immediate aftermath of the shooting. In a state of panic, in the dense fog, he had mistakenly "recognized" him as Doug, the crazy father who'd made all the threats; the memory of Doug and his threats was ingrained from all the fuss that had gone down during Paul's trial. It was a natural mistake.

But it set Doug up to take the fall for it.

He should have considered all of that more carefully. But you couldn't do everything perfectly all the time.

It was a shame that Doug had to pay the

penalty for his mistakes, and Paul, too, but that was life.

And that was death.

In the end, Doug wasn't anybody's idea of a saint or a hero. He was a flawed guy who'd had more than his share of bad luck, but in many ways he'd made his own karma, and his karma was essentially what had gotten him killed.

He was nearly certain that the woman — Julia — would not decide to call the police immediately. She'd have to mull it for a while before she would act. It was already late at night, and she'd lived with her suspicions now for over a week. She'd undoubtedly sleep on it, maybe call someone in the morning.

And really, even if she made the call, what was she going to say?

But of course he couldn't take that chance.

33

The big question, Juhle thought, was how far they should let the scenario play out. What they needed was something overt, something that betrayed their suspect's guilt in an undeniable fashion — but this equated to something now truly dangerous, especially in light of Abe Glitsky's information about his suspect's MO in taking out his victims. A door opens to his knock and the minute he sees his target, he shoots him in the head; the assumption could be made that not so much as one word was exchanged in any of those attacks.

Outside, Juhle knew, Jack and Jill had driven back here and parked around the corner on Octavia. They had taken an obscure route from his house and gone as fast as they could without lights and sirens so they could beat him to his expected destination on Green Street. And, successful, now they were directly across the street tucked into one of the doorway porticos.

Waiting.

A male figure appeared at the corner on the other side of the street, and Jill whispered to Jack, "Back up." They both moved in closer to the doors, out of the reach of the streetlights.

They watched as he walked, apparently aimlessly, not hurrying at all, up toward Julia's building. He didn't appear to be watching out for anything. Wearing tennis shoes and one of those Giants heavy jackets designed for the late-inning fog, he strolled with his hands in his pockets. When he got to ground zero, he didn't even slow down, but continued on past the building and out of their line of sight.

Jill dared stepping halfway out of her hiding place. The man got to the corner of Franklin and turned left and out of sight. She blew out heavily and said, "False alarm."

"You want to get a little closer?" Jack asked. "Not much time if he turns in."

Jill shook her head. "We can't let him see us."

"So we stay here?"

"Probably better."

"Damn."

"I know," she said, glancing back to her left, at the corner of Gough. "Uh-oh. He's back." Whispering urgently now. "Same guy. Walked around the block." Reaching out her palm, she pushed her partner back again, all the way up against the doors. "Gotta be him."

Grabbing her cell phone, she hit the Recents button and let it ring once, their signal to Juhle. "Gotta be him," she muttered again.

The man strolled as he had before, coming toward them on the opposite side of the street. This time, when he reached the stairs leading up to the landing at Julia's building, he pulled his hand out of one pocket, reached for something else with his other one. Climbing the six stairs, he stopped at the landing and, reaching out, pushed one of the buttons.

"Shit," Jack barely breathed. "The front door locks. Shit."

"We can't move till he's in."

From across the street, they clearly heard the buzzer that unlocked the main door to the building. And the automatic light turned on in the hallway.

"We gotta," Jack said. "No choice. Go go go!"

■ ■ ■ ■

"Who is it?"

"Julia?"

"Yes."

"This is Nick Halsey. We need to talk."

"Hands up! Police!"

Two of them stood silhouetted in the outside doorway. Where the hell had they come from? Halsey half-turned, the gun already out, ready to fire, in his right hand.

"Drop the weapon!"

"Easy, easy. I'm good."

"Now! Now!"

Turning a quarter of the way around, he held up his empty left hand, hiding the sight of his right. Then he suddenly whirled and dropped to a knee, extending his right hand. He pulled the trigger once, twice, a third time.

Glitsky, standing literally at the inside knob of Julia's front door, his own weapon racked and ready in his hand, barely had time to register what he was hearing out in the hallway; then, on opening the door, seeing and registering what was going on.

Nick Halsey huddled on the floor of the

hall, turning to face Abe, his gun now coming up, firing with no hesitation, the round slamming into the wood of the door right at Glitsky's face. He felt a deep burning in his cheek, but it barely registered before another shot echoed in the hall and Halsey grunted, but he wasn't finished yet, as he brought his gun to bear on Glitsky.

There was no time for Abe to think, only to react.

The next two shots were perfectly simultaneous: Halsey made some inchoate noise as Glitsky's bullet hit him in the top of his chest.

Abe felt the hit in his own chest. It backed him up a step, then he went down in a heap, the blood spouting from somewhere on him into the hardwood floorboards.

34

When Treya opened the door to him at eight o'clock the next morning, Hardy told her that they had to stop meeting like this, but she was out of even the most perfunctory of smiles. Instead, she touched his arm a bit protectively and said, "They tell me it looks worse than it is, which is supposed to be good news. If he's back to sleep, you might want to leave him be." She was guiding him over to the hall that led back to their bedroom.

"Will do. And thanks again for calling me."

She shrugged. "I thought you'd want to know."

"I guess he never got around to that bed rest we were talking about yesterday."

"Yesterday? That couldn't have been just yesterday."

They stopped at the doorway. Glitsky lay covered up, his sheet up over his head.

"Beat up one day," Hardy said, "shot the

next. He's working on a bad week."

"I can hear you, you know," Glitsky said. He pulled down the sheet and propped himself up against the headboard. "How you doing, Diz?"

Seeing him, Hardy grimaced. "Ouch. Just a quick first impression, I'd say I'm doing better than you."

Abe gingerly touched the bandage that covered half his face. "I'm lucky," he said. "Another inch, I would have lost an eye or maybe worse."

"Just what you need, though, another scar to match the first one. Maybe this new one will look better on your face."

"It's really not so bad."

"Yeah, I can see that."

"The ribs hurt worse, and talk about lucky." Tapping his chest, he said, "Kevlar works, thank God."

Hardy looked across at Treya, a question.

She nodded.

Coming back to Abe, he said, "I thought it was just your face."

"Naw. That's just some shrapnel from the door. Wood chips. The chest one could have done a lot worse, but it punched me pretty good. The face bleeds a little more, though."

"A lot more," Treya corrected him. Then, to Hardy, "Eleven stitches."

"Nice scar material," he said. "Maybe next you can get a tattoo and really scare people."

"Good idea."

"Thank you. I had another one, too. Good idea, that is. It was only just yesterday, something about calling you off the Rush case."

"I must have missed that memo. And a good thing I did."

"I wonder if Jack and Jill would agree with you."

It was Glitsky's turn to grimace. "They were okay, stable, when I left the hospital. All three of their wounds were extremities. Jack one, Jill two. They're going to be all right. Uncomfortable for a while, but basically fine. Which is more than I can say for Nick Halsey." He closed his eyes briefly and drew a deep breath.

Treya reached down and touched his leg. "Hon?"

"Good," he said, opening his eyes again. "I don't believe that Doug would have given Nick up at the trial. He didn't have to shoot him. He didn't have to do anything and he could have gone on finding guilty exonerees and putting them down. But he'd gone around the bend with this whole vigilante thing, and anybody who got in his way had to go. First Doug, and then there's no doubt he would have shot this woman Julia last night if we hadn't been there."

"You're talking about the hippie woman who originally let us into Doug's apartment?" Hardy asked. "How'd she get involved in the sting in the first place?"

"She had an on-and-off thing with Doug, and I realized that it was totally plausible that she would have seen the two of them — Doug and Nick — leave together on the night. Because that's what did happen; they did leave together. Anyway, true or not, she sold her story to Nick, so he had to take her out, too. And I can't say he didn't try."

"Can I ask you another one?"

"You're going to anyway, whether or not, so sure, hit me."

"How'd you finally get it whittled down to him? Halsey?"

Without naming Martin Dozier, Glitsky laid out the connection to the possibly guilty exonerees, the New York/Chicago/Atlanta/San Francisco murders, all with a similar MO. It didn't take him long.

When he finished, Hardy was frowning. "That's a fairly long string of coincidence, Abe. I mean, you flushed him out and it worked, but . . ."

"I agree with you. I knew it wasn't enough. But then I was talking to Jack and Jill, and

Jill just happened to mention about there being no evidence, it was as though a cop had done it. Which put the idea in my brain. Was there a cop out there who was a close enough friend to Doug Rush to convince him to drive out to the park with him and talk trial strategy or whatever the excuse was in the middle of the night? Well, lookit here, boys and girls, there sure was."

"Nick Halsey."

Glitsky nodded. "Couldn't have been anybody else. But still, I had no proof and probably wasn't going to get it even if I could get a warrant to search Nick's place. So on a hunch — really, nothing much more than that — I went down to Records and found out what I needed to know.

"It turns out that Nick was on vacation on every week that one of these guys got killed. That was just too much to be coincidence. And even if it might have gotten him arrested, I figured it wasn't going to be enough to convict, so for me there was no more doubt. We had to try to flush him, as you say. Sting him. And Devin agreed. And here we are."

"And if you all don't mind," Treya said, "I think that's enough for now. Somebody does need to get himself some rest if he's ever going to get better. I'm talking real, live, uninterrupted sleep. Do you think we can do that?"

It did not escape Ken Yamashiro's attention that if he and Eric Waverly had still been working the Paul Riley/Doug Rush case, either or both of them might now have been lying in their respective hospital beds, shot. Or perhaps in the morgue, dead. He didn't know if there was a lesson there, but at least the circumstances bore reflection.

Maybe the cosmos was trying to tell him something.

In the four-plus weeks that he'd been on admin leave, he had kept himself in shape with an intense workout and jogging program. He'd also cleaned up his diet, cut his drinking way back. He'd lost twenty-two pounds.

He hadn't laid eyes on or talked to his former partner. He wished him luck, but he was no longer going to be around to take another fall for Eric Waverly.

When they decided that they wanted him back, he was going to be the perfect police officer for the rest of his career.

When Juhle had called him this morning requesting a meeting, he felt that he knew what this had to be about, and he was ready. It made sense, he thought, that they would reach out to him now, when Jack and Jill were clearly going to be unavailable for at least another month or two while they recovered from their bullet wounds. This left the homicide detail short of inspectors, and Ken was ready to step back up and do the job.

He had been tempted to call Eric to find out if Juhle had called him, too. But in the end he decided to play his own hand and let Inspector Waverly do the same.

At 11 a.m. sharp, Ken knocked on Juhle's open door and poked his head in, then stepped over the threshold and saluted.

The lieutenant pushed his chair back from his desk; seeing him, Yamashiro was forcibly struck with the reminder that Juhle was coming off what must have been an exhausting night of little to no sleep. His shoulders sagged and his face was sallow, and he simply nodded in greeting, a great sense of weariness flowing off him.

He neglected to return any portion of Yamashiro's salute, instead indicating with a nod that he take one of the folding chairs in front of Juhle's desk.

When Ken was seated, Juhle exhaled heavily and nodded again. "I'm afraid," he began, "that there's no way to put a positive spin on what I'm about to tell you. And you're only hearing it from me first because I asked the chief — since we've always gotten along — if I could be the one to break it to you. The department, the powers that be, have decided that you're going to be let go, effective immediately."

Ken felt the blood draining out of his face. "What do you mean, let go?" he asked stupidly.

"I mean terminated. Fired."

"No, but wait." Yamashiro couldn't find any words. "You mean out of Homicide?"

"Not just Homicide. There's just no tolerance anymore for the kind of behavior that you and Eric had demonstrated on that tape. You've probably seen the YouTube of it a hundred times. You two guys look like the Gestapo. That was just a complete breakdown in protocol. And I have to say that it didn't help it turns out that Doug Rush wasn't guilty of shooting Paul Riley."

"How do you know that?"

"Well, it's complicated, but the events of last night made it crystal clear. Rush didn't do it. And you and Eric just beat the shit out of him. And there's zero tolerance anymore for that sort of behavior."

"He just went off on us, Devin. Out of nowhere."

"No, the point is, Ken, that you and Eric

both overreacted. And everything you did was caught on video."

"Which shows we were acting in self-defense, Devin. He flat-out attacked us."

"That's not the interpretation of the chief or, frankly, the mayor either."

Yamashiro grimaced. "I'm going to appeal this, Devin. The union will never let it fly."

It was Juhle's turn to make a face. "Well, that's the other reason why the chief wanted it to be me who broke this to you. Of course, you can appeal to whoever you want, but wherever you go it's a long and winding road. I've been instructed to tell you that as long as you go along with the department's decision here, there'll be no further discussion about the possible loss of your pension and benefits — they'll still be guaranteed. But if you choose to fight this out, then those benefits will be on the table as something you could potentially lose. And between me and you, I have to tell you that I fought very hard with the chief, who was not inclined at all to let you keep your benefits under any circumstances, but I told her that you had always been better than just another good cop —"

"What about Eric?"

"I'll be making him the same offer when I see him."

"And when will that be? Today?"

"I don't know. I haven't been able to reach him. Have you talked to him?"

Ken shook his head. "Not since you sent us home last month."

This clearly surprised Juhle. "Not once?"

"Not even. We needed to take a little break from each other. No — not a little one, a complete breakup. He's got to have some serious counseling, Dev, whatever else happens with all this. Frankly, he needs to be in rehab."

"I was going to suggest that."

"So you knew?"

"It wasn't like he tried to hide it, Ken."

Yamashiro took a beat. "Okay, then, not to throw my ex-partner under the bus, but I want you to know that when they shot the video with Doug Rush, Eric was at the very least on some pain medication, some prescribed, some not, if not a little alcohol to go along with it, too."

Juhle's mouth grew tight with anger. "If I see a way to bring up these medical and psychological issues when I speak with him, I will. But whatever I do with Eric, I'm sorry, but it's not going to speak to your own situation."

"What I'm trying to say, Dev, is that none of this bad arrest or getting physical with

Mr. Rush would have happened at all if Eric hadn't been in some kind of altered state. I've seen that YouTube, as you said, about a hundred times. It's obvious that nothing would have happened if Eric hadn't been so bad off. He basically threw Rush at me after they were already into it, so what was I going to do? I just wanted to get him in the car behind the screen and out of danger. He jerked up and smacked his head. And this is what I'm getting canned for? I didn't do this, Dev. Not the way it looks on the video."

"Yeah, well, I'm afraid that's the way it looked to the powers that be. And going off with dirt on your partner isn't going to win you any allies here at the Hall, Ken. Trust me on that. You've got to simply let it go and move on."

"It's just so fucking wrong, Dev. I know you see that. It's all politics and bullshit. This is twenty-five years of my life we're talking about here. It's completely unjust."

Juhle let out a breath he'd been holding. His lips ticked up at the corners in a grotesque attempt at what was evidently meant to be a conciliatory smile. Whatever, it quickly faded. "This just in," he said. "Injustice abounds. Get used to it."

■ ■ ■ ■

Gina Roake walked up the long stairway to the third floor of the Freeman Building, crossed the landing, and knocked on, then pushed open, the door to Wes Farrell's office. Her friend and law partner was sitting canted forward, his elbows on his knees, the picture of dejection. He looked over and started to smile, but gave up on it.

"You wanted to see me?" she asked.

"I did. I do. Thanks for coming up."

She came in and sat catercorner to him on one of the stuffed wing chairs. "Anytime, as you know." She paused. "Are you all right?"

"Not so much, as it turns out. You know I knew Nick Halsey?"

"I don't think I did know that."

"Yeah. Back in the day, when I was the DA and he was in Homicide. He was a good guy. We did some fun stuff together. I'm having trouble thinking he was capable of killing all those people."

"I guess he thought the system was broken and he could correct it. And they weren't people to him anymore."

Wes sat in silence. "You remember how this whole thing started?"

"When they arrested Doug Rush?"

Shaking his head, he said, "Back when I decided he was guilty before I knew any of the facts. I'm thinking I shouldn't ever have taken the case. And I was just so completely wrong. If I had just believed him . . ."

"Would you have done anything different?"

"I don't know. Maybe everything different. Doug knew how I really felt — I didn't make any secret of it — and it made him desperate somehow. I mean, if his own lawyer thought he did it, how's that work? If I'd for a minute thought that there was some other murderer out there who'd killed Paul Riley, I would have taken all kinds of different precautions and been a lot more careful. And Doug might still be alive today. To say nothing of that poor couple down in Miramar, and even Nick."

"I think that this falls under 'stuff I can't control,' Wes."

"At least it's a pretty good smack upside the head. I shouldn't be doing what we are supposed to be doing here as defense attorneys if I don't buy into the program."

"That's probably true. And good to hear. But we're never going to be perfect."

"I hate that part. I was sure I was."

"That, my dear Wes, is always the first mistake."

ACKNOWLEDGMENTS

After finishing my previous book, *The Rule of Law,* I decided that after twenty-five books in the past twenty-five years, I would take a sabbatical and let my creative batteries recharge. Over the next year, I was amused yet gratified to hear from many of my readers, concerned and wondering if I was retiring, or — perhaps more to the point — if Dismas Hardy and Abe Glitsky would once again find their way into another novel. I wasn't really in any hurry to bring my gang back onto the stage, but these things sometimes take on a life of their own, and *The Missing Piece* is a perfect example.

In the summer of 2019, before the pandemic had arrived, I still hadn't come up with a plot or a theme, and I found myself in a post-dinner conversation with my *consigliere* Al Giannini, and my son, Jack. As it turns out, both of these guys are working attorneys — Al a lifelong prosecutor and

Jack a public defender. Not too surprisingly, the talk turned to law, and particularly to the work of the Innocence Project.

As one may imagine, argument ensued.

And I had my book.

So thanks, Al and Jack, for providing the theme that would propel this story about self-doubt, the elusive nature of proof, and the lure of vengeance. Many times over the next six or eight months while the book came together, I went back to the well and tapped these sources for further (and often conflicting) opinions, details, and insights. (Did I say "often" conflicting? I meant "always.")

The pandemic's arrival allowed me to clear the decks for full-time writing, but there was still day-to-day work to be done, and keeping things moving on that front, as she has done for the past twenty-some years, is my assistant Anita Boone. Also laboring in the promotional world to keep readers up-to-date on social media is the fantastic Madiera James (xuni.com). My two "personal" editors, Peggy Nauts and Doug Kelly, always step in at the last minute to make sure that there are as few errors — technical, typographical, factual, or otherwise — as possible.

Also, in the day-to-day category, keeping

the creative and joyful fire alive even as the pandemic threatened to put it out, were Josh and Justine Kastan (and Cora and Wolf), Max Byrd (buy his books!), Tom Hedtke, Alan Heit (in whom some see a resemblance to Abe Glitsky), Rob Leininger (buy his Gumshoe books!), Glenn and Julie Nedwin, and Abe and Gillian Hajela. It's great having great friends!

Two generous readers have donated character names in this book. These donors, and their respective charities, are: Natalie Keeve (Gold Country Wildlife Rescue) and Terry Brown (Music in the Mountains).

At Simon & Schuster/Atria Books, I am blessed with a truly remarkable creative team. Here's a huge "thank you" to editors Peter Borland, Daniella Wexler, Jade Hui, and publicist David Brown. Working behind the scenes for the success of these books is the top-flight sales group of Janice Fryer, Wendy Sheanin, Colin Shields, Gary Urda, and Paula Amendolara. It is a pleasure and privilege to work with all of you. For all that you do, thank you so much.

No acknowledgments would be complete without including my literary agent and dear, dear friend, Barney Karpfinger. Barney is everything that an agent should be, and then so much more — a sensitive and perceptive editor, a brilliant negotiator, a shrink when I need one, and a true pal in every sense of the word.

Finally, I love hearing from my readers. Please feel free to stop by my website and say hello — I really do answer my email.

And finally, thanks to you all, dear readers, for buying my books!

ABOUT THE AUTHOR

John Lescroart is the *New York Times* bestselling author of twenty-nine previous novels, including *The Rule of Law, Poison,* and *Fatal.* His books have sold more than ten million copies and have been translated into twenty-two languages. He lives in Northern California.

The employees of Thorndike Press hope you have enjoyed this Large Print book. All our Thorndike, Wheeler, and Kennebec Large Print titles are designed for easy reading, and all our books are made to last. Other Thorndike Press Large Print books are available at your library, through selected bookstores, or directly from us.

For information about titles, please call:
(800) 223-1244

or visit our website at:
gale.com/thorndike

To share your comments, please write:
Publisher
Thorndike Press
10 Water St., Suite 310
Waterville, ME 04901